ONE LAST CHANCE

Matty batted her eyes.

"Something wrong?" Cooper T. asked, frowning. "Something in your eye?"

She shook her head. "No."

Why hadn't she paid better attention when Phoebe flirted? Phoebe knew all the secrets, but Matty badly needed guidance in the art of seducing a man. And now she had no time to learn. All the nights she'd spent alone on the trail with Cooper T. came down to one night, this one last chance.

"We'd better go," he said in a raspy voice. "I don't completely trust myself alone with you."

"Why?"

"Because when you look at me with those big eyes, I get weak. When I look at your lips, I want to kiss them."

"I want you to kiss them, too," she whispered.

"Oh, good God," he said. Then, with a groan, Cooper T. swept her into his arms.

HEAVEN SENT

SANDRA MADDEN

LEISURE BOOKS   NEW YORK CITY

*To the family who freed me to travel west
and the friends who always believed:
Susan, Virginia, Hy and Meg.*

A LEISURE BOOK®

January 2002

Published by

Dorchester Publishing Co., Inc.
276 Fifth Avenue
New York, NY 10001

If you purchased this book without a cover you should be aware that this book is stolen property. It was reported as "unsold and destroyed" to the publisher and neither the author nor the publisher has received any payment for this "stripped book."

Copyright © 2002 by Sandra Madden

All rights reserved. No part of this book may be reproduced or transmitted in any form or by any electronic or mechanical means, including photocopying, recording or by any information storage and retrieval system, without the written permission of the publisher, except where permitted by law.

ISBN 0-8439-4955-4

The name "Leisure Books" and the stylized "L" with design are trademarks of Dorchester Publishing Co., Inc.

Printed in the United States of America.

Visit us on the web at www.dorchesterpub.com.

HEAVEN SENT

Chapter One

June 10, 1868

"My Winchester's pointed right at your heart, mister. So don't go makin' any funny moves," Matilda Rose Applebee warned in a sharp, raspy whisper. She aimed to sound rattlesnake mean. "If you can't be brought back nice and peaceable, I'd just as soon shoot you on the spot and have done with you."

The man on the bed groaned. Like most folks in the small southern California mission town of San Juan Capistrano, he was sound asleep. Or passed out.

One candle flickered in the cold, stark room of the Gold Dust Hotel. Her horses had better sleeping accommodations, she thought, looking around. A layer of dirt coated the thin curtains, cobwebs in assorted sizes clung in corners, and the holes in the walls, punched or kicked by rowdy cowboys, were plentiful.

Up until an hour earlier, Matty had watched and

Sandra Madden

waited out in the corridor, hunkering in the shadows until the low-down snake known as Cooper T. Davis staggered from the downstairs saloon up into this room on the second floor. He hadn't bothered to lock his door behind him. Matty reckoned that in his inebriated state he'd been lucky to reach his room.

She'd bided her time until she figured the fast-talking drummer had passed out. No more than a silver-tongued swindler, he drifted from town to town selling patent medicine. Until now. Matty was about to put an end to his nefarious career. With the element of surprise on her side, she'd slipped into his room, Winchester at the ready.

The man was snoring loud enough to cover the noise of a herd of stampeding cattle, let alone one small woman.

Matty had tracked Davis down as if she was following the tracks of a poaching bobcat. But unlike that wily four-legged creature, this hunted man hadn't caught a whiff that she was on his trail.

She hissed in his ear.

He moaned and pulled the pillow over his head.

"Git up, varmint."

"Go away," he moaned.

"You're comin' with me now to marry my sister or I'm makin' her a widow. Take your choice."

"Lady, what are you talking about? I don't know any widow women. Go away," he mumbled.

Before she could stick the rifle in his ribs to show him she meant business, the shad-belly rolled over, away from her. He didn't even bother to open his eyes. One arm flopped over the side of the narrow bed. Except for his boots, he slept fully dressed. He smelled of whiskey and leather, which she didn't find at all pleasing.

"Unless you're ready to die, I'm takin' you to a wedding. And don't you think I'd have any regrets about puttin' the family jewels out of commission either," she growled. "One wrong move and it's over. Frankly, I'd just as soon pull the trigger now and be done with it—except poor Phoebe is needin' you."

Matty wished Cooper Davis would at least open his eyes, see her rifle, and know she meant business.

Edgy, frustrated, but determined, she strode to the opposite side of the bed, sat on her heels, and pressed the cold metal muzzle of the rifle against his nose.

He opened his eyes.

She had his attention.

The closeness of the muzzle caused his eyes to cross. His dark irises widened as he focused on the metal pressing against his nose.

"Git up and git your boots on," she ordered, forcing her voice to a low, gruff tone.

Frowning, he pushed the gun barrel away. He didn't appear the least bit alarmed. He seemed more baffled than anything, like a man who didn't believe in ghosts confronting an apparition. He narrowed his eyes—heavy-lidded, apple green, indolent eyes. Even in the dim light, she could see they were cloudy with sleep and the aftereffects of a long night in the saloon.

"Do you think you could point that shotgun in another direction before you hurt someone?"

Matty stood up and backed off. Finding a new target, she aimed the barrel of her Winchester right between his eyes. "Rise and shine now . . . and don't be up to any tricks."

With a low groan, Cooper T. Davis sat up, swinging

his legs to the floor. He was a tall, rangy one. Staring at the wide planked boards, he scratched the back of his head in an absentminded way. He didn't act like a worried man, like a man who, with one wrong move, might meet his maker in a matter of seconds.

He sighed and raised his eyes to hers. "You know, it's not ladylike to break into a man's hotel room, wake him from a sound sleep, aim a gun at him, and tell him he's gotta get up and get married. That's downright bad manners."

He ran his fingers through his thick, disheveled hair. The color of black coffee, his wayward locks fell over his ears and curled up at the nape of his neck.

Matty blew out an impatient puff of air and rolled her eyes. "Look who's bellyachin' about manners."

This was her first real close-up look at Cooper T. Davis. Truth was, he was giant-sized. All muscle and metal, he looked to have the strength of an ox. She reckoned the man had won his share of barroom brawls. He might possibly pose a problem or two.

The drummer's features were easy enough on the eyes, all in proportion and squared off like the hero in a Brontë novel. She was especially taken with the deep cleft in his chin.

"Maybe you better start from the beginning, lady. What's your name? Who's your sister? Where the hell did you come from?"

She didn't mind obliging him, but she kept him in her sights. "My name is Matilda Rose Applebee. My sister's name is Phoebe Pearl Applebee, and you know her a mite too well."

"I don't know who you're talking about, woman. I don't know any Phoebe Applebee."

"Just let me refresh your memory, Mr. Cooper T. Da-

Heaven Sent

vis. I didn't expect you to do any confessin' right off."

"Please do. Refresh my memory." Closing his eyes, he began to rub his temples in a slow circular motion, the way a man suffering from a bad headache would.

Matty couldn't help but take a certain amount of pleasure in his discomfort. He deserved to feel pain. Poor Phoebe had fallen into deep mental distress over her condition. A condition brought about by this low-life no-account.

"Not more'n two months ago, you came upon a neighborly social on the Silver Star Ranch. You were invited to stay and you did. You availed yourself of my daddy's hospitality. Do you recall that occasion?"

He frowned in a one-eyed wince. "Come to think of it, I do."

"You also availed yourself of my sister."

His closed eye opened. He stared at her wide-eyed. "What? Are you crazy? No. No, I did not avail myself of your sister, or anyone else's sister." His hands flexed into fists. He cocked his head, giving Matty a long, hard, sizing up. "I think I would recollect such an event."

"You wouldn't be the first man whose memory failed him after he put a woman in the family way."

"My memory is just fine. I remember stopping at the Silver Star after passing through Santa Barbara."

"Selling snake oil is what you were doing!"

"My product is not snake oil!" He grimaced in pain. Pain no doubt brought on by raising his voice, Matty thought with absolutely no sympathy. Davis shook his head and waved a hand as if he was brushing away a pesky fly. "Lady, would you mind putting that gun down and telling me straight out who you are? My head's a bit of a muddle right now."

She waved the rifle in a menacing manner. The Winchester was heavy, but early on she'd learned to handle the weapon with the ease other women possessed with a needle and thread. "I'll never put this gun down in company the likes of you. And don't you think I don't know how to use it, 'cause I do. And I told you before the name is Matilda Applebee. Miss Applebee to you."

"Miss Applebee," he repeated. She wasn't expecting the wry, lopsided grin he slanted her way. Nor the flop of her stomach in response. "Would you happen to be related to the aforementioned Phoebe Applebee?" he asked.

There was no denying Cooper T. Davis was a good-looking man, Matty thought. Especially when he smiled. His eyes crinkled at the corners like a man who laughed, or squinted, a lot. His lips drew out fine and nice. She suspected he sold a goodly amount of his patent medicine and seduced a mighty lot of innocent women along his route—just as he'd done to poor Phoebe. But he sure was thickheaded. He must have lost a good part of his brain function from drinking too much of his own tonic and rotgut whiskey.

"Of course I'm her sister, varmint," she replied with an exasperated roll of her eyes. "I've been tellin' you. And you spent the night at our ranch. The night we were celebratin' Phoebe's eighteenth birthday."

Because Matty didn't care for parties and dancing, she'd spent most of that evening avoiding the festivities. She'd lingered in the indoor kitchen, one of the few rooms in the ranch house she didn't care much for. She sat at her daddy's table listening to him and his cronies discussing the ranch business. Despite her daddy's declaring she couldn't and wouldn't, Matty aimed to run the Silver Star Ranch by herself one day.

Heaven Sent

Long about midnight, she'd wandered back out to the party, hanging in the shadows, observing. Matty saw Cooper T. Davis dancing with Phoebe. Her sister was all smiling and batting her eyes, as if she had something stuck in her lashes and couldn't get it out. Drawn to the tall dark stranger—by curiosity, she reckoned— Matty watched them dance for a while. She heard his deep belly laugh, and it had made her smile. She'd wondered what Phoebe had said to make the man laugh like that.

Cooper T. Davis stood out from the rest of the cowboys at the party. He was taller than the others, with shoulders as broad as the barn and a grin as big as sin. He had the kind of straight-out smile that made you feel warm all over, as if you were lying naked under the summer sun—as Matty sometimes did, unbeknownst to anyone but the birds and the beetles.

And his eyes were downright riveting, gleaming like a wild cat on the prowl. A little bit dangerous and a lot exciting. Matty had seen him, all right. Who could miss him? Whoever could miss Cooper T. Davis? He filled up acres.

"As I remember it, Miss Applebee, I spent that night in my wagon, not in the bunkhouse, not in the main house. I slept in my wagon, alone. The next morning I moved on—"

"Hightailed it out of there is more like it."

"Lady, you've got your facts mixed—"

"You don't recall spending time with Phoebe—in your wagon?"

"No one was in my wagon that night." He shook his head, as if he was dealing with a slow-wit—an attitude that only served to aggravate Matty further.

She might not have beautiful brown eyes and a heap

of blond ringlets like Phoebe, but she had a quick mind and a dead-on aim.

"I didn't expect you were the kind would tell the truth," she told him in a tone dripping with scorn. "But how could you even pretend to forget Phoebe? My little sister is the most beautiful girl west of the Mississippi. And you, you low-lyin' dog, took advantage of her."

"Whaaat?" Cooper reacted with a jerk of his head. The quick motion obviously caused him some pain. His eyes squeezed shut. "Is your sister accusing me of taking advantage of her?"

"How would I know if she hadn't told me? My sister is with child and you're the only one could have done it."

He jumped up from the bed. "You are just plain loco, lady. Crazy."

She took two quick steps backward, aiming the Winchester directly at his heart. But he'd stopped. With a wince of pain, he rocked on his heels.

"I'm right as rain," she crowed. He deserved to suffer. Matty had come a long way to capture this polecat.

"That's your opinion, lady. I've got another that says you've been riding in the sun too long. And I'm not in any condition to be discussing this . . . or anything else with you."

"Your opinion doesn't mean a thing to me, Mr. Cooper T. Davis. You're coming back to Silver Star Ranch and doin' the right thing. You're gonna marry my sister Phoebe."

Through the lone window of the hotel room, the first pale cinnamon rays of sun streaked the sky to the east. Cooper shook his head, an especially bad habit this morning. Every shake and wag of his head kicked a dull ache into throbbing pain.

Heaven Sent

This was as real as a nightmare could get. He had a bad hangover, and a mule-headed woman dressed like a man was pointing a rifle at him. Damned annoying.

In other circumstances he might have thought the hellcat attractive. Despite the men's clothes, the dim light, and the wide brim of her hat, it was evident Matilda Rose Applebee was worth a closer look. If you could get beyond her startling eyes. She had eyes an angel would envy, a luminous shade of lavender blue fringed by long, dark, curling lashes. Eyes that rolled with impatience. Bright, alert eyes. Disconcerting eyes . . . that followed his every movement.

Who would have believed the soul of a harridan hid behind that sweet, heart-shaped face? The petite gunslinger was a bundle of contradictions.

Dressed in a man's buckskin from shirt to trousers, she looked like a short, skinny desperado. Not a particularly dangerous woman. Dark wisps of hair fell along the nape of her neck. He supposed the rest must be tucked up under the wide-brimmed hat she wore. From the top of her hat to the tip of her lizard boots, Matilda Rose presented a portrait of pure pluck.

In a flash of hangover-induced madness, Cooper calculated that it might be interesting to discover if a woman's body was hidden beneath the layers of men's clothing. Gut instinct told him he wouldn't be disappointed.

Fact was, if a man made allowances for her turned-up nose and sun-bronzed skin, he might think the rifle-toting, pistol-packing woman a comely little thing. Even with a head full of hornets, Cooper hadn't missed the fact that she wore a holster on her hip.

He could only guess she'd been fed a pack of lies by her sister. There was no mistaking Miss Applebee's eyes spitting fire when she spoke of what he'd supposedly done to Phoebe. Her contempt warned him the time was not propitious to employ sweet-talk.

"So, your sister sent you after me, did she?"

"It was my idea, not hers. She's a sweet, shy thing—as you very well know. The kind who can be taken advantage of unless there's someone around to stick up for her."

"Big sister to the rescue."

"She didn't want me to come."

"Because I'm an innocent man and she knows it."

"Because she was afraid for my safety."

"So am I."

"Phoebe's beautiful in every way," she insisted. "You should consider yourself a lucky man."

"Right." Trying to reason with this hardheaded woman was like talking to a mule. Just a waste of breath. "It's at least a nine-day trip back to your ranch," Coop pointed out, thinking a heavy dose of reality might bring her to her senses. "How are you going to keep me from killing you and making my escape? Are you prepared to stay awake day and night on the trail with that gun aimed at my head?"

She lifted her chin and raised her eyebrows, haughty as a plains princess. "Don't you worry. I've got the trip planned. Besides, from what I heard you have a fresh wound. Someone got to you before me. You're not going to be runnin' too hard."

He had to hand it to her. The little vixen had done some investigating. She might be small, but she had a brain. He just hoped she wasn't trigger happy.

He'd always thought he'd end up wounded or dead from some shootout. Instead, he'd taken a bullet in his left thigh two nights earlier just sitting in the Harbor

Heaven Sent

Saloon, minding his business. He'd been relaxing for the first time in months, playing poker and drinking whiskey. The same as he'd done this evening. Tonight, evidently, he'd had a little too much whiskey. His head felt three times its normal size.

Coop didn't know what being a gimp meant to his future. But he knew the trail he'd been following had gone cold. In a day or two, soon as he was strong enough, he intended to head back to San Francisco, where he'd started from two months ago.

Might as well go part of the way with the girl. She was obviously sun-addled or worse. Maybe he'd deliver her safely to her ranch and go on his way.

Not that he had the time to dally with a misguided cowgirl looking for adventure. In order to save his job and maneuver a transfer, he had to reach the San Francisco headquarters before month's end.

"All right. A man knows when he's bested. But I'm not admitting to anything untoward with your sister, you understand."

She rolled her eyes again. Damned annoying habit she had.

"We'll get this all straightened out before we reach your ranch," he assured her. "In the meantime, you've got yourself a prisoner, Miss Applebee."

An hour later, mortified beyond measure, Matty rode out of town on the drummer's garish wagon for all the world to see. Purple scrolls and gilt cherubs emblazoned each side of the bright red wagon. Flourishing black script proclaimed Dr. Angus Van Kurem's Good Health Tonic. Smaller block letters declared that the invigorating bitters provided fast relief from most internal complaints. If bloodletting didn't work, Dr. Kurem's would.

She was grateful they passed no other travelers as Cooper T. guided the cumbersome, creaky wagon along the dusty bluff road running north along the Pacific. The two Appaloosas pulling the wagon were slow, swayback, and old.

Matty had hitched her sweet pinto, Spirit, to the rear of the wagon, along with the big black gelding the drummer called Traveler.

She rode up front on the bench beside her prisoner, her Winchester at the ready. He'd insisted on driving. She hadn't been about to give him any choice.

"This way you can shoot me if I make a run for it," he'd said.

She wasn't worried. It looked to her as if he could barely walk, let alone run. Akin to a chameleon's hide, Cooper's complexion changed by the minute, from a frightening shade of yellow to an eerie green, to pale, pale white. Matty found the phenomenon rather fascinating.

"You're hung over, Cooper T."

"No fooling, and each bump in the road just makes me more irritable. So don't chatter."

"I don't chatter. I don't do silly female things like that." Matty prided herself on never behaving like a weak, simpering miss. She held a shotgun in one hand, a pistol rested in her holster, and she'd tucked a parlor gun into the top of her boot. "You're not dealing with an everyday woman."

He snorted. "Ain't that the truth."

"How's your leg?" she asked. She required distraction. They were forced to sit closely, and not a mile from town she'd discovered the warmth generated by

Heaven Sent

Davis's body to be mildly disturbing. He gave off a musky male heat that seemed to seep through her pores. She felt it agitating beneath her skin like an itch she couldn't reach. All-fired mysterious, it was.

"It's just a flesh wound," he answered, oblivious to her discomfort. "Grazed my thigh. Nothing to slow me down any."

"Don't you feel ashamed of yourself?"

"For what? For getting in the way of a stray bullet from some drunken cowboy?"

"No. You—"

"I told you I didn't put your sister in a family way," he snapped.

Obviously Cooper T. was a sick man. The rocking, rolling, and pitching of the wagon most likely made him feel worse with every mile. She allowed herself a small smile.

"Well, now, Phoebe said you did, and Phoebe Pearl never tells a lie."

"Phoebe Pearl told a whopper this time. You've got the wrong man."

"We'll just see about that. Besides, I wasn't talking about what you did to her. I was talkin' about this tonic. Aren't you ashamed of sellin' such stuff? Or maybe you just don't have a conscience like normal people. Promisin' folks a tonic that will cure them of anything. My daddy says patent medicine does nothing but line a drummer's pockets."

"For your information, Angus Van Kurem's tonic has helped a lot of folks. If you're going to continue to jabber, I'll be requiring a dose myself. I'm feeling a trifle peaked this morning."

If he expected her to commiserate with him, he'd way misjudged her. Cooper T. had no one but himself to

19

Sandra Madden

blame for feeling peaked. "How did you get into the patent medicine business?" she asked.

"Sort of accidental."

"How long have you been drivin' from town to town, always on the move? Don't you ever get tired of all the travelin'?"

"No. I'm a rover. It's in my nature to see new places, meet new folks."

"And tell your poor innocent victims lies about Dr. Van Kurem's tonic—"

"Miss Applebee, I'm plum out of patience today—"

"Is it your hangover still botherin' you?" Matty asked cheerfully. Cooper Davis deserved his pain for what he'd done. What's more, he needed to take responsibility and make an honest woman of her sister. Unfortunately, apart from being a good-looking devil, he wasn't exactly prime stock.

Her sister could have made a better choice than to bed down with a drifter . . . a drummer who sold useless tonic to an unsuspecting public. A man with a fondness for whiskey and gambling just wasn't good enough for Phoebe.

"No, my hangover's not bothering me," the polecat answered after a spell. "You are, Matilda Rose."

"You can call me Matty."

"I can think of a dozen things I'd like to call you. Matty isn't one of them."

She ignored him. "Poor Phoebe. I hope she can train you into a good husband."

"Train me?"

"A man that drinks, plays cards, sells patent medicine, and takes advantage of innocent women is not exactly a prize, Cooper T."

Heaven Sent

He shot her a sidelong, narrow-eyed glance. "Can I be honest with you?"

"Of course." She doubted honesty ran in Cooper Davis's blood.

"You're right. Frankly, I'm not fit to be anyone's husband. Got adventure in my blood. Settling down doesn't hold any appeal for me. I'd rather die."

"And you might."

"How'd you get so stubborn, woman?"

"Everyone needs to settle sooner or later. A piece of land beneath your feet and a roof over your head will bring you to your senses."

"That's what women think."

"It's what we know."

"You're wrong, then. Dead wrong," he argued. "Look, lady. You aren't going to change me just to suit your purposes. I've been roamin' too long. I'm the man that mothers warn their daughters against."

"You'll like it once you get used to it."

"If your sister's gone and got herself in the family way, why don't you just send her back East to visit relatives?"

"We don't have any relatives in the East."

"In your case, one of a kind is probably a good thing," he muttered.

"Believe me, Cooper T., once you settle down on the Silver Star, you'll never want to roam again. Even if I were to travel the whole entire country, from coast to coast, I know there's nothin' more beautiful, nothin' better in the world. I've lived at the Silver Star Ranch all my life, and I'm never going to leave. It's a piece of paradise here on earth. You'll learn the truth about settling down soon enough."

"Never."

21

Sandra Madden

"What was that?"

"Just how long did it take you to reach San Juan after you left this paradise to track me down?"

"Five days, with good weather all the way. Billy Bowed-Legs is waiting at Peach Creek. He helped me find you."

She couldn't have trailed Davis without the help of Billy Bowed-Legs. Billy worked for her father as a wrangler, but he missed the old days when he rode as an outlaw rustler. Talking the old man into accompanying her hadn't been difficult.

Cooper's tone dripped with sarcasm. "Well, I'll certainly give Billy Bowed-Legs my personal thanks."

"I hope Daddy's not too mad," she said softly, talking more to herself than to the disgruntled man at her side. But even as she spoke, Matty knew her father would be livid. "I left a note for him, sayin' I had somethin' important to do. For Phoebe's sake, I didn't tell him what I was up to. Figure you'll be long hitched before she begins to show, and maybe Daddy will never know. It would pay you to stay on the good side of him."

"More'n likely your daddy's happy to have a few days without you chattering his ear off. If you don't mind, Miss Applebee, my head is aching something fierce. I'd appreciate it if you would reach under your seat and get me a bottle of tonic."

"Here you go."

"Thanks. Now then, I'd appreciate it even more if you would rest your tongue for a stretch."

"How long a stretch?"

"Until we reach Los Angeles. About four days."

"On top of everything else, you're insultin'."

A slow, crooked grin spread across Cooper T.'s face.

22

Heaven Sent

"I reckon if you can be still for three hours I'd be a happy man—and less insulting."

With a sniff of outrage and a sting of hurt, Matty tossed her head, tilting her chin to an extraordinarily high angle, even for her. Cooper T. Davis could suck green apples. She'd rather chat with an Apache. She wasn't about to talk to him.

"Tarnation!"

He hiked a mocking eyebrow. "Watch your language, Matilda Rose."

"Look at that, Cooper T.! Look at the sky. We're heading straight for a bad storm."

"Are you cursed, by any chance, woman?"

Chapter Two

Cooper took a long, hard study of the oncoming storm. The thick purple and black clouds rolling toward them didn't bode well.

"We can't turn back and hope to outrun the weather, so we'd better find a place to ride it out."

"Ride it out!" Matilda's extraordinary eyes widened, as if he'd just suggested a romp in the meadow.

"We'll rest a spell in that copse over there," he said calmly, turning the horses.

"No! We'll be hit by lightning." She clutched his arm, digging in her fingers with surprising strength.

Cooper figured she was scared to death and too proud to confess it. Well, he'd do his best to calm her nerves. A woman's nerves were fragile things. He could only imagine how much more she chattered when nervous. It gave him chills. He was a quiet man.

"We'll wait the storm out in the back of the wagon. The lightning won't get us," he told her.

Heaven Sent

Her eyes fixed on his, fiercely intense. "Turn back to town, Cooper. Hurry."

"Matilda Rose, how fast do you think this old wagon can go?" he asked in a soft voice. "It's a heavy load for the horses."

She let out a puff of steam. "I don't know how you talked me into riding this . . . this pitiful excuse for a wagon."

"In case you haven't noticed, ma'am, I have a way with words." Cooper shot her a teasing grin and tipped his hat back off his forehead.

But she remained unmoved and uncooperative. "Let's leave the wagon here and ride the horses back to town."

"Leave my wagon? This splendid drummer's wagon is my legacy. I'm not leaving it anywhere. Dr. Angus Van Kurem left it to me when he passed on to the great healing place in the sky. No, ma'am, I'm not leaving it. Not unless you're aiming to put a bullet between my ears."

"Don't tempt me, Cooper T." She folded her arms beneath her breasts. He could feel the anger seething under her skin. "I say we head back."

"I say *you* head back if you're of such a mind. Unhitch your pony back there and go."

"And let you escape? Forgit it. I'm not goin' back to town by myself," she said, slanting him a look that could kill fresh grass.

"Matilda Rose, although I'd like nothing better than to go on without you, I'm not leaving you alone in the wilderness. After the effort you made to find me, I feel responsible for delivering you safely to Billy Bowed-Legs. It's the least I can do. Besides, these storms never

Sandra Madden

last long. It'll pass in an hour or two and we'll be on our way."

"I don't like this," she grumbled.

"Then it's settled. We have all the comforts of home here in this old drummer's wagon. Plenty of room for the two of us in the back with the bottles of tonic and my provisions."

"No way I'd ever be comfortable in your company, Cooper T."

"How many times do I have to tell you? I am not a womanizer, a rake, a rogue, a rounder, a philanderer, or anything of the sort. You have nothing to fear from me. Why can't you believe me?"

"Why?" She rolled her eyes, as if she was dealing with a simpleton. "Because you're a man. And Phoebe never lies."

"Ah, yes. Of course."

If he wasn't careful, he'd be rolling *his* eyes soon. With a shrug of his shoulders and a shake of his head, Coop turned his mind to more pleasing thoughts. Before long, he would be enjoying a whiskey and a cigar in the back of the wagon. Smokes and his beverage of choice might be the only things he could look forward to until he ditched Matilda Rose and her bow-legged partner.

"I'll sit in the back of the wagon with you, Cooper. But if you so much as *try* to touch me, I'll kill you," she warned, narrowing her eyes and patting her rifle to stress her intent and assert her toughness.

She was beginning to get on his nerves. Never one to show his full hand, however, Coop gave her a grin. "Let me tell you something, Matilda Rose. I've never yet touched a body dressed in men's clothing."

She made that *harumphf* sound again.

Heaven Sent

"You can get in the back now," he told her, after pulling the wagon to a halt under a thick canopy of scarlet oak trees.

"First I have to see to Spirit, best I can," she said, jumping down before he could help her. It was quite a drop, but she landed on her feet.

The girl had gumption, he had to give her that. "Your horse has never been out in the rain before?"

She made a face at him. But at least she didn't roll her eyes. " 'Course she has."

"Just checking."

The rain started just as Cooper finished securing the wagon horses. He took off his old Stetson and knocked the rain off before hauling himself into the wagon. Closed against the elements, it was dark and cozy, he thought.

Already perched on a low wooden case on the opposite side of the wagon from him, Matilda Rose held the lantern, inspecting their quarters. Her wrinkled frown shrunk her forehead to half its natural size. And her eyes had gone as dark as mulberries in the rain.

"How do you like it?" he asked, knowing what her answer would be. "Comfortable, isn't it? And cozy."

"It's a mite cramped, Cooper. Appears you haven't sold much snake oil lately."

"Recently bottled a new supply from Van Kurem's secret recipe," he lied, hunkering down. He never actually peddled the tonic. He only sold it when someone asked, and he never guaranteed results.

Because of his height, Coop pretty much had to fold himself in half when he sat in the back of the wagon. "Now let me ask you a question: Does your daddy know you go around wearing men's clothes?"

"He knows. I handle the horses on the ranch, and

Sandra Madden

ride out after stray cattle. You can't do those things in a skirt."

Coop looked at her across the lantern she'd placed between them. The darn thing was low on oil. "Did it ever occur to you that as a woman you're not supposed to break horses and ride herd on cattle?"

"No."

"Of course not."

The wind howled through the trees and moaned against the wagon. It seemed each gust loosened boards, which clapped in a furious beat against the sides of the wagon. The light rain grew heavier, pelting the roof like hail.

"Are you sure it's safe in here?" Matilda Rose asked, scrunching herself up and wrapping her arms around her legs as a frightened little girl might.

Aiming to ease her fear, Cooper assured her with more confidence than he felt, "The quarters are a bit tight, I'll give you that. But the wagon is safe."

At that moment the heavens opened up. Heavy rain became a raging downpour and the wagon rocked from the impact of the rain and wind.

Eyes round as wagon wheels, Matilda Rose lifted her gaze to the roof. She held out her palm. Her brows knit together as she studied her hand. "Your wagon leaks!"

"Just in a few places," Coop soothed. "Now, how 'bout forgetting the weather for a while and having something to eat? Look in that barrel behind you."

Obviously unhappy, she narrowed her eyes on him. It was clear he was not winning her esteem. His eyes fell to her sulky mouth, lips moist and appetizing. If he kissed her, she might forget the storm, the leaks, the delay.

And she might make good on her threat to kill him.

Heaven Sent

Coop lowered his head and ran a hand through his hair.

Matilda Rose turned away.

Except for the rumble of thunder and the rain pummeling the roof, all was quiet while she rummaged in the barrel.

"Whiskey, jerky, and raisins," she reported with a wag of her head and a quick roll of her eyes. "Is this what you call fixin's for a meal, Cooper?"

"Emergency rations are what I call them. That's the finest jerky a man can buy. If you'd rather drink water than whiskey, you'll find good spring water in the small barrel."

Coop watched her surreptitiously. After taking only one bite she gave up on the jerky, and she barely nibbled at a handful of raisins. She'd finished before he'd begun.

"How'd you get shot? A jealous husband?"

"No. I told you it was an accident. You've got the wrong idea about me, Matilda Rose."

"Stop calling me that. Matilda Rose. It's like your makin' fun of me or something."

"What would you like me to call you?"

"Applebee or . . . Matty."

He nodded.

She yawned.

"Why don't you get some sleep? Take a little nap," he suggested. "You must have had a hard night, being there in my hotel room to wake me up before dawn this morning."

"Sleep? You expect me to go to sleep? Why, you'd just steal my rifle and run!"

"I told you I'd take you to wherever this Billy Bowed-

Sandra Madden

Legs is staked out. Whether you believe it or not, I'm a man of my word."

"The trouble is, you left Phoebe *without* a word."

Coop needed a smoke. "You've got a one-track mind, woman."

"If you leave me, I'll track you down. I found you once; I can do it again. I'll trail you to the ends of the earth. To San Francisco. Anywhere. 'Cause you're gonna make my sister an honest woman."

"I'd say that possibility already was a lost cause. A man can't make a woman honest who ain't."

Matilda Rose raised her rifle. "Don't you ever say a mean thing about Phoebe again."

Her loyalty to her lying sister was commendable, and frustrating. "Do you mind if I have my cigar now?"

"Yes, I mind. It's too close in here to smoke that smelly thing."

Coop wondered if her fiery spirit extended to the bed. If she was as much of a maverick in a man's arms, she might be worth fighting for. In the next heartbeat he chastised himself for entertaining such preposterous speculations.

"Matilda Rose, just say your prayers and go to sleep. Give my ears a rest."

"I'm gonna do it. But you've been warned." She scowled.

He nodded and scratched the back of his head. "I'm shaking in my boots over here."

Her *harumphf* was soft, but he heard it before she took off her hat and unleashed a mass of glorious chestnut hair. A thick tangle of silky curls, streaked with gold, fell past her shoulders.

And took his breath away.

He stared. Without her hat, Matilda Rose's face

Heaven Sent

seemed sweeter, her full lower lip more tempting. With her attitude, Coop doubted she'd ever been kissed. Maybe that was what the high-strung filly needed to tame her. A good loving.

"What are you lookin' at?"

"Nothing." Coop's fingers itched to wind their way through the soft curls gleaming in the lantern light. How could he tell her he wanted to feel a fistful of her hair in the palm of his hand? She'd shoot him.

"Just don't be lookin' at me that way."

He had an idea the *way* she meant was maybe a glint of lust caught in his eyes. He needed a distraction. Urgently. "If you'll pass the lantern, I'm going to read a book while you nap."

"Fuel's getting low in the lamp."

"There's more right . . ." He hadn't gotten the words from his mouth before the wagon plunged into darkness. A momentary lull in the storm caused everything to be quiet.

Except for Matilda Rose's soft giggle.

The storm stalled right over the drummer's wagon, lasting way longer than Cooper T. Davis had predicted. More exhausted than she cared to admit to her prisoner, Matty slept through most of it.

True to his word, the smooth-talking drummer did nothing to disturb her. Instead of being relieved, Matty awoke feeling a mild edge of irritation. He'd said he'd never touched a body in men's clothing. However, he didn't say he hadn't wanted to.

His gaze kept falling to her lips. And when Cooper T.'s eyes met hers with that piercing green gaze of his, Matty's stomach tumbled to her toes.

She hated herself for being disappointed that he

hadn't even tried to steal a kiss. What sort of horrid human being was she? Beyond his physical... vigor and twinkling eyes, he hadn't a thing to recommend him. She ought to be drowning in shame. Drawn to a lowlife drummer, the man she was taking back to marry her sister.

It promised to be a long trail ahead.

Cooper poked his head in from the rear of the wagon. "Horses are hitched. You want to ride back here, Matilda Rose, or up front—where you can keep an eye on me?"

"Right beside you. That's where I'll be ridin'."

Chuckling, he held out his arms to help her down.

"I can do it myself."

"Reckon you can, but it will be easier with my help."

Before she could protest further, his hands circled her waist, strong and warm. A bolt of heat surged like warm molasses through Matty before her feet touched the ground.

Struggling to retain her composure, she gave a little puff of indignation and marched to the front of the ugly old embarrassing conveyance Cooper called his legacy. She scrambled aboard before he could help her again. Sitting straight and prim on the bench, she settled her rifle beside her.

In just a matter of time, they would arrive at the cabin where Billy Bowed-Legs waited, where she could relax. With just a few more hours of sleep, Matty knew she could shake the raw restlessness gnawing at her innards. Since she'd never experienced the feeling before, she could only blame Cooper T. Davis and his lazy smile for her disconcerting state.

Billy waited for her in a cabin near Peach Creek, a mere two-hour horseback ride away. If it hadn't been

Heaven Sent

for the slow old contraption disguised as a drummer's wagon and the sudden spring storm, they would have been there by now. Billy would be worried about Matty for sure.

"Can't you make this hay wagon go any faster?"

"Disparaging remarks won't get us where we're going any sooner," he answered dryly, shooting Matty a wry grin. "Take a look at the scenery. Unless you're hankering to handle the reins."

"I'm not."

Back on the road overlooking the Pacific, the scenery was, indeed, magnificent. But Matty was convinced that nothing could compare with the acres of breathtaking beauty of the Silver Star Ranch.

She slanted a covert glance at Cooper. Wearing his hat down low, shading his eyes, he chewed a toothpick. No doubt about it, he was a good-looking man. Matty could almost understand why Phoebe had let him have his way with her. Even with a dark stubble of beard, the strong set of his jaw and the steady gaze of his eyes could stop an unwitting woman in her tracks.

Phoebe's innocence had led her astray. Fortunately, Matty knew far too much about Cooper T. Davis for her head to be turned. That slightly wicked grin of his would never melt her candle.

But she was spending too much time thinking about the man who sat beside her, indifferently invading her senses with an overpowering dose of male virility. As if he didn't know it! Some poor man had been passed over and Cooper T. had gotten twice his share of masculinity.

Thinking to divert her mind from what were surely devil-induced thoughts, she took out her harmonica.

Cooper snapped to attention. "What's that?"

Sandra Madden

"What do you think it is? A mouth organ. Billy taught me how to play."

Cooper's disapproving gaze went from the harmonica to her mouth and back again. "Are you planning to blow on that thing all the way to the mission?"

"Don't have anything better to do. Is there a tune you'd like to hear?"

He shook his head in the solemn manner of a man who'd just lost his best friend.

The sun was just about to set when they pulled up at the cabin on the outskirts of Mission Gabriel. Billy was nowhere to be seen.

"Billy! I've got 'im," Matty called as she jumped down from the wagon. "I've got Cooper Davis."

Relief and eagerness to see her old friend bubbled up within her as she ran into the cabin.

Billy lay asleep, dead still on the narrow bunk. Eager to share the triumph of her capture, she knelt down beside him. "Billy, wake up," she whispered. "I'm back, and I brought Cooper Davis with me. Billy?"

The grizzled old man with a nose tip in the shape of a walnut didn't stir. Matty shook him gently. "Billy, wake up."

He remained absolutely still. She brushed his cheek with the back of her hand. Cold. She gasped. The air whooshed from her lungs as if she'd been struck. Her heart screamed in agony. For a moment Matty could only stare as painful realization spread from her brain to her bones.

"Billy!" Numb with grief, she threw her arms across the man who had been like a dear uncle to her since she'd first learned to walk. "Wake up, Billy. Wake up!"

The next thing she knew, Cooper was beside her,

Heaven Sent

quietly urging her away from Billy Bowed-Legs's lifeless body. "Come on, Matilda Rose. Come away now."

"No, no, no." Fighting to hold back a woman's tears, she could not breathe. She felt as if she was suffocating, drowning in a dam of unshed sorrow.

"He's gone. Old Billy's passed," Cooper soothed in a hushed tone. Gently pulling Matty away, he wrapped an arm around her and guided her to a chair by the fireplace. "You sit a spell while I take care of things. We'll give him a decent burial. Don't you worry."

The next few hours passed in a haze of grief. Cooper dug a simple grave while she picked wild flowers by lantern light. He recited the Twenty-third Psalm with her. She played Billy's favorite song on her harmonica, "The Girl I Left Behind Me." Tears Matty could not control rolled down her cheeks. She didn't think she would ever be able to stop crying.

When the simple ceremony ended, Cooper led her back inside the cabin. "I'll get the fireplace going and fix you some tea."

"Did Indians kill him?"

"No. Looked like old age did Billy in. His heart just stopped. He would have waited for you if he could."

"It's my fault for insistin' he come with me. This is my doin'. He wouldn't be dead if I hadn't made him come."

"That isn't so. His time came and he happened to be out on the trail. Couldn't think of a better place for an old cowpoke to meet his maker."

"When my daddy was away from the ranch, which used to be a lot, I followed Billy around. He taught me most things I know."

"Where was your mama? Why wasn't she teaching you what a girl's supposed to know?"

Sandra Madden

"She ran off with an actor. I was five years old at the time. Phoebe was only three. I can hardly remember Mama, except for her blond, blond hair. Like summer sunshine, it was. Phoebe has Mama's hair."

"I'm sorry, Matilda Rose. That's bad luck—and a shame. A woman's not supposed to run off and leave her babies."

"Billy helped raise me, and I've tried to be a ma to Phoebe. Now Billy's gone and it's my fault." She couldn't hold back the fresh onslaught of tears. Matty buried her face in her hands and bawled like a baby.

Cooper came round and raised her to her feet. Limp and drained, she didn't have the energy to resist. He could have done anything with her. She felt his arms go around her. He rocked her, comforting her. Cradling her, he swayed very slowly from side to side.

"You go on and have a good cry, Matilda Rose. It's healthy to let your sorrow go. You don't want it tearing you up, penned up inside you like a wild mustang."

His arms were strong. She felt sheltered and safe, unashamed of her tears. With her head resting on his chest, she could hear the steady beating of his heart.

He smelled of leather and tobacco and man. The very real sound, smell, and feel of him gave her consolation. And she hated herself.

No matter what Cooper T. said, she had been responsible for Billy's demise, and now here she was in the arms of her sister's future husband.

She sobbed uncontrollably, hiccuping at regular intervals.

"I know what you need," Cooper said. "Don't know why I didn't think of it before. A couple of swallows of Dr. Angus Van Kurem's tonic will make everything seem almost right again."

Heaven Sent

After ushering her to the bunk, he dashed out to the wagon for the tonic. When he returned, she eyed the bottle doubtfully.

"I don't know, Cooper."

"Well, I do." He gave her a full-out grin and a wink of assurance. "A few swallows of Dr. Van Kurem's tonic and a good night's sleep is what you need."

"Just what's in this tonic?"

"Can't be disclosing the secret ingredients. Don't know you well enough yet," he teased. "Just drink it down."

Out of pure desperation Matty took a long swallow, hoping it would ease her heartache. The tonic tasted like a bitter combination of licorice, old hearth ashes, and wood alcohol. She gagged and sputtered out half the foul stuff.

"Maybe another swallow for good measure," Cooper coaxed. After she complied, too depressed to argue, he continued. "Now, I'm going to put my bedroll over there by the door so you don't have to worry about a thing. We'll get an early start for the Silver Star tomorrow."

Matty didn't remember much more after that until she woke the next morning.

Alone in the cabin.

She hurried to the door. The drummer's wagon and all the horses were still there. But where was Cooper?

Most likely off attending to nature's call, she thought, running a hand through her tangled hair. Lordy, she was a sorry mess. She needed a shampoo, a bath, and a change of clothes something fierce.

The bloodcurdling howl came while she stood in the doorway attempting to remember the direction of the creek.

Cooper's cry echoed through the hills.

Chapter Three

Matty ran toward the sound of Cooper's cry. No way was she going to let the man die before he married Phoebe. She was not over Billy Bowed-Legs's passing either. Not by a stretch. But before she fell asleep last night she'd thought about what he'd want her to do. She thought about Billy up in heaven watching over her like a guardian angel. A bearded, wrinkled, bow-legged angel.

The old cowboy would hate it if he caught her sobbing like a schoolgirl. She had to make him proud. The first way to do that was to single-handedly get their prisoner back to the Silver Star—just as she and Billy had planned to do.

But the prisoner sounded to be in trouble.

Hair loose and flying behind her, Matty scrambled up the bluff to the thick brush lining the embankment. From behind a row of prickly bushes, she heard the rush and trickle of Peach Creek. And Cooper moaning.

Heaven Sent

He lived.

"Cooper T.!"

"Here!" he shouted, his voice husky with pain.

The mile-high varmint lay near the wide, rushing stream—his left foot caught in the jaws of a steel trap. She ran down the embankment. Shirtless and braced on his elbows, he grimaced as he surveyed the bloody damage. Three small trout flopped on a string beside him.

"Tarnation, man! What have you done?"

"What does it look like?" he barked. "Got my foot caught in a damned fox trap."

Matty wanted to say something about him being outfoxed, but from all appearances he'd lost his sense of humor. She pushed her hair back with one hand.

"That looks mighty painful."

"Matilda Rise." He breathed heavily, speaking slowly and deliberately. "Go back and get my whiskey. I need some strength to get out of this damned thing."

"I can get your foot out of there. Billy Bowed-Legs showed—"

"Just once do as I ask without yammering about it!"

She recognized his pain, but he didn't have to snap at her. She wasn't responsible for this particular fix. The drummer definitely displayed displeasing tyrant tendencies, and was an arrogant sidewinder to boot.

If Phoebe's reputation weren't at stake, Matty might give up on Cooper T. here and now. Why should she bring back a man who sold snake oil for a living and growled like a mean old mountain cat to be her sister's husband? She answered her own question: because Cooper T. was better than no man for a woman in Phoebe's delicate condition.

"What are you waiting for?" he demanded. Despite

the cool morning air, perspiration beaded his forehead.

"Rest easy, Cooper T. I'll have you out of there and fixed up in no time. I'm not inclined to bring my sister back a wreck of a man."

"Go!"

When Matty returned, the reluctant bridegroom seemed to be breathing easier as he fiddled with the trap. He must have been bathing in the stream earlier while he did his fishing. His hair, wet and dark as a moonless night, was slicked back behind his ears.

"This will help," she said, pouring the contents of one of the bottles she had brought over his trapped ankle.

"What the hell?"

"Dr. Van Kurem's. It says right here on the label that it's good for tired blood, dyspepsia, rheumatism, cuts, bruises, and constipation. You're cut."

His eyes narrowed. "Where's my whiskey?"

She shook her head. "Hasn't it crossed your maverick mind that you drink too much of the stuff? Besides, you don't need it as long as we've got Dr. Van Kurem's patent medicine. As much as I hate to say it, the snake oil helped soothe me yesterday evenin'. Take a swig."

"It's not snake oil; quit calling it that."

After handing him a fresh bottle she sat on her heels and examined the damaged ankle. "This isn't the same leg as you got shot in is it?"

"Yes, it is," he replied tersely through his teeth.

"My, my, my. As it happens, for my twelfth birthday Billy Bowed-Legs gave me a gift that was meant for occasions like this. We'll have your ankle free in no time."

"No!" His eyes rounded in horror.

"What's wrong now?"

Heaven Sent

"Be careful with that knife, Matilda Rose. Be very careful."

"If it'll comfort you any, this isn't the first time I've worked with a Bowie. This old blade has come in handy through the years."

Matty waited 'til his shudder passed before starting to work.

If she didn't have to keep her eyes on the trap, she'd be staring at Cooper's chest. It wasn't as if she'd never seen a man's bare chest before. She had. Difference was, the cowboys on the ranch weren't built like Cooper T. Davis. The cowboy chests she'd been exposed to were either attached to flabby midsections or lean to the point where she could count their scrawny ribs.

Based on Matty's experience, limited to be sure, Cooper T. had a perfect chest. The broad muscular expanse narrowed down to a tight stomach and trim waist. And he didn't have so much body hair that a grizzly bear would sit up and roar with envy.

"Yeow!"

She'd sprung the trap open.

"Your ankle's free."

Cooper T. took a long haul on the bottle of tonic he held.

Matty bent closer, gently probing his ankle with her fingers to feel for any broken bones. "It's a little bloody down here. A mite raw," she reported. "But I reckon you'll be just dandy in no time." Whipping a neck scarf from her back pocket, she marched down to the stream just a few yards away. "I'll just clean up your ankle and you'll be right as rain."

He hadn't been right as rain for twenty years.

After Matty washed the wound she helped him to his feet. With one arm over her shoulder, he slowly hobbled back to the cabin. His thigh throbbed and his ankle stung like a wildfire burned in the bones. Meanwhile, the little woman supporting him, with no mind for his pain, chattered, too cheerfully, all the way to the cabin. She obviously thought his wounds would slow him down, make him easier for her to handle. Well, she was wrong about that too.

"Look at this beautiful blue sky, and the brush so new and green. It's a wonderful day for travelin'," she prattled. "I'll get you to a spot where you can put your foot up, and while you're restin', I'll cook those fish you caught this morning."

"Didn't figure on trappers. Just thought you'd like something better than jerky and raisins to eat."

"You thought right. That's why Billy and I brought some provisions with us. Beans, coffee, and bread are waitin' in the cabin—as well as rock candy."

"A feast," he said dryly.

She rolled her eyes, but this time she smiled. A light, soft smile that made his skin tingle. A smile that touched him almost as much as her tears of the night before, when he'd held her small body, wracked with sobs and hiccups, against his chest. Confronting her pain, his heart had squeezed up into a tight searing knot. Billy's untimely death had shattered her spunky front like fragile crystal. And Coop had been at a loss.

Matilda Rose Applebee was a contradiction. She confused him. When she'd examined his ankle, her fingers had been warm and gentle. For a few precious minutes the rifle-toting, swaggering cowgirl had been replaced by a sweet, nurturing woman. Or was he hallucinating?

He was grateful when they reached the cabin and he could finally rest on the bunk. Coop had his pride. De-

Heaven Sent

pending on a woman for support of any kind soured him. And she was only a little bit. He weighed twice as much as she did, if he didn't miss his guess.

He felt dumber than a mule for walking right into that trap. He should have known trappers would have an area near the creek staked out. He should have been more watchful.

Matilda Rose bustled around like a hen with too many chicks. She propped his leg up on a nest of blankets she'd made and offered him another bottle of tonic. "You might want more. It does dull the pain. At least pain of the heart."

Coop could tell by her frown, by the shadow that darkened her eyes, she was thinking of her friend Billy. "If I finish that bottle, we aren't going to be doing any traveling today," he pointed out.

"It's got alcohol in it, doesn't it? The snake oil?"

"A little," he admitted.

"A lot. But never mind, I have coffee brewin'. And besides the provisions we brought, there's a clean shirt in my saddlebag. So while you're dealin' with the pain and feelin' a little woozy—"

"Are you trying to make me feel worse?"

"Why would I do that?" she asked with a smile a bit too bright for Coop's liking. "Anyway, while you're laid up and can't be sneakin' a peek, I'm goin' down to the stream and take me a bath."

"Whatever gave you the idea I'd want to sneak a peek?"

"You're a man," she declared, giving a soft *harumphf* before marching out.

She was right. Coop would have sneaked a peek if he could. He'd give every silver dollar in his saddlebag to see what lay beneath that buttoned-up shirt and

43

baggy trousers. A man couldn't help but wonder when tallying her obvious attributes. Her lavender-blue eyes—eyes that apparently could read into his mind. Her sweet, saintly face—her most misleading feature. In Coop's mind it only stood to reason Matilda Rose possessed a body to make a strong man weep.

But she wasn't the kind of woman you loved for a night and walked away from. Oh no, not without risking a bullet in your back. And he didn't care for the kind of woman who masqueraded in the clothing of man. Not that he'd met all that many.

Coop liked women who were proud to be women. Women who weren't afraid of sharing themselves for a mutually satisfying time. He'd never stayed in one place long enough to promise a woman his forever and he never intended to settle down. Roving was in his blood. Angus Van Kurem had seen to that.

He pretended to be asleep when Matilda Rose returned and nosily began to prepare breakfast. Pots and pans banged and whomped. After a while the aroma of coffee and frying fish made his stomach gurgle and his mouth salivate.

"Are you ever going to finish cooking that breakfast?"

"Just about done," she replied, adding a soft *harumphf.*

"I heard that."

"Get up here to the table."

"I thought you might feed me in my bunk, like a real nursing woman would."

"Never been a nurse except to a couple of colts."

She'd tied her thick mass of wet chestnut hair back with a wide crimson ribbon. Her clean clothes were no more revealing than what she'd worn before. She'd

Heaven Sent

dressed in a man's light blue workshirt, laced at the neck, and loose-fitting dark blue trousers. A less observant man might forget she was a woman. Her choice of getup could easily discourage the average cowboy.

"You smell good," Coop told her.

"It's essence of rose . . . soap. It does smell real good, doesn't it?"

He nodded. "Like a blooming flower."

She might not look like one, but at least she smelled like a woman now.

"I would have let you borrow my soap, Cooper T., if you'd have woke me before you went to the stream this morning."

"I wanted to surprise you with breakfast and show you what a good-hearted man I am. Not the devil you take me for."

"You'd have to do a lot more than make me breakfast to prove you're a good Samaritan."

"Yeah," he acknowledged ruefully. "Pretty foolish of me to think I could win your heart with fresh fried fish."

She smiled at that. And then got serious as she dug into her breakfast. "The only heart you've got to think about winning is Phoebe's."

"Not interested."

"For the baby's sake."

"What baby?"

Matilda Rose lowered her eyes and let out a long sigh. He couldn't tell if her sigh signified that she'd given up on his feeble mind or that she regretted she wasn't the one to be marrying him.

"Yours and hers," she said quietly. "It's bound to be a comely young 'un . . . what with Phoebe's looks," she added hastily.

Sandra Madden

"What's it gonna take to convince you that you've got the wrong man?"

"Hearin' it from my sister's lips."

Cooper would bet the wagon that wasn't going to happen in the next hundred years. He groaned. No use arguing with a hardheaded woman. He wasn't about to sweet-talk this stubborn little female into reason. Instead, he offered a compliment as she wolfed down her breakfast. "This is mighty good. Best coffee I ever drank."

"Billy showed me camp cookin'."

"He taught you well. He must have been a good man."

"The best. I said some prayers by his grave after my bath." She raised her eyes to his, regarding him intently. "Thank you for what you done for Billy last night."

"No thanks necessary. I'd want someone to do the same for me."

She nodded, and swallowed hard. "He always looked after me, and now he's up there doin' the same job."

For a fleeting, disconcerting moment Coop wondered if Matilda Rose was going to start praying to Billy Bowed-Legs. "I reckon. Everyone needs someone to look out for them."

The way her eyes grew all misty, he figured she was fighting back tears. Because he didn't know if he could handle her crying again, he chose to distract her. "We might be able to make it to Canton today."

She gave a sad wag of her head. "It's a half a day's ride from here. At least it was for Billy and me. But we had no patent medicine wagon painted with plump little cherubs to slow us down."

"I'm just as interested in making time as you are,

Heaven Sent

Matilda Rose. Like I told you, I have to be in San Francisco by month's end. My job is more or less on the line, and the director's gonna be there."

"Why's your job on the line?"

"Haven't been making my quotas recently. Think maybe I'm bored. I'm wanting a transfer to the railroads. Jesse James and his gang are holding up the trains and robbing folks faster than a man can blink. That's the kind of adventure a detective like me needs. A big capture."

"A detective? Are you tryin' to tell me you're a detective?"

"Yes."

"No. Do you think I was born in a barn?" Matty obviously didn't believe him for a minute. "Like *I* said, you're comin' with me to the Silver Star, where you're gonna marry Phoebe Pearl and light a spell."

"You can't make me—"

"Maybe then you can be on your way. Phoebe might not want to keep you. And my daddy might not favor the idea of you being a drummer. He might send you on your way once you've made an honest woman of my sister," she added.

"I am not a drummer."

"Why are you drivin' a drummer's wagon then? If a bird has feathers, waddles, and quacks like a duck—that bird's a duck."

"Besides being my legacy, my inheritance from Angus, the wagon's good cover for a detective."

"What were you doin' down by the border? Plannin' to slip away?"

He hung his head. It was his most embarrassing assignment to date. "I was on the trail of a bigamist."

"Did you catch him?"

Sandra Madden

"Crossed into Mexico before I could catch up. But who am I fooling?" He paused and shrugged. "My heart wasn't in the chase. I can't get worked up about a man who's married one too many women. Not the way I can about going after the James gang."

She gazed across the table at him as if he was daft to even think she would believe a thing he said. "How did you meet Dr. Van Kurem? Were you after him too?"

"No. He hired me on as his helper when I was just a boy."

"How old?"

Damnation, the woman was nosy! But he knew the next few days on the trail would go easier if he told her what she wanted to know. Whether she believed him or not was another matter.

"Ten years old."

"And your ma and pa let you go with him?"

"I had nobody. I was an orphan. Angus was a mite frugal, but he gave me a good life. I slept in the wagon as we traveled from town to town, and had three squares to eat every day. Maybe that's why I can't settle down now. Been traveling for so long. I'm curious about what's around each bend in the road."

"If you had a real home, you'd feel different."

"Can't imagine being tied to one place. It would be like being behind bars . . . in prison."

She shot him a sly little smile, her eyes sparkling with a potentially enchanting light. "Oh, I reckon you'll like being married to Phoebe better than bein' behind bars."

"I'm not a marrying man."

Her smile faded and Matilda Rose nodded, all serious again. "We'll just see about that."

"Yes, we will." What would it take to convince her

that he would have to be gagged, drunk, and hogtied to marry a woman he didn't even know?

"What happened to Angus?" she asked.

"He raised me 'til I set off on my own at sixteen. I always knew where he was, and I visited on a regular basis. Helped him out. He died a year ago. Just keeled over like Billy Bowed-Legs. Sudden and without pain is better than wasting away for old men who've lived good lives."

"You're right about that, I suppose." She raised her eyes as if she expected to see Billy Bowed-Legs floating above on angel wings.

"The old doctor left me the wagon."

She pushed out her chair and stood up. "You tell a good story, Cooper T."

"I work for the Pinkerton Agency out of San Francisco."

"You really expect me to believe such hogwash?"

"It's the truth. I'm a Pinkerton detective."

"And I'm Susan B. Anthony."

His ankle ached without letup, piercing pain shot through his wounded thigh at regular intervals, but Coop took the reins and drove the wagon. The three mounts were hitched behind.

Streaks of creamy clouds slashed across the brilliant blue sky and a gentle breeze cooled the air just right for traveling. Now and then you could see a glimpse of the ocean, splashing against the rocks below.

Matty played her harmonica. "Would you like to hear 'The Streets of Laredo,' Cooper T.?"

"No, can't say as I would. As a matter of fact, I'd like to listen to the birds and the bees for a while. If you

Sandra Madden

can hold yourself back from playing that mouth organ, I'd truly appreciate it."

Playing the harmonica made her feel closer to Billy, but she put her instrument aside and stared ahead at the long, empty road. She knew Cooper T. was in pain. The old thigh wound and the fresh trap bite had to be hurting. But she had to give him credit; the drummer didn't bellyache. He just snapped like an old turtle.

After seeing her prisoner's bare chest this morning and feeling a strong inclination to reach out and touch it, Matty was more aware of his body than the day before. She was more aware of the powerful heat radiating from him as he brushed against her, and the scent of his own dangerous essence. An essence more potent and memorable than rose soap.

By dusk, they'd reached the outskirts of town. Cooper T. looked a bit gray about the face, but Matty figured he'd be all right after a night's rest in a hotel bed. Oh, tarnation.

"Cooper T.!"

"What?"

"We're gonna have to share one room tonight. Much as that disturbs me, I can't take the chance of you up and leavin' me here. Now that Billy's gone, I'm gonna single-handedly have to keep a close eye on you."

"How could you keep a closer eye? Didn't we share a room last night, in a manner of speaking? Did I make any ungentlemanly moves? Did I jump you then, when my ankle was good?"

"No . . ." She rolled her eyes. "But I was grievin'. Just remember, seein' as how Billy is up there watchin' over me, he's watchin' what you do too."

"I'll try not to forget that."

"See that you don't."

Heaven Sent

"Matilda Rose, I told you I'd take you to the gates of the Silver Star Ranch and deliver you safe and sound. I meant with your virginity in tact."

"Cooper T.!" she gasped in shock. Except for Phoebe Pearl, no one had ever spoken the word *virginity* aloud in her company before.

"But I am *not* staying to marry Phoebe," he continued, seemingly oblivious to her reaction. "I'm telling you for the last time, I don't know the woman."

"You might not know what she likes to eat or play on the pianoforte, but you know my sister all too well . . . in the biblical sense."

He lowered his head and groaned.

But Matty paid no mind. She had her eye on something else. "What's that movin' . . . that big cloud of dust up ahead?"

The unhappy drummer lifted his head, squinting into the horizon. "Pack of horses. Maybe a posse."

But it wasn't a posse. Matty held her breath as, minutes later, the wagon was surrounded by five men. Her heart pounded as if it were preparing to fly from her chest.

When the dust settled, she could see the men all wore neck scarves secured over their noses to hide their identity. And they all held pistols aimed at her and Cooper.

"Tarnation!" she whispered under her breath. "What now?"

She glanced over at Cooper T., who didn't reply . . . he only rolled his eyes.

Chapter Four

"Let me do the talking," Coop warned under his breath, as the men waved their pistols menacingly.

"But—"

"Not a word, Matilda Rose."

The gang surrounding the wagon looked tough, and smelled the same. Coop figured none of the five had bathed in days. Only their eyes showed above bandana masks, dark eyes, light eyes, small, average-sized, and squinty eyes.

All five senses were on high alert as Coop forced a hard smile. "Howdy, gentlemen."

"Throw down whatever you got of value."

The order was given by a cowboy who sat tall in the saddle and wore round wire-rimmed glasses. When he removed his hat to wipe the sweat from his brow, he revealed a shock of red-orange hair that would stand out in any crowd. The bandit leader's carelessness took

Heaven Sent

Coop by surprise. Round-rim glasses and a carrot-top mop of hair would make the crook easily identifiable in the future.

Coop shook his head. "Not much of value, I'm afraid."

But Carrot-Top ignored him, issuing further orders to his gang. "Mule and Bud, get back there to the rear and search the wagon."

"Not much in the wagon either," Coop drawled. "You're welcome to a case of Dr. Van Kurem's, though."

The bandit grunted in disdain and redirected the aim of his revolver from Coop's head to his heart.

"Trust me, it isn't that bad."

The leader of the ragtag band of villains remained unmoved.

But not the little lady who sat beside Coop. He should have known Matilda Rose's continued silence was too good to hope for. "What are you bein' so all-fired polite about?" she demanded, flashing an angry sidelong glance.

Before he could answer, she jumped to her feet, clutching her rifle. "You're nothin' but big bullies," she lashed out, giving Carrot-Top and his men a pint-sized put-down. "Why don't you just move on and pick on someone your own size?"

"Put a bridle on it," Coop growled without moving his lips.

The smallest bandit, who resembled a scarecrow in height, stature, and haircut, laughed. "Could we take the gal with us, Josh? She's a high-spirited filly, she is."

With a soft gasp, Matilda Rose sat back down on the wagon bench, closer to Coop than she'd ever come before. Her eyes were wide and unnaturally bright.

Sandra Madden

Coop couldn't do much to comfort her at the moment, but he made a mental note that Carrot-Top's name was Josh. This might possibly be the dumbest bunch of bandits he'd run into since he'd become a Pinkerton.

"No," Josh snarled. We're not takin' the woman. That's just askin' for trouble."

"You're right about that," Coop offered. "This woman's been nothing but trouble since the day I met her."

He felt her body stiffen.

Carrot-Top Josh nodded sagely. "Knew it. Now back off, Luke."

"What's yer name, woman?" Luke asked, undeterred.

"None of your business," she hissed.

"Is that right? Well, I'm jest gonna make it my business." Luke moved a leg to dismount, his dark bushy brows gathered in an ominous frown.

"Matty . . . my name is Matty." Her voice broke as she spoke her name the second time. She inched closer to Coop until she pressed against him, until he could feel her warmth and smell the faint sweet aroma of roses.

Giving a curt nod, Luke, the scarecrow bandit, settled back in his saddle. "That's better. Don't take to no woman sassin' me."

Coop stole a glance from the corner of his eye. This was the first time Matilda Rose had given any indication that she wasn't as brave as she pretended. But she gave a good show. Her chin stuck up at a defiant angle, and stiff as a stick, one hand still rested on her rifle. She'd balled the other into a fist on her lap. Her eyes

54

Heaven Sent

were raised to the sky. Probably praying for divine intervention—from Billy Bowed-Legs.

The little hellion's attempt to conceal her obvious apprehension unexpectedly tugged at Coop's heart. He laid a hand across her balled-up fist and felt her trembling. She did not make a move to push him away. With his free hand, he withdrew a pouch from his shirt pocket.

"This is all I have," he said, tossing the pouch of coins to the ever-vigilant Carrot-Top thief. "Didn't sell much of the medicine at the last stop."

"Don't expect to sell much at yer next stop neither. That town is smaller than spit," he grumbled, counting Coop's coins.

"Sorry to hear that. Especially considering you're taking all that's left of our money."

"Yeah? What about you, woman? You got any money? You can hand it over or I can let Luke search yer body."

Without a word, Matilda Rose withdrew a small velvet pouch from the pocket of her trousers and threw it to the ground. "It's all I got," she mumbled, tight-lipped and sullen.

"My Mary would like the gal's boots." The fifth, and up until now silent, bandit spoke up. Overweight by at least thirty pounds, the husky cowboy-gone-wrong was sweating profusely, as was his horse.

Coop had noticed the chunky villain had been staring at Matilda Rose's lizard boots for a long time. He'd begun to worry the no-account had some kind of fetish.

The two thugs who'd been sent to search the back of the wagon returned. "Nothin' back there worth any money."

Coop nodded. "Told you so,"

Sandra Madden

"Can't carry snake oil," Josh muttered.

"Even they think it's snake oil," Matilda Rose bristled.

"But you can have the boots, Clyde." Carrot-Top scowled at Matilda Rose. "Take off your boots and pitch 'em down here."

She grabbed Coop's arm with a life-or-death grip, forcing him to look down into those angry, frightened, magnificent lavender-blue eyes. "I don't have another pair of boots with me, Cooper T. Tell these varmints they can't have my boots," she hissed under her breath.

"Precious, take off your boots and toss them down to the nice men so they will go on their way and we can be on ours," he replied quietly, with more patience than he possessed.

"And travel all the way home barefoot?"

"This is not a good time to argue."

"That's 'cause they don't want *your* boots," she bit back. Her eyes glittered with hostility.

"Is there a problem, lady?" Josh growled.

"No, no problem," Coop assured him. He lowered his voice. "Matilda Rose, I will get you a pair of new boots in town. We're thirty minutes away from Canton. You can go barefoot for thirty minutes."

She raised her chin belligerently. "These boots don't come off easy."

"I'll help you."

Matilda Rose closed her eyes and bit down on her bottom lip. The band of unwashed thieves snickered and chuckled, as if they were watching a show. But Coop ignored them all as he wriggled and pulled on the lizard boots until they slid off.

"Henpecked," Clyde noted with satisfaction.

Heaven Sent

"The little woman gots yer wrapped around her finger," Luke half snarled.

But Josh hurled the final insult. "Must say, it was hardly worth our time, stoppin' you, drummer dude."

Head drooping, eyes lowered, Matilda Rose stared at her stockinged toes. Coop caught a glimpse of misty eyes when he handed her smart lizard boots over to the round, grinning Clyde.

"Good luck in Canton. You're gonna need it," Josh called as the sorry bunch of ruffians rode away.

Cupping Matilda Rose's chin in his hand, Coop gently lifted her head, gazing directly into her amazing eyes. Dark mulberry eyes, filled with sadness at the moment. "Don't worry. I'll see to it that you have new boots within the hour."

"They took all our money. How you gonna buy boots now?"

"What kind of detective do you think I am? Knowing how to outsmart the bad guys is what keeps me alive. I have a secret stash of coins hidden in back."

His revelation seemed to reassure her, and she settled back, staring at her bootless feet, wiggling her toes.

Henpecked? Wrapped around her finger? Coop sure had the sorry gang fooled if that's what they thought. Of course, those men were dumber than a duffer.

Canton's main street consisted of five ramshackle wooden buildings and a wide, dry dirt road. As they rumbled into town the horses kicked up more sand and dirt than could be found in the entire Mojave, Coop figured. Matty choked and coughed beside him.

Once a boom town, the dismal spot had fallen on hard times five or so years earlier and had become just a stop on the road. Mayor Eli Canton predicted a rebirth of his town before the end of the decade. He was alone in his thinking.

The Canton general store, the only store in town, carried only one pair of ready-made boots. Cooper T. bought them.

"They're two sizes too big," Matty complained.

"We'll find something to stuff inside and fill the empty space."

"How am I gonna walk like that?"

"We're ridin', remember?"

"How could I forget! If we hadn't been ridin' on that contraption you call a wagon, we wouldn't have been stopped by that smelly gang of bandits. If we had been on horseback, they never would have caught us."

"They didn't get all our money, did they?"

"They got all of mine," Matty grumbled. Bringing Cooper T. back to the Silver Star became more of a challenge every day. More trouble than she'd reckoned at the start. But she'd do whatever she had to do to save her sister's name.

Concentrating on keeping the oversized boots on her feet by curling her toes, Matty silently hobbled down the dusty street alongside her captive companion.

It wasn't much to see. She and Billy Bowed-Legs had only passed through Canton on the lookout for Cooper T. But the small town didn't give a body any reason to stop. Matty expected Canton would be a ghost town in a few years.

"Don't you worry about money. I've got enough for both of us, Matilda Rose."

"I don't want your money."

He grinned down at her. "Consider it a loan."

Depending on her prisoner was truly irritating. Made her feel mean-spirited and cranky. She looked for

Heaven Sent

something to cheer her. "At least they didn't get Billy Bowed-Leg's ring."

"His ring?"

"Billy's most prized possession." She'd looped the golden nugget on a string and hung it around her neck. The ring fell snugly between her breasts. "He won it in a rodeo."

"Where are you keeping it?"

She patted her chest.

He hiked an eyebrow. "There?"

She nodded solemnly.

His gaze focused on the area of her breasts. She flushed.

"Close to my heart," she explained.

After a few long, silent moments, Cooper raised his eyes to hers and shrugged. "Seems safe enough. Now let's get something to eat and a place to sleep. Got to send a telegram to the home office and let them know I'm on my way to San Francisco."

"Hold on. Not so fast! You're on your way to the Silver Star Ranch. Nothin's happened yet to change that."

"Right. San Francisco by way of the Silver Star Ranch."

She rolled her eyes. She'd never met a more stubborn man. Poor Phoebe was gonna have her hands full with Cooper T. "Where's the hotel?"

"Well, now," he drawled, "Canton doesn't have a real hotel."

"What do they have? Billy and I just watered our horses and rode through. We didn't see much."

"That's because there's not much to see. I'm partial to one establishment that serves vittles and rents beds. Right here, Bridget's Irish Emporium." He swooped an arm toward the two-story wooden building with swinging doors. "Proprietress, Bridget O'Brien."

Doubtful she was going to approve of Cooper T.'s choice, Matty followed him through the swinging doors. Once inside, she immediately identified the inn as a saloon.

Dust from the street mingled with sawdust on the floor. In a scattered fashion, several bulletholes nicked the wood paneling. A variety of names—some rude—had been carved into the long bar. She could barely see her reflection through the film of dirt coating the mirror behind the bar. And one whiff of the musty odor mingled with strong whiskey could send a faint heart into a swoon.

No one needed to tell Matty that the girls who lounged at tables around the room played more than the piano; and the rooms were often rented by the hour.

She turned on her heel, ready to leave, when a tall, big-boned, amply endowed woman sashayed out from the back. "Coop!"

"Bridget O'Brien! My favorite Dublin lass," Cooper T. boomed in greeting.

While Matty watched, Bridget welcomed Cooper T. with open arms. Some might consider the Irish proprietress a pretty woman. Her thick mass of dark curls had been swept to the top of her head and seemed to be anchored by the big red ribbon perched there. Fair-skinned and heavily rouged, the woman in the fancy low-cut red dress hugged and kissed Matty's prisoner as if he were some kind of returning hero.

Matty's blood boiled. Did Cooper T.'s tall, muscular figure and lazy smile blind women to his character flaws? He chuckled with pleasure as Bridget's girls

Heaven Sent

flocked around him. Just like a rooster in a henhouse. She expected him to crow any minute.

"Ma'am." Matty tapped Bridget on the shoulder, forcing the woman to stand back from Cooper T. "Ma'am, we're here to rent a room and get some dinner."

Bridget's deep blue gaze bounced off Matty right back to Cooper T. "Is the little cowgirl with you?"

Cooper T. grinned, pulling Matty to his side. "Yes, she is. A ways back Matilda Rose lost her escort. I'm taking her safely home."

"I'm taking Cooper T. Davis back to the Silver Star," Matty corrected him quickly.

Coop shot her a condescending smile. "We need a place to stay for the night."

"One room, so I can keep an eye on him," Matty added.

Bridget snickered. "I know what you mean, honey. I'd keep an eye on Coop too if I was travelin' with him."

Matty's stomach constricted. She knew she shouldn't judge on first impressions. But she did. And she didn't like Bridget O'Brien at all. The Irishwoman had a lilting accent, big breasts—that she flaunted shamelessly—and a narrow waist. She was a bold hussy, to boot, batting her eyes and pawing Cooper T. like he was made of gold.

"We can sleep on the trail if you don't have a room for us," Matty declared, hands on hips, out of patience.

"Oh, but I do. Follow me."

The stairs squeaked as Matty and Coop followed Bridget to what she claimed was the finest room in the house.

The fine room was similar to the closet Matty had

found Cooper T. bunked in at the start of all this back in San Juan Capistrano.

Overlooking the street, the room boasted one bed covered with a faded quilt. Three hooks, two kerosene lanterns, tattered curtains, and a washstand with a small cracked mirror above it comprised the furnishings. The sketch of a beautiful—but naked—female angel hanging by the bed added a homey touch.

"Make yourself at home," Bridget purred, flirting wildly with Cooper T. "Supper will be ready shortly."

Matty breathed a sigh of relief when Cooper at last closed the door behind the Emporium's proud proprietress.

"This is what I get for ever leavin' the Silver Star," she muttered. She reckoned she'd get scraps for her meal while Cooper T. ate steak.

"What are you mumbling about, Matilda Rose?"

"You wouldn't understand."

"Not much I've understood about you so far," he agreed cheerfully. "While you freshen up, I'm going out to the telegraph office. Is there anything you want?"

"What would I want? We already know you can't git anythin' in this town," she snapped impatiently. " 'Sides, you aren't goin' anywhere without me."

"Matilda Rose, do you think I'm going to make a fast getaway on my wagon? If I'm not back in thirty minutes, you can come after me and catch me in a hurry."

"That's true." Tired and disheartened, she could use some time alone. "But be back in thirty minutes."

He winked as he left.

She longed to sink into a bathtub but settled for a lukewarm hand bath, using her rose-scented soap. Feel-

Heaven Sent

ing almost human again, Matty brushed and plaited her hair in one long thick braid.

Being with Cooper T. took a lot out of a woman. She could bite the sights off a six-shooter, her nerves stretched so tight. But she couldn't afford to let her guard down. Cooper T. posed danger either way, escaping or staying.

Almost to the minute he said he'd return, the door opened and the drummer strode through. Grinning from ear to ear, green eyes twinkling, he was as handsome as any man Matty's eyes had ever rested upon. Her heart thumped unnaturally fast.

"Wait'll you see what I found for you." He brought his hands from behind his back and brought out a pair of black leather slippers.

"Slippers! Where did you find them?"

"Never mind. Just sit down and let's try them on your feet."

Matty perched on the edge of the bed. Slippers weren't boots and couldn't protect her feet or do the same work in the saddle that boots could, but they sure were comfortable, and these fit as if they were made for her. Looking down, she held her feet out and wiggled her toes. The black kid slippers felt soft and enclosed her feet like a worn glove. She leaned closer. They were worn. They definitely looked used.

"Where did you get these, Cooper T.?"

"Looked Bridget's girls over 'til I found one with feet your size. As it happened, Annie just received them from mail-order. They've hardly been walked in."

Matty rolled her eyes.

Looking Bridget's girls over was a job he no doubt enjoyed. "And she just gave her slippers to you?"

"Not exactly."

63

Sandra Madden

He'd paid for them! "I'll see you get everything I owe you when we get to the Silver Star, Cooper T."

The crooked, wry smile he aimed at her caused a quick shiver to run up and down her spine. "I'll be counting on that, Matilda Rose."

My, oh my, my, my. He was a dangerous man. Matty quickly lowered her eyes from his devastating smile to gaze stoically at her feet. "Strumpet slippers."

"Your feet won't know the difference."

"Reckon you're right about that. Th . . . thank you."

Casting her a mocking smile, Cooper T. bowed down low. "My pleasure."

Feeling faintly confused, she turned away. "Right now, I'd better get somethin' in my stomach before I pass out."

"And . . . I found you something for after supper."

Curious, Matty spun back to him.

He winked and withdrew a small sack from his shirt pocket.

Wary, she opened the package slowly. What she saw made her mouth water. "Oooooh."

"Do you like them?"

"Rock candy and gumdrops are my favorites." How had he known?

"Good. Enjoy them."

"I . . . I will." Matty wasn't used to getting presents and didn't know how to accept what she was loathe to admit appeared to be his generosity, his thoughtfulness. "Hope they don't make me fat."

"It hasn't been an especially good day . . . or two. I hoped having the candy and slippers might bring a smile to your face. You've got a real pretty smile, Matilda Rose."

She knew what he was doing now! He was buttering

Heaven Sent

her up, so he could wear her down. So she'd let him go. She knew what the wily drummer was up to. But a rooster never bested a fox. Raising her gaze to his fine laughing eyes, she smiled. Nothing wrong in letting him think he was winning her over. He was underestimating her again. Something he no doubt would regret.

Matty was forced to take small soft steps when she and Cooper T. went downstairs to dinner. Striding briskly as she usually did proved impossible wearing strumpet slippers. It didn't feel right.

The nice supper Bridget promised consisted of thick hunks of beef that had only been passed briefly over a fire. A heaping mound of baked beans and fresh baked bread completed the meal.

Bridget and her three girls hovered constantly, always asking if he needed something more, something else.

"When are these girls going to leave you alone so you can eat?" Matty huffed during a minute alone.

"They're just lonesome for new company."

"Are they what I think they are?"

"And what is that?" he asked drolly.

"Strumpets," she whispered, seeking confirmation.

"Would I put you in such notorious company?"

She nodded. "Yes, you would."

"You wound me, Matilda Rose. You really do. Just be grateful I found us a place where we can afford to eat a filling meal and enjoy a bed to sleep in tonight."

She shook her head and silently asked Billy Bowed-Legs to give her strength—if he was anywhere close by watching.

Cooper T. ate with a hearty appetite. Matty pushed

Sandra Madden

the food around on her plate, dreaming of rock candy and gumdrops.

After serving steaming mugs of coffee and bread pudding, Bridget sat down with them. "So will you be havin' cards and whiskey with us tonight, Coop?"

"You bet."

"No."

Bridget shot Matty a disapproving frown. "Just who are you, lass? Why are you dressed in men's clothes? And what are you doing with Coop?"

"I'm Matty Applebee from the Silver Star Ranch just north of Santa Barbara. My clothes are comfortable and cover my body. So no man can be gawkin'—"

"Honey, it ain't so bad to have a man gawkin'," Bridget interrupted with a laugh. "That's what you want a man to do."

"Says you." *An adventuress, a harlot,* Matty added to herself. "I'm bringin' back Cooper T. to marry my sister."

"Marry?" The color drained from Bridget's face. The Irish saloon owner looked as if she was going to faint dead away. "Is that true, Coop? You going to get married?"

"Matilda Rose is a bit confused," he explained. "I'm traveling along to the ranch in hopes of straightening things out with her sister—who is also confused."

Bridget fanned herself. "Didn't suppose you were a marryin' man."

Matty narrowed her eyes. "We're gonna straighten things out real good . . . for Phoebe's sake."

"Phoebe?"

Cooper T. scratched the back of his neck. "Her sister, the prevaricator."

"Harumphf!"

Heaven Sent

He leaned toward Matty with a quirk of his lips. "Does that mean you're ready to retire to our room, precious?"

Since when had he started calling her precious? Just another way to rile her. No man in her experience had ever riled her so easily, had been able to cause such prickly feelings . . . akin to being stuck in the stomach with cactus.

Then he grinned. A smile as broad as a buffalo's back, blinding as the sun glinting on a gun barrel.

A woman with less fortitude might fall into the vapors at the sight of that smile. But not Matty. Beyond a momentary weakening of the knees she felt nothing.

She looked him dead square in the eye. "I am good and ready."

Once in the room, Coop could hardly wait to get back downstairs. As soon as Matilda Rose was bedded down, he'd return. He deserved a good cigar, a whiskey, and a couple of poker games.

Bridget looked pretty good to him tonight too. Though she'd offered herself to him at no charge in the past, he'd never taken her up on her Irish hospitality. Tonight he felt just edgy enough to do it. He'd been with the poor man's Calamity Jane two days too long, he figured. Matilda Rose had him all on edge.

"I'll take the bed, and you can lay your bedroll by the door like you did before," she announced.

"Do I ever get a turn at the bed?" he grumbled. "I'm getting mighty tired of sleeping on the floor."

"You're my prisoner."

"How could I forget? Just remember, I haven't officially surrendered yet."

"I'll make a note," she said, munching on gumdrops.

"Maybe I'll just sleep in the wagon tonight."

She stopped chewing. "Then I will too. It would disturb me somethin' awful to wake up and find you long gone."

"The only time you're going to find me gone is when we reach the gates to your ranch," he said, just barely controlling his aggravation. "Then I'll be gone in a flash. Until then, understand this: I will not abandon you."

"Can't trust anything you say," she pouted. "That was Phoebe's mistake."

She plunked to the edge of the bed and began to undo her long thick braid. Sun-streaked strands of her silky hair glinted in the lantern light.

"Never mind. I'll sleep here," he said, giving in to the innocent, vulnerable girl he glimpsed now and then. Gazing at her hair, he wondered how it would feel if he were to untwine the thick shiny plait. He shook off the strange thought. "But first I'm heading downstairs for a night of entertainment."

"I'll go with you." She stood up. Chestnut curls spilled to her shoulders. Her slightly parted lips were moist and inviting, her forget-me-not eyes spellbinding.

For a fleeting instant he stood mesmerized. An ache flared deep inside him. A throb of indeterminate origin. Instinctively Coop knew it would not be wise to linger in the small room with her.

"No. A saloon is no place for a girl like you."

He started toward the door.

She followed. "I was just there."

"That was different." His hand was on the doorknob, and his palm was sweating. "That was earlier in the evening. Now it's men only."

"Where you go, I go," she insisted with a toss of her

Heaven Sent

head. She stepped closer. A small woman with spirit, and stubborn as a one-legged mule. "Think of me as your shadow. If Billy Bowed-Legs was here, he wouldn't let any prisoner of his go traipsin' off."

Coop frowned. "Do you think your pal Billy would want you in a saloon with cowboys who haven't had a woman in months? There's lust in those cowpoke hearts."

She was quiet for a minute. He drew in a deep breath of relief.

"I'm dressed in men's clothes; no one's gonna lust after me."

"Now, I just wouldn't count on that. In that getup you might stir a man's curiosity."

"How?"

"A man might start to use his imagination, want to see for himself what that big shirt and baggy trousers are hiding."

She pursed her lips. He could feel her mind churning.

"Matilda Rose, surely you can see that I can't be responsible for protecting you in a room full of inquisitive men."

She regarded him in a steady, unnerving gaze. "I'll take my Winchester along."

"Bridget doesn't allow weapons in her place."

"What?"

"Yep. It's the truth. Men get careless after a few drinks. They get trigger happy. Look, I just want a cigar, a whiskey, and a little fun."

"We have to get an early start tomorrow."

"Don't worry. I'll be ready to roll at dawn."

He turned the doorknob. She took another step closer, so close she brushed his back. He inhaled the essence of rose... and sweet woman. Coop turned back.

Matilda Rose stood a breath away, her eyes flashing, stubborn and defiant. "Don't move," she breathed.

Something hard and cold nudged his ribs. He looked down.

She held a derringer against him.

"Oh, no," he moaned. "Is that parlor pistol loaded?"

"What do you think?"

"Put it down."

"Sorry, but I have to do whatever it takes to keep you in my sights."

"Whatever it takes?"

She shot him a puzzled frown. Wary, suddenly and obviously nervous, she pursed her lips. Full, pink lips nearly puckered in the kiss position. Lips that had been tempting him from the first time he set eyes on her.

Before she could protest, Coop swept her into his arms. The gun fell to the floor with a clunk as he brought his mouth down on hers.

Chapter Five

The room rocked. The floor vibrated. The deep rumble of a locomotive engine enveloped them, overriding all other sound.

Matty had no idea a man's kiss could have such an impact! Dizzy and disoriented, she clung to Cooper T. for dear life. Beset by startling new sensations emanating from deeply private parts of her, she made no attempt to free herself from his arms or from his lips. Lips that smothered hers with astonishing urgency. My, oh my, my, my. The drummer was truly dangerous—and delicious. Her mind couldn't hold a thought. Her body couldn't move. As if they had a will of their own, her lips answered his.

She marveled at the salty, spicy taste of him, the tingle in her belly, the furious beating of her heart. The bruising intensity of his mouth on hers alternated with a gentleness that both enthralled and bewildered Matty. Her knees went to mush. Tarnation!

Sandra Madden

Cooper T. moaned, crushing her fiercely against him, drinking from her lips as if consumed by an insatiable thirst. Matty struggled to understand the contradictory feelings jolting her body. The surging glorious warmth. The prickly alarm. How had she come to this?

And then the world crashed down around them. A shattering of glass marked the fall of the washbowl. Distant screams and howling dogs echoed through the room. Finally, the sound of a lantern smashing to the floor at her feet brought Matty to her senses. Pushing against Cooper T.'s chest, she dragged her mouth away.

"What have you done?" she demanded breathlessly.

Before he could reply, the roar subsided, the quaking and shaking of the room ending as quickly as it had begun.

Cooper T.'s slightly glazed gaze focused across the room. Setting Matty gently aside, he dashed toward the lantern, which had sent slivers of fire everywhere. Snatching the quilt from the bed, he beat out the fires.

Shouts of "Earthquake" rang from the corridors of Bridget's Irish Emporium. Of course. An earthquake. Matty felt like a fool for believing this had anything to do with Cooper T.'s kiss. Nonetheless, she trembled from head to toe.

"Are you all right, Matilda Rose?"

She nodded her head, her lips quivering, unable to speak. She wasn't all right but couldn't be certain why. It might be the aftereffects of the earthquake . . . or the aftereffects of Cooper T.'s kiss.

"You sure do pack a wildcat kiss for a little woman." He chuckled, flashing one of his disturbing grins. The kind that took her breath away.

He had no right to be charming after what he'd just done, after what had just happened. The arrogant drummer was only days away from marrying Phoebe Pearl.

But all she could muster was a pathetic little squeak.

"I'm going to check downstairs," he said, guiding her back to the bed. "Stay here, precious. I'll be back in a few minutes."

Head still spinning, she nodded. He strode out the door, for all the world like a man on a rescue mission. She had to hand it to him: Cooper T. acted quickly to douse the sparks that might have ignited a major fire. A woman could feel safe with a man who thought fast. But not Matty. Obviously, she wasn't safe with Cooper T..

She should feel burning shame right down to her strumpet slippers for enjoying his kiss for even one second! She was lower than a worm, clearly unworthy of a sweet, innocent sister like Phoebe. A sister who trusted her and would never wrong Matty. Nothing she could do about it now but make sure it never happened again. Never.

The world settled into eerie silence. One lantern still swung from its hook, casting shadows but giving Matty enough light to retrieve her derringer and straighten up the room.

As the quaking in her heart slowed, she started to think rationally. In the next instant she understood what had happened. From his heavenly perch somewhere up above, Billy Bowed-Legs had caught her kissing Cooper T. The old buckaroo had seen her doing nothing to fight off the devil's kiss. It was plain to her now—Billy's anger with Matty had obviously manifested itself in the earthquake. Enough of a quake to put a stop to the kiss, to warn her away from the man who would soon be her sister's husband. It had been a

Sandra Madden

sign from Billy to beware of Cooper T.'s wicked heart.

No matter how powerful an inclination she felt toward Cooper T., she had to remember that he was a snake in the grass who would do anything to avoid marrying Phoebe—including wooing Matty.

"I'm sorry, Billy," she whispered aloud. "It won't happen again. I'm not gonna let some fast-talkin', two-timin' man draw me in with his tricks and honey tongue. Cooper T.'s big shoulders and silly grin don't affect me none. None at all. You'll see. From here all the way to the Silver Star, I'm gonna stay good and clear of that man."

Having apologized to Billy Bowed-Legs and with the room put back to rights, Matty decided to venture downstairs to help Cooper T.

She took the stairs slowly. Tables, chairs, and cards were strewn about the main room that served as restaurant, saloon, and poker parlor. A glass chandelier had fallen, and broken bottles littered the floor. The place smelled like sour whiskey.

A dozen men, Bridget, her girls, the bartender, and two Chinese helpers had been caught in the chaos. Matty pitched in, working beside Cooper T. to bandage heads, clean cuts, and soothe bruised nerves. The girls who worked for Bridget were hysterical and more in need of assistance than the macho male customers, who kept up a stoic front. " 'Twasn't nothin'," the cowboys muttered to no one in particular.

For once her tall, teasing prisoner didn't argue with her, seeming to understand Matty's need to be with other folks. When she finally became too exhausted to move, Cooper T. sat her down. He and Mick the bartender put the chairs and tables back on their legs. Bridget swept broken glass and cussed.

Heaven Sent

An hour later, back in the room, Matty sank to the bed once again. "I suppose you're more in need of a good cigar and a strong whiskey now than you were before, Cooper T."

"That's the truth." He wagged his head and scratched behind his ear. "But I'd better stay with you. There'll be an aftershock or two coming."

She looked up into his eyes. Soft, green, tired eyes. "I'm not afraid of an old aftershock."

"Good. But I'm staying just the same."

He turned and spread out his bedroll by the door. The room was as quiet as a church. The only lantern still intact burned low.

Matty perched on the edge of the bed. "For a snake-oil peddler, you're not all that bad," she said softly.

He turned, shooting her a wry smile. "Was that a compliment?"

"You helped a lot of folks tonight. And you put that fire out real quick."

"Now you're seeing the true me. I knew you were an intelligent young lady." He grinned full force, sending her heart into a wild rhythm. "I knew you'd come around."

"Didn't say anything about coming around."

"You will."

Matty straightened her shoulders and lifted her chin. "There's somethin' you oughta know."

"What's that?"

She spoke softly and firmly. "If you try and kiss me again, I'll blow your head off, Cooper T."

The corner of his mouth quivered. "Is that any way for a lady to talk, Matilda Rose?"

"I reckon it's the only language a varmint like you can understand."

"Well, now, I can't deny I'd like to kiss you again. But I won't do it unless you say so."

"*Harumphf!*" No man had ever told her that he'd like to kiss her again. Truth to tell, no man had ever kissed her smack on the lips like that. "You won't ever hear me say so!"

"Ever?"

"Ever."

Matty lay down. Eyes half shut, she watched him turn settle onto his bedroll. "And I'd appreciate it if nothin' was said to my sister about . . . that kiss."

"My lips are sealed."

"It never happened."

"Never."

When she heard him chuckle, irritation flared like bad chili in Matty's belly. Beyond natural curiosity, a man had never stirred any feelings one way or another inside her. Until now. And now she didn't understand those feelings. Matty was still wrestling with her disconcerting emotions when he began to snore softly. Only then did she give up questioning and give in to sleep.

She'd just drifted off to sleep when a heavy jolt woke her. She bolted upright in the bed.

"It's an aftershock," Cooper whispered in the dark.

"I know that."

"Are you all right?"

" 'Course I am."

"I don't know as you'd tell me if you were frightened or hurting," he observed quietly.

"Well, it wouldn't be any of your business."

"Do you want me to come over there and offer some comfort?"

She didn't miss the teasing tone in his voice. "Don't

Heaven Sent

even think about it. Remember Billy Bowed-Legs is up there watching over me . . . which means he's watching you too."

"Well, now, that's a frightening thought, Matilda Rose."

Coop took the reins just after dawn the following morning. His pint-sized companion took up her mouth organ shortly afterward. The sight of her lips on the harmonica reminded him of how her lips felt beneath his, soft and pliant. He didn't know what he'd expected, but he hadn't expected the earth to move when he'd kissed her. He hadn't expected his heart to fly, the pit of his stomach to fall. He hadn't expected the sweet and tangy gumdrop taste of her to whet his appetite for more.

Coop's feelings weren't open for discussion. They never had been. Old Angus Van Kurem fed, clothed, and educated Cooper, but any expression of feelings had been strictly forbidden. According to Angus, great men didn't talk, they acted. Strong men didn't fret or cry, they toughed out their pain—physical or otherwise. Intelligent men denied any emotion that might make them appear weak to another man, or to a woman.

Now, not knowing what to say, or how to say it, Coop listened to Matilda Rose play every tune she knew on her harmonica. She started with "The Old Chisholm Trail." Fortunately, by midmorning she'd played herself out and ended with a rousing rendition of "Rye Whiskey."

When the sun blazed overhead, he pulled the horses to a stop. "We're going to rest our animals and eat that lunch Bridget packed up for us now. Figure that sycamore over yonder will be a good spot to spread a blanket."

"A picnic!" Her lavender-blue eyes lit up as if he'd announced a gold discovery. Her smile was as warm and bright as the sun.

His heart kicked up at her obvious pleasure. "Just like we were a courting couple," he drawled.

Her smile turned to a frown. "Don't ever get that idea, Cooper T. Even if there was no Phoebe, you'd be the last man in the world I'd get hooked up with. A woman would have to be plum crazy to get caught up with a patent medicine man who did nothin' but drift from town to town."

He gave her a wink and lowered his voice to a confidential aside. "I thought you were a little loco from the moment we met."

With a puff of exasperation, Matilda Rose jumped from the wagon and spread her arms to the sky. "This is a glorious day. We'll have a wonderful picnic."

She is glorious. Coop's thought took him by surprise. Where had that come from? Damnation. He scratched the back of his neck, wondering what was happening to him, wondering if Matilda Rose realized that more often than not, she behaved just like a woman.

She spread a blanket beneath an ancient sycamore tree overlooking the Pacific. A salty breeze blew from the ocean as Coop wolfed down biscuits the size of plates, thick slices of honeyed ham, chunks of cheese bigger than his hand, and chocolate cake.

"Bridget packed a fine meal," his picnic companion admitted, licking chocolate from her fingers.

A job he watched with envy. "She was grateful for the help we gave her," he said, leaning over to brush a

Heaven Sent

chocolate crumb from Matilda Rose Applebee's cheek. A silky bronze cheek.

She bucked back. "Have you known her a long time?"

"Been passing through Canton for a few years. Mostly on business. Always stop in to say hello when I do."

"You didn't try and sell any snake oil while we were there."

"How many times do I have to tell you? Peddling the medicine is not my business. I only sell it when people ask, and half the time I give it away. Like I said, I'm a Pinkerton."

"Without any identification to prove it."

"Stolen in Tijuana."

"You're tellin' me you've been robbed twice and shot once since you left San Francisco?"

"All in the line of duty. Traveling subjects you to a certain amount of danger, and that's what I like. The excitement keeps my blood hot and stirred." Coop gave her a lazy smile. He didn't expect her to understand. Besides, his thigh ached a little less each day. He'd be back in fighting form by the time he reached San Francisco.

"I know how that feels. Excitement. My blood gets stirred when I'm ridin' the ranch, pickin' up strays. That's when I know I'm alive."

He rolled a toothpick between his teeth. "You are one of the most alive women I've ever met."

She frowned suspiciously. "Was that a compliment?"

"Take it however you please."

Shaking her head, she pushed to her feet and dusted off her hands. "A swim would please me. I'm going to wash off these dirty old clothes and grimy skin."

Sandra Madden

"You can't take a bath in saltwater," he objected.

"Watch me. It's better than nothin'. I'd suggest you do the same or I'm soon goin' to be ridin' on Spirit *beside* the wagon."

He wanted to feel offended but didn't. "You're not an easy woman to get along with. Has anyone ever told you that?"

She grinned an impish smile that melted whatever resistance he might have had to a cold bath in the Pacific Ocean. Seemed Matilda Rose smiled more of late, perhaps because they were getting closer to her home. Coop kind of wished she smiled even more.

He helped her down the bluff, holding her hand as they walked, stumbled, and slid to the beach.

Yelping, she grumbled about her slippers. "This would go better if I was wearin' boots."

"I'll be happy to carry you," he offered.

"No, thank you," she retorted crisply.

The rocky bluff sloped to a small sandy beach bordered by a stretch of rocks as far as the eye could see. As they reached the beach, Coop used his heels to slow down, but Matty slid into him. Cheeks flushed, she righted herself quickly, as if singed by his touch.

Coop pulled off his boots and tossed his shirt on the rocks. "The water's going to be cold," he predicted. He had no problem about taking a bath, but he didn't care to do it in the icy ocean.

"A brisk swim will be refreshin'."

He nodded. There'd be no talking her out of this crazy notion. It was a good day for a swim. Nary a cloud could be seen in the brilliant blue sky. Slivers of sunlight glinted on the sand and danced on the water.

Matty ran into the sea fully clothed, knowing her trousers and shirt would weigh her down but not car-

Heaven Sent

ing. She loved to swim in the ocean, to ride the waves as if she was a child again. Bracing herself for the chilly water, she took a deep breath and plunged into the ocean.

"Are you a good swimmer?" Cooper T. called.

A series of chills washed over her as she stood.

"I swim like a shark," she boasted, turning toward him with a grin. Up to her waist in the water, Matty stopped short. Her smile dissolved; her feet sank into the sand.

Cooper T. stood several yards away. He'd taken off his shirt, leaving nothing between her eyes and her imagination but solid muscle and flesh. Her eyes fixed on his broad shoulders and thick biceps. His tanned, sculpted body shimmered with strength and power. And for a moment, Matty stood mesmerized. Sucking in her breath, she realized the rugged virility radiating from him was as natural to Cooper T. as breathing.

Despite the cold water, she felt her body growing warm. Embarrassed by her shameful reaction to the towering mountain of a man who would soon become her brother-in-law, she lowered her gaze. But not far enough. Her eyes locked on the drummer's mat of crisp dark chest hair, glistening with beads of water. My, oh my. Matty's heart palpitated wildly.

"Is something wrong?" he asked.

Her heart was getting ready to explode. That was what was wrong. He'd started some kind of craving inside her that she didn't understand and couldn't satisfy. She swallowed hard. "Nothin,' nothin' at all. Been swimmin' since I was four years old."

"Did your mama teach you, or your pa?"

Matty ducked under the chilly water before answering. She came up cooler. "Billy Bowed-Legs taught me."

"Was there nothing that man couldn't do?"

"Nope." Her heart began to beat regular again. She barely knew what they were talking about. All she knew was, she couldn't be letting her gaze wander back to Cooper T.'s lusty, astonishing body. She kept her eyes on her hands, ostensibly looking for signs of puckering.

"Well, let's find out just how good a swimmer you are, Matilda Rose." Grinning, he ran a hand through his dark wet hair. "Are you prepared to race?"

She didn't hesitate. "Parallel to the big rocks and back to the beach. Ready?"

"Ready."

"Go!" She gave a whoop and threw her body full force into the water.

Cooper T. didn't exactly glide through the water with grace. His strokes were heavy, and with more splash than substance. However, he had the advantage of strength and surged to shore in the final minutes. Matty collapsed on the sand in the shallow water, breathing heavily.

Cooper T. sat on his heels beside her, close enough for her to reach out and touch him where she'd never touched a man.

Tarnation! She hoped Billy Bowed-Legs hadn't heard her thought, or read her mind. The sigh that escaped her was pitifully wistful. As her breathing returned to normal and the sand warmed her, the hankering to run her fingertips over Cooper T.'s chest grew so strong it scared Matty. Her palms itched, her toes curled. Her pulse quickened.

She reckoned she must be close to having sunstroke.

Heaven Sent

"I believe congratulations to the winner are in order."

"You beat me fair and square," she gasped, pushing the hair out of her face. "It was my clothes holdin' me back. They're too wet and heavy."

Giving her a lopsided grin, he raised a brow. "Take 'em off and we'll race again."

For a long moment his gaze locked on hers. She held her breath without realizing, immersed in the soft twinkling depths of his eyes.

Light-headed, and close to swooning right then and there, Matty shook her head. Something was happening. Something to do with Cooper T. Davis. Something scary.

"It's time to move on," she replied, prim and proper as a schoolmarm.

"We'd better dry off on the beach first."

"Maybe." Her wet shirt and pants stuck to her skin in a downright annoying manner. If she'd been by herself, she wouldn't have been wearing any clothes. Back home, Matty swam in the ocean and sunbathed on the beach in the altogether. Her body was bronzed all over.

If she avoided looking at Cooper T.'s bare chest, she reckoned she'd get over the strange feelings he'd provoked.

Sitting on the sand, braced against a smooth rock, she rested her hat over her face to shut out the sun. Within minutes the brief respite and dry-out she'd planned were lost to warm, contented sleep.

The buzzing woke her.

"Cooper T.?"

His reply was groggy, as if she'd woken him. "Yeah?"

"What's that buzzin' by me?"

"Looks like a wasp."

Sandra Madden

"Tarnation! I'm allergic."

"Then you'd better lie real still, Matilda Rose."

"And wait to get bit?!"

"Hold on, I'm coming." A few seconds passed before he spoke again, close to her. "Well, I'll be. Sure enough. A wasp on the beach. It's circling your head just like you were a daisy and it was a bumblebee looking for honey."

There was only one thing in this world Matty feared, and that was a wasp or hornet sting. She'd seen a ranch hand swell up and die after being bit by an angry swarm. Not long after, she discovered she suffered from the same allergy.

She'd been running barefoot near the Silver Star's flower garden and was bitten on her big toe. It was before her mother left. Matty remembered clearly how her mother paced, wringing her hands and cursing life in the wilderness. Meanwhile, Matty's toe swelled to the size of a saddle horn. From that moment on, she'd avoided wasps and hornets as if they were rattlers.

"This isn't funny. Kill it, Cooper T."

"Do you want me to use my rifle or my Colt?"

"I don't care what you use, just kill it!"

She felt a breeze, heard a flapping, and the buzzing stopped. Slowly, she slid her hat back. Cooper had used his shirt to wave the wasp away.

"Let's be goin'," she said, heaving a sigh of relief. "That old wasp was more 'n likely a sign from Billy not to be lollygaggin' on the trail."

Cooper T. rolled his eyes. "Old Bowed-Legs speaks in mysterious ways."

Matty's damp clothes chafed against her skin, her mind all confused. She wanted to be home on the Silver Star where things were familiar and life was peaceful.

Heaven Sent

Ever since she'd taken the drummer captive, one dilemma had followed another.

Back on the wagon and out on the road, Matty bounced until her body ached. The gaudy gilt wagon lumbered over a winding dirt road high above the ocean. Silent companionship replaced conversation as Matty and Cooper T. took in the breathtaking scenery. A cooling afternoon breeze carried the scent of salt and pine.

Coop drove the wagon as fast as he dared. Sometimes he actually saw the road ahead; sometimes he saw Matilda Rose's wet clothes clinging to her body. Which was disturbing.

He was as anxious to reach San Francisco as she was to return to the Silver Star Ranch.

The kiss he stole in Canton had made him even more aware that beneath those baggy clothes she was all woman. Given the proper circumstances, he might even be in danger of losing his heart to her. He'd feel a lot safer in another state laying plans to capture the James boys.

At sunset, Coop pulled off the road to make camp in a small clearing adjacent to the rutted trail. Rocks and thick brush to the north and east of the clearing protected them from the wind that had grown increasingly strong throughout the afternoon. A clear cold stream wound along the south side of the open space.

By the time he and Matilda Rose finished the leftover ham and biscuits, a crescent moon dangled like a silver charm against the ebony sky. In the distance, they could hear the pounding waves of the incoming tide. Between them, the fire snapped and crackled.

Matilda Rose sat Indian style with a blanket wrapped

around her to ward off the cold night air. She slowly brushed her long chestnut mane.

"Tell me about your sister," he said, tired but not ready for sleep. Sparring with Matilda Rose always proved entertaining. "Who is this woman you'd have me marrying?"

She smiled, obviously pleased he was at last showing some interest in her younger sibling. "As you well know, in appearance Phoebe Pearl is perfect. Her pretty blond ringlets and clear blue eyes turn heads wherever she goes."

Coop twirled a toothpick between his teeth. "Between you and me, a woman's looks fade as she ages, Matilda Rose. Does Phoebe have any . . . talents?"

" 'Course! What do you think? I've heard folks say she makes the best apple pie in the state of California."

"Sticks to a man's ribs, does it?"

"The crust is so flaky it melts in your mouth. And when Phoebe Pearl mends, she sews little tiny stitches a body can hardly see."

"That's important to a man like me," he intoned dryly. "Tiny stitches."

"Well, it will be!"

"Does this paragon of virtue keep a clean house?"

"Tarnation, yes! Phoebe's been in charge of our house since she was fifteen years old. She supervises the housekeeper and plans all the menus with the cook. Not only that, but she keeps the household accounts too."

"How can I expect such a paragon of virtue to tolerate my shortcomings?"

"She will . . . with my help. You are a blessed man to be gettin' Phoebe. My sister has worked at acquirin'

Heaven Sent

the skills to make her a good wife since she put her dolls aside."

"Does she talk like you?"

Matilda Rose's dainty brows bunched up again in a wary frown. "What do you mean?"

He sighed, leaned back, and braced himself on one elbow. "You know, the cowboy lingo. The tough talk. Has Phoebe Pearl received an education from anyone other than Billy Bowed-Legs?"

" 'Course! We both had tutors raisin' up. Then we went away to finishin' school."

"Did you graduate, Matilda Rose?"

She lowered her eyes, hanging her head sheepishly. "I got bored after the lessons were done. I didn't care to know how to serve tea. So I left finishin' school before they were quite finished with me."

He couldn't help chuckling, couldn't help feeling charmed by her honesty and her slight embarrassment.

"But I know how to talk right and ladylike. It's just I'm never around ladies much, 'ceptin' for Phoebe, and she's used to me."

"What about a fellow?" he asked, needing to know and doubting he could be the first man to see through her shield of contentiousness. "Hasn't there been a man you liked to impress with your sweet talk and social graces?"

"No, can't say there has been." She stared into the fire. "There might never be. My heart belongs to the Silver Star."

"Your ranch can never give you what a man can."

"I don't need a man like Phoebe does. She'll be happy to see you, Cooper T."

"Yeah." He stood up and stretched. "What sort of wife will Phoebe Pearl be?"

"The best." Matty inclined her head and began to braid her hair. "The best a man like you could hope for."

Coop hitched a thumb under his belt loop and slung out a hip. "The way I've heard it, a good wife sees to her husband's needs in all things. Including the way she warms his bed."

She dropped her half-plaited braid and shot him a fierce frown. "Are you askin' me if my sister will warm your bed?"

"Yes, I am," he replied, straight-faced.

"Nothin' any decent man would be askin' his future sister-in-law," she huffed. "But you can rest assured, Phoebe will do her wifely duty."

He added wood to the fire. "That's not good enough, Matilda Rose."

"Tarnation! You're lucky you're getting a prize like Phoebe."

"There's more to marriage than apple pie. I want a wife who's going to like the feel of my body next to hers, a wife who warms my lips with her kisses. A woman with a soft, willing mouth . . . like yours. A woman who can't get enough of me, a woman who'll be a wildcat in the bedroll."

Across the fire, a flushed Matilda Rose stared at him with her mouth wide open.

He leveled the most sincere gaze he could muster. "Do you think Phoebe Pearl will be that kind of wife?"

She leaped to her feet. "I think you've been touched by the sun!"

"A lady in the parlor, a tramp in the bedroom. That's what I want in a wife."

"Phoebe's no tramp," Matty bristled, hands on hips. "Despite what you did to her!"

Heaven Sent

Before he could answer, Coop heard a sound. A sound beyond the crackling of the fire and the rushing tide.

Cocking his head to listen, he raised a finger to his lips.

"What is it?" she demanded, all steamed up and obviously prepared for battle.

"Did you hear that?"

"What?"

"Someone, or something, is over yonder by the rocks."

Chapter Six

Matty's heart thudded. Her stomach constricted. While straining to hear a telltale sound her lungs refused to take in air, or let it out. Immobilized, she mentally prepared to take a stand—or run like wildfire. She stared into the thick black night, peering into the dense brush and beyond the jagged rocks where the sound had come from. But she was unable to discern any movement and heard nothing but her own labored breathing.

With the stealth of an Indian warrior, and as casual as the switch of a cow's tail, Cooper T. made his way to her side. And then in one swift, deft motion he spun Matty around behind him and grabbed her Winchester from the ground.

He aimed the rifle toward the rocks and brush. He spoke softly and calmly. "I've got you covered. Throw your weapons toward the fire and walk out with your hands behind your head."

Heaven Sent

"Who are you talkin' to?" Matty rasped beneath her breath.

Lowering his voice, Cooper T. spoke easy. "Now, nice and slow, Matilda Rose, make for the wagon."

This was one time she wasn't about to argue with her prisoner. She tiptoed back to the garish wagon in her silent strumpet slippers while her prisoner marched forward toward the unseen enemy.

"Come out real friendlylike," Cooper T. ordered, leveling the Winchester. His voice boomed harshly in the quiet night. "I've got a rifle aimed your way, and my pardner's ready to cut you down with a Colt."

Even from a distance Matty could feel his tension. Unblinking, on guard, body taut and stalking his prey. This was yet another aspect of the man. A man more complex than she'd at first thought. The easygoing, twinkling-eyed drummer she knew had vanished in the blink of an eye. Far as she could tell, at the moment Cooper T. Davis wasn't even breathing.

Matty reached the back of the wagon with her pulse racing as if she'd run fifty miles or more. Never taking her eyes off Cooper T., she pushed the doors of the wagon open, climbed up, and claimed her Colt.

That was when she heard the low, fierce growl. Trembling, Matty held her breath, hoping that whatever wild beast had dared approach their camp could not hear the thunderous beating of her heart. Another growl, louder, more menacing, came from the darkness. It might be any of several different kinds of big cats that prowled this territory. Cooper T. was in serious danger. Fear lodged in Matty's throat like a lump of dry clay. Nerves all a-prickle, she jumped from the wagon. Who would help the crazy fool drummer if she didn't?

Still another warning growl sliced the night, quickly followed by the snap of twigs, the rustle of leaves.

Before the scream left her, she saw the flash, the spark. Cooper T.'s shot echoed in the wilderness.

And then came the thump.

Matty scurried after Cooper T. as he ran toward the brush. Just below the rocks, a bobcat weighing at least two hundred pounds lay in a thin ribbon of moonlight.

"You're a mighty fine shot," Matty breathed. Even Billy Bowed-Legs would never have been able to stop a wild cat in the dark, just listening to the sounds alone.

"Why, thank you, Matilda Rose." Cooper T. grinned and dipped his head her way. "I appreciate any compliment when it comes from you."

She stepped back as he poked the cat with the barrel of the rifle to make sure the animal was dead.

"You saved my life tonight. I . . . I am not ungrateful."

He'd shown real courage when he'd stood his ground, not knowing if it were a wild man or a wild animal concealed in the dark brush.

And it was still fresh in her mind that he'd kept the bandits at bay. The sidewinders who held them up outside Canton might have gotten away with her boots, but the skinny one, Luke, had wanted more. He'd wanted her. The way Cooper handled the situation, only Matty's pride had been hurt. A small price to pay.

Truth was, her hostage was protecting her. A fact that made her uncomfortable. A bad mix of battling emotions drummed in her head, swirled like sour lemons in her stomach.

"I'm just going to drag him off a ways and then we

can settle in for the night," Cooper T. said. "Unless you'd like some bobcat for breakfast?"

"Cooper T., that's disgustin'!"

"Well, I don't know. You put up a tough front for a girl. No telling what a woman like you desires."

Her chin shot up as if it had a mind of its own. "I'm a woman like any other."

Cooper T. gave a wag of his head. "Matilda Rose, believe me: You are unique. I've never met a woman quite like you in my life."

He might have been making fun, but his smile appeared genuine. Her heart skipped inside her, real peculiarlike. Not knowing quite how to respond, she turned on her heel. "I'm goin' to the wagon and I'm sayin' good night."

"And I'm going to bury our bobcat. Sweet dreams, Matilda Rose."

She heard him chuckle as she stomped away.

Once in the wagon, out of the cool night air and snug beneath the blankets, Matty thought about Phoebe Pearl being married to Cooper T. The match was akin to a hummingbird mated with a hawk. The drummer possessed a certain strength of will, while Phoebe had none at all. Her sister swayed in whatever direction the current wind blew.

While Cooper T. favored excitement, Phoebe functioned as a creature of habit. Every day she played the same pieces on the pianoforte. She ate the same breakfast day after day, wore the same frilly dresses.

Matty had to face the truth: Although she'd heard opposites attracted, this was not a union made in heaven. She was bringing together two people completely unsuited to one another. But she had no choice. For the sake of her sister's unborn child and to save

Phoebe's reputation, the unlikely couple must be wed. It wouldn't be the first such marriage of convenience.

She wondered what kind of woman would attract a man like Cooper T. Would Bridget O'Brien be more to his taste for a bride?

One thing Matty knew to be true; *she* wasn't his type. He'd been downright insulting and too honest to suit her when he criticized her manner of speakin'... speaking. He didn't like her clothes, or the way she walked either. Yet she had noticed him staring at her mouth a few times, gazing at her eyes, contemplating her hair when it was loose. Maybe there was something about her he liked.

Not that she cared.

The good-looking drummer was far from being Matty's kind of man. However, these last few days she'd found some things about him she liked. His body stood as tall and beautiful as one of those drawings of Greek statues in the finishing-school books she'd studied. The man appeared to have been molded to perfection by a loving hand.

And he took things in stride. He didn't get riled or go flying off the handle. Standing up to the scalawags in Canton and taking on the bobcat tonight showed him to possess a fair amount of courage. A commendable trait.

Matty hoped her sister would recognize Cooper T.'s favorable qualities—despite the fact that he'd stolen Phoebe's virtue and moved on. She planned to ask her sister to forgive him, and to overlook his shameful occupation.

Selling patent medicine couldn't be a trade to inspire pride, but his current profession would be behind him shortly. Soon Cooper T. would be working alongside

Heaven Sent

Matty on the Silver Star Ranch. Making a good living for his wife and child.

With that thought, her heart squeezed into a hard brittle ball. It hurt.

When she heard steps outside the wagon, she'd already made up her mind. She should be, and could be, nicer to her future brother-in-law without compromising her position. After all, he'd just saved her life. And he would soon be family.

"Cooper T.," she called out. "You can sleep inside the wagon tonight, if you want. It's nice and warm in here."

"What?"

"I said I wouldn't mind havin' you in here."

"Really?"

She'd figured he'd be surprised by her offer, but something didn't sound quite right. Matty reached for the Colt beneath her pillow. "Cooper T.? Is that you?"

"Ahh, no," came the hesitant reply. "The name is Hawkins. Horace Hawkins."

Matty threw back her blankets, lunged to the back doors of the wagon, and pushed them open. A man seemingly unperturbed stood by the fire warming his hands.

She jumped down.

The man who'd identified himself as Hawkins turned as she advanced on him in her stocking feet. For a fleeting moment, she didn't know if he was a man or a grizzly bear. Horace Hawkins owned a face full of dark hair, including bushy side whiskers, mustache, and beard. He had no upper lip that she could see, and his lower lip was all but covered with beard. His somber black frock coat and trousers were torn and dirty.

Sandra Madden

She aimed her revolver at his heart. "What did you do with Cooper T.?"

"Do? Cooper T.?" The stranger smiled uncertainly, his brown, hound-dog eyes focused on the muzzle of her Colt. "I've done nothing with anyone, my dear. I have not seen a soul in days. Not since my horse died. Who is Cooper T.? The person you were inviting to share your bed?"

"I was not!"

"I beg your pardon. My mistake."

"You better not be makin' any more mistakes."

"I will do my best, my dear."

"What direction did you come from?" she asked warily, assessing the man. Horace Hawkins looked to be middle-aged. Tarnation! He even had a full growth of hair sprouting on the back of his hands.

He pointed toward the ocean. "I was walking on the beach when I spotted your fire."

The crunch of underbrush announced Cooper T.'s arrival. "Matilda Rose, what have you found?"

Before she could answer, Hawkins replied with a smile, "A man of God."

A preacher! And he heard Matty inviting Cooper T. to spend the night in the wagon. Matty's breath caught in her lungs. She felt her cheeks fire up.

"Pleased to meet you. I'm Coop Davis and—"

"And I'm his sister, Matilda Rose," she interrupted hurriedly. If she claimed to be Cooper T.'s kin, the preacher would have to believe her innocent of any sinful intent. Which she was. Her invitation for the drummer to spend the night in the warm wagon had simply been an act of kindness.

She had no doubt Horace Hawkins had been sent by Billy Bowed-Legs. Billy was still up there, watching

Heaven Sent

over her. No way was he going to allow Cooper T. to sleep in the same wagon with her. Billy always told her she was too trusting. What had she been thinking? Just because Cooper had saved her life a few times was no reason to share the wagon's warmth with him. Even if it was his wagon.

"Sister," Cooper T. repeated, scratching the back of his neck.

"The Reverend Hawkins's horse died," Matty explained.

"Three days ago. I've been walking and living on berries ever since."

Cooper T. gestured toward the fire. "We've got some extra grub, and the coffee's still warm."

"Jerky and raisins are what we have," Matty added.

"I appreciate your generosity. Raisins and jerky will taste like a feast to me."

Soon she was sitting by the fire again, with the drummer and the preacher. Hawkins gulped fistfuls of raisins and tore at the jerky.

"It's most inconvenient for a circuit rider to be without a horse," he said between mouthfuls. "You cannot know how happy I am to have met up with you. When I saw your fire, I knew it was a sign. I fell to my knees in the sand and gave thanks."

"Well, we'll be glad to take you along," Cooper T. said. "We're headed for Los Angeles . . . my *sister* and me."

"We even have an extra horse that you can ride," she offered.

Hawkins raised his eyes to the sky and gave them a saintly smile. "Someone is indeed watching over me."

"You bet." Matty raised her eyes. Billy Bowed-Legs. She could just hear the whoosh of his flapping wings.

Sandra Madden

Cooper T. crooked his finger. "Sis . . . I'd like to have a word with you."

Matty smiled at the circuit rider. "Excuse us."

She followed Cooper to the back of the wagon, where he narrowed his eyes and lowered his voice. "What's going on?"

"Horace Hawkins is a man of God. It doesn't look good, me bein' with you . . ." she declared, chewing on her lip. "Alone. It's not proper. I don't want him to think a single, unwed, respectable woman like myself would be traveling alone with a male . . . a peddler of patent medicine like yourself."

"Propriety? Matilda Rose, when did you develop a sense of propriety?"

"The minute I thought that if he knew the true circumstances, Hawkins might insist on marrying us. He might not understand how everything is on the up-and-up and I'm taking you home to marry Phoebe."

"You and me? Hitched?" He laughed. She hated that he laughed. "Now that's an interesting thought."

"And only a featherhead would think it! I'd rather marry the devil," she snapped before turning on her heel and marching back to where the circuit rider rested by the fire. "I'm sayin' good night now. This time for good."

His chuckling rang in her ears as she marched away.

Coop and Horace agreed to take turns watching through the night. Coop took the first watch. Not knowing what other wild animals lurked on the bluff, he built up the small campfire until it blazed. With a twinge of envy, he watched Horace Hawkins snuggle into his bedroll beneath the wagon where Matty slept. Coop didn't mind sharing with the circuit rider, but he felt tired and drained.

Heaven Sent

Until he'd heard the bobcat growl earlier, he hadn't known if he was facing man or beast out there. Once he realized what it was, he hadn't fancied the thought of the big cat dining on Matilda Rose. She had her faults, but she didn't deserve to be dessert.

He took a deep breath. The cool night air seemed alive. Coyotes howled, crickets chirped, owls hooted. The pale moon looked as lonely as he felt, and an overcast sky hid the stars. Coop bit down on his toothpick and stirred the fire.

Horace Hawkins snored. Maybe Billy Bowed-Legs was looking after Matilda Rose. Coop wasn't sure he could have resisted temptation if it had been just the two of them alone tonight.

He wanted a peek, just a peek at the body beneath Matilda Rose's oversized cowhand's clothes. Instinct, and the way her shirt and trousers clung to her during their ocean bath, told him she had curves to take a man's breath away. He'd give the rest of his gold to taste her lips again, slip his tongue deep into her mouth. Coop would be a happy man if he could just run his hands through her shiny chestnut curls, to bury his head in the silky locks. He wanted to lose himself in the essence of rose, Matilda Rose.

All the yearning and hankering he was doing was getting mighty painful. He could feel it in his groin, his chest, his stomach, even his mouth. He was grateful when it was time to get some shut-eye and turn over the watch to Horace Hawkins.

Coop woke in the morning to the smell of strong coffee and off-key whistling. His eyelids were barely open before he understood why his mouth had felt sore the night before. He had a damn toothache.

Sighing, he dragged himself out of the bedroll and

over to sit by the fire to pour a tin mug of coffee.

Matilda Rose regarded him as if he'd grown another head. "Cooper T., you've got a chipmunk cheek!"

"Thank you for bringing that to my attention." His jaw throbbed with pain. It was all he could do to keep a civil tongue.

The hairy circuit rider sat on his heels in front of Coop. "Let me take a look at your mouth, young man."

"No, no. Ow'll be fine once we get to Los Angeles and find a dentist." He felt as if he had a mouthful of hot pebbles between his teeth. He couldn't speak without slurring his words.

But Coop's pained protest didn't stop the preacher. "Open wide."

"What'd you see in there?" Matilda Rose asked, peering from behind the preacher.

"The Lord has seen fit to test you this morning, Cooper." Horace turned to Matty. "Your brother's got a mouth full of inflamation and a bad, bad tooth in the back right side of his jaw."

Coop lifted his gaze to where Matilda Rose stood over him, hands on hips, frowning at his jaw. "Not a word . . . sissy."

"I wasn't goin' to say anything like . . . you're bein' punished for your evil ways. Would I say somethin' like that when you're hurtin' like a snake out of its skin?"

The preacher reprimanded her mildly. "This is no time for sibling bickering."

She rolled her eyes.

"Looks as if that tooth will have to come out," Hawkins continued. "It's loose in there as it is."

"No," Coop said. "Ow'll see a dentist in Los Angeles."

Heaven Sent

"I don't recall a dentist bein' in Los Angeles," Matilda said with a deepening frown.

Coop's mouth hurt so bad the pain felt as if it were spreading to his head.

"Riding the circuit, I've done my share of birthing babies and pulling rotten teeth. If you don't get that bad tooth out of there quickly, young man, it's going to poison your system."

"Could he die?" Matilda Rose asked in a breathy voice.

Her tone puzzled Coop. He didn't know if she was afraid he'd croak or she hoped he would.

Hawkins nodded solemnly. "It's possible."

Coop shook his head. "Naw."

"Show me what to do, Reverend Hawkins. I'll help you. Just don't let . . . my brother die."

"Damn ot—"

Horace laid his hands on Coop's shoulders. "Save your strength, young man. Don't talk. Do you have anything we can use as antiseptic, Matilda Rose?"

"A bottle of Dr. Van Kurem's will do fine," she told him and dashed away.

The Reverend Hawkins whistled as they waited, off-key but rather cheerfully for the occasion.

Coop cupped his swollen jaw gently. He didn't have the energy to argue. He wanted coffee but was bound to get Van Kurem tonic.

"How are you goin' to take the tooth out?" Matilda Rose asked when she returned with two bottles of tonic.

"I'll need a knife and a strip of rawhide."

"You can use my knife, and there's rawhide in Billy's saddlebag."

Whistling "Abide with Me," Horace Hawkins

propped Coop against the trunk of a wide old oak tree and forced him to drink the tonic, and then to gargle with it. Coop didn't know which hurt worse, his mouth or his ears—from having to listen to the bearish preacher's out-of-tune whistling.

"Do you have anything stronger than this to dull the pain, young man?"

"No." He shook his head as much as he dared. Just when he needed it most. His misery doubled. "All out of whiskey."

A brisk morning breeze rustled through the trees, carrying a trace of salt from the nearby sea. A profusion of golden buttercups sprinkled the hillside by the stream. A perfect day to travel, Matty thought, rummaging through Billy Bowed-Legs's saddlebag. Billy always prepared for trouble at home or on the range.

She found a fistful of rawhide strips and two red bandannas that would serve to stop the bleeding. She reckoned there would be plenty of bleeding.

Poor Cooper T.; he'd been a model prisoner. He'd protected her from ruthless bandits and a savage beast. He'd comforted her when Billy Bowed-Legs took the big jump and passed on to cowboy heaven. And when the earthquake gave her a fright, he'd given her comfort. Plain and simple, he didn't deserve to suffer.

She returned to Cooper T.'s side, experiencing stomach spasms she could only think were sympathy pains. But a full bottle of Dr. Van Kurem's had relaxed the drummer to the point where he wore a lazy smile between spasms of pain.

"Hold his mouth open," Horace ordered. The circuit rider pointed with the knife. "His mouth."

Matty did as he bid and watched in horror as Haw-

Heaven Sent

kins lanced around Cooper T's tooth with Billy's whittling knife.

Cooper T. moaned. His gum bled something fierce.

Matty gritted her teeth. Her insides squeezed up tight in commiseration. She watched as Horace wound a rawhide strip around the bad tooth. Her stomach felt like she'd taken a blow from a cowboy's fist when the grim-faced preacher yanked at Cooper T.'s bad tooth. And yanked. And yanked a third time.

Chills spiraled down her spine.

For a moment, Matty thought Cooper T. had passed out. The blood drained from his face, and his eyes rolled back in his head.

The fourth and firmest yank brought out the tooth.

Matty fell to her knees beside Cooper T. "It's over. The tooth is out," she told him softly.

"Jus' let me die," he groaned.

"You're going to live, young man," Horace pronounced in the hearty tone of success.

"You're gonna be right as rain, Cooper T.," Matty assured him. "I've got some cool stream water on this cloth and I'm gonna press it against the hole to help stop the bleedin'."

"Wan' more tonic."

The preacher nodded his head in agreement. "I think a touch more tonic would be in order."

"But he's bleedin'!" Matty protested.

"A touch."

When she complied, Cooper T. murmured. "Better. Numb now."

"No more," Matty said with authority as she worked the cool cloth into his mouth.

Within an hour, most of the bleeding had stopped.

Sandra Madden

The swelling had begun to dissipate and some color had returned to Cooper T.'s face.

"Let's go. Let's get on with our endless journey," he said, struggling to get up.

Matty objected. "I don't think you're strong enough."

"Don't worry, I'm fine."

"Don't push yourself on my account, young man," Hawkins kindly interjected.

"No pushing required. Let's go."

"I don't think you should drive, Cooper T.," Matty argued. "I'd be happy to handle the reins."

"Have you ever driven a wagon before?"

"No, but I'm sure I can." *And drive it a lot faster.* He claimed his contraption wouldn't go any faster because Cooper T. wasn't in any hurry to get to Phoebe and get hitched. He was dragging his feet. Matty knew she could hustle that old drummer's wagon and two big horses on its way.

"No one drives my wagon but me."

This trip had strained Matty's nerves from the start. A few hours ago, she'd thought everything was at last under control. But now, caught up in still another quarrel with Cooper T., sick as he was, she lost her temper. "You are stubborn as an old mule, Cooper T. Davis, with all the sense of a mail-order cowboy!"

Hawkins laid a hairy hand on her arm. "This is not the time to be locking horns with your brother, if you don't mind my saying so."

Unable to rail at him as well, by virtue of his profession, Matty simply glared at the interfering preacher.

"Precious," Cooper T. added hoarsely, "the preacher's right."

"Well, we'd better git goin'," she bristled impatiently. "That is, if we're goin' to reach the Silver Star in this century."

With a quirk of his lips he turned to Hawkins. "Horace, you ride Billy Bowed-Legs's mount."

"Nice little mare," Hawkins said, running a hand over the horse's neck.

Cooper T. nodded. "Her name is Feller. Matilda Rose will sit up here with me."

"I'll play my mouth organ," she offered as they got underway. "Music soothes."

"Not always. Not today."

"I found a book of sonnets in the back of the wagon. Would you like me to read to you?"

He shook his head. "No, quiet will do fine."

"Surprised that you read Shakespeare. Do you really, or do you keep this book for show?"

"Dr. Kurem educated me while we were on the road. You might be astounded at what I know, Matilda Rose."

"Harumphf."

"All right. Go on. Read."

" 'It was a lording's daughter, the fairest one of three, that liked of her master as well as well might be . . .' " Matty read.

And she did not stop until Cooper T. passed out.

Chapter Seven

Cooper T. slumped over suddenly. His head fell with a thunk to Matty's shoulders.

"Tarnation!" she shouted, grabbing for the reins. The pigheaded drummer had croaked!

Or maybe not. Heart hammering, keeping an anxious eye on the unconscious man, Matty managed, with Horace's help, to guide the big Appaloosa team off the road and into a small glen. Bracing herself just about cut through the soles of her feet. It was a miracle she could do anything at all in her skimpy kid slippers.

She listened for any sign of life while the circuit rider dismounted and strode to the wagon.

"He's not dead, is he?"

"No, dear girl." The burly preacher cast a condescending smile as he swung Cooper T. over his shoulder and carried him down from the wagon. "Your brother simply misjudged his strength."

"The man is as stubborn as a long-eared mule," she

Heaven Sent

declared, puffing a sigh of relief. He gave her a fright, all right. Her stomach squeezed up tighter than a lasso when Cooper T. gave out. Why had he insisted on going on when he wasn't fit? She didn't want him joining Billy-Bowed Legs in cowboy heaven. Foibles aside, he was too young and too good-looking to die. Besides, what would Phoebe do for a husband if Matty didn't bring the drummer back alive?

She helped the Reverend Hawkins settle Cooper T.'s long, muscular form beneath the shelter of twin oaks. Dousing her bandana with Van Kurem's tonic, she placed Cooper's head in her lap and gently patted his perspiring face. A decidedly pale face, shadowed with stubble. Peculiar, that even sick as a dog, Cooper T. looked better than most men on their finest day. Unconscious, he was as almighty striking as when he was awake awinking and agrining.

"Shouldn't we be doin' something for him?"

"No, my dear. Your brother simply needs to rest and regain his strength."

But Cooper T.'s stillness scared her. Despite Hawkins's assurance, Matty held her fingertips at his throat, feeling for a pulse. She searched for tangible signs of life, a deep breath, a flutter of eyelashes. Something. Her scrutiny drifted from the deep laugh lines fanning his eyes to his narrow nose and strong square jaw. Was it possible for a handsome man to get better looking with each passing day?

Tarnation, no! She'd been on the trail too long.

If they were destined to spend another night camping, this flat grassy area seemed a good spot. Wide leafy oaks offered shade, and she could hear the rushing water of a creek close by. Most importantly, they were within a day's reach of the City of Angels.

From there it was only another few days to the ranch. Soon she would be home where she belonged. Soon Cooper T. would be Phoebe's husband. Her stomach knotted. It was the worrying she was doing over the arrogant peddler. He was making her sick.

At Matty's request, Horace helped lift Cooper T. into the back of the wagon, where he could rest more comfortably. The preacher then built a fire so she could cook up some beans from Billy's saddlebag and make tea for their patient.

"I'll stay with—my brother—in the back of the wagon tonight. Seems as if he's gonna need some nursin'."

"If it will make you feel better, my dear. I'll keep watch out here. Don't worry about a thing." His dull brown eyes fixed on hers. He nodded his hairy head, agreeing with himself as he spoke. "Glad to see your feelings have taken a more kindly turn, Matilda."

"Well, he's . . . he's sick."

"We must always strive to love one another. That includes brothers and sisters."

"Yes, sir. You've been a mighty help to us, Reverend Hawkins. Thank you."

He smiled widely. "Don't mention it."

She knew, sure as the sun rose in the east, Billy Bowed-Legs had sent the circuit rider to help Matty in a dire time of need. She never could have pulled the drummer's tooth, or stopped the Appaloosas by herself. She could not deny the truth. As much as she hated to admit it, it was clear to Matty now that she possessed neither the strength nor the stomach necessary to do all the things a man could do on the trail.

Cooper T. took some tea early in the evening, but then he fell into a restless sleep. Matty cooled him with

Heaven Sent

water from the stream, and held him while he sipped the tea. She held his large warm hand in hers, and long about midnight he finally drifted off into a deep sleep. Hearing his soft rhythmic breathing, Matty was finally convinced he would live. Soon after she fell into her own exhausted sleep.

When she woke up in the morning, Cooper T. was gone. She jumped out of the wagon to find her prisoner sauntering toward her from the creek.

"Good morning, precious. Thought you might be planning on sleeping all day."

He strode toward her, looking strong and right as rain. The crooked half-smile on his lips caused her pulse to get up and gallop like a mustang on the run.

"Mornin' Cooper T. It appears you're back on your feet."

He chuckled. "Takes more than a bullet to the thigh, a derringer in my ribs, an earthquake, a pulled tooth, and an ornery cowgirl to do me in."

Grateful to see him back on his feet, she took no offense. A tingle of something akin to happiness shot through her. She smiled. "Reckon you're tougher than rawhide."

As he drew closer, Matty noticed the swelling in his jaw had gone down considerably. The devilish sparkle had returned to his eyes, and the wry grin to his lips. Her heart turned over; a leap of relief, she reckoned.

Dragging her gaze away, she looked to where the fire had gone out. "Where's the Reverend Hawkins?"

"Apparently he rode away at dawn this morning on Feller."

"What do you mean?"

"He's gone."

"The circuit rider stole Billy Bowed-Legs's horse? Is that what you're sayin'?"

"He must have tired of our company, *Sissy.*"

"A preacher? A horse thief? Can't be."

"Oh, but it can," he said with a rueful smile and a wag of his head. "It doesn't take a Pinkerton to figure this one."

"A horse thief!" Indignation ignited like fire in the pit of her stomach. "And a preacher to boot!"

"Hawkins may have felt Billy Bowed-Legs didn't need Feller anymore."

Matty dug her fists into her hips, blinking back tears. "I promised Billy, out by his grave, that I'd take care of Feller. Always."

Cooper T. popped a toothpick in his mouth and nodded his head slowly. "Don't worry, Matilda Rose. I'll get Billy's horse back." He gave her a disarming wink that served to bring her anger up short. "Soon as I catch Carrot-Top and his gang of sidewinders."

"Aren't you forgetting something?"

The drummer who still claimed to be a detective cocked his head. "What?"

"Phoebe Pearl."

He rolled his eyes.

If Billy Bowed-Legs enjoyed a second life as guardian angel to Matilda Rose, he wasn't doing such a good job in Coop's estimation. Seemed like anything that could have happened to them on the trail had.

He guided the wagon into Los Angeles to the tune of "Buffalo Gals." It wasn't that he minded listening to the mouth organ mile after mile, but he knew a much better place for Matilda Rose's lips. Smack beneath his. Her mouth could be playing a far different tune. But

Heaven Sent

he wasn't a man who dwelled on things that couldn't be changed. With a resigned sigh, he turned his attention to the bustling pueblo before him.

Once a sleepy mission village, Los Angeles was now a growing cow town, though still a good deal smaller than San Francisco. The Spanish and Mexican influences could readily be seen in the low adobe buildings. The flat roofs were covered in black pitch brought up from the tar pits.

Acres of open fields sprouting wild grasses and alfilerilla for forage gave a man a sense of space and freedom. Vineyards, orange and apple orchards dotted the landscape, bearing witness to the rich soil. Cattle ranches and farms for miles around depended on the services offered in the City of Angels.

"Looks as if we're just in time for the Fourth of July Independence celebration," he said as they rode beneath one of the bright red, white, and blue banners strung across the main street.

Her eyes lit up. "I'm partial to fireworks."

The light in her eyes warmed his heart, his gut, in some mysterious way. Coop figured there was enough fire in Matilda Rose to light up more than her eyes. Hell, she could light up the entire City of Angels. Nothing he could mention to her, of course. Instead, he pointed up the road.

"There's a hotel up ahead where we can get us a room for the night and possibly a bath."

"Two rooms," she said.

"Two rooms?" He couldn't believe his ears. "You trust me enough that I can actually sleep in my own room in a bed for a change? Matilda Rose, we haven't been separated for a second since you swept me off my

Sandra Madden

feet—at gunpoint. Why would you agree to two rooms now?"

"You've . . . you've shown yourself to be trustworthy—in a certain sense. I reckon it has somethin' to do with Billy Bowed-Legs. The angel bein' him, workin' through the devil . . . bein' you."

"A trustworthy devil." Coop scratched the back of his neck as he thought that one over.

He had a difficult time imagining the man he'd buried as an angel. In his mind, the bearded, craggy old face of Billy just didn't look right framed by huge white feather wings.

"But make sure our rooms are side by side," she added, "so's I can hear your comin' and goin'. No sense encouragin' any temptation you might have to fly."

He didn't answer right away, debating, weighing a confession. Somehow the crazy cowgirl had worked her way under his skin. She tempted him every day. He decided on ambiguity.

"I've been living with temptation every day, Matilda Rose."

Her head snapped around. Her wide blue eyes locked on his. "I knew it!"

No. She'd mistaken his meaning, as he thought she would.

"Don't get riled. I promised to see you safely to the Silver Star, and I will . . . *Sissy*. It's the devil in me tempting me with dreams of a good cigar, smooth whiskey, and a winning hand of cards."

"*Harumphf.*" Her familiar sound of disapproval was followed by the tilt of her chin. "Should have known."

"It's a man's dream."

"And don't call me Sissy. There's no need anymore."

"Even if you become my sister-in-law?"

Heaven Sent

"No *if* about it," she snapped and turned her attention back to the passing street scene. "You'll never find the circuit rider in a crowd like this," she said. "Everyone for miles around has come to town to celebrate the Fourth of July."

"If he's here, I'll find him, and I'll find Billy Bowed-Legs's horse. Remember, I'm a detective, a Pinkerton."

"I'm Amelia Bloomer."

"Wouldn't surprise me."

" 'Spect with all these folks in town you can sell a ton of snake oil."

"Just let it go, Matilda Rose."

She grinned at him. A full-out, teasing smile that made Coop's throat go dry, and his breath to catch. Sensuous lips and sparkling eyes rendered him momentarily oblivious to all else. It took him a few seconds before he remembered he was driving a big team on a busy main thoroughfare.

A man had to be careful in the city. He had to concentrate. Folks in a hurry dashed out in front of wagons. He couldn't be mesmerized by a smile that slowed the natural rhythm of his heart, by eyes as purple-blue as the twilight sky. Something damned disturbing was happening to him.

"I reckon if you find Billy's horse, I might be persuaded you're a real Pinkerton, Cooper T."

"Before this day is out, you'll have your proof. I'm going to telegraph the San Francisco office and have them send a telegram addressed to you stating I am who I say I am."

"Good. Phoebe will feel much better knowin' she's marryin' an honest, professional man."

"You just said I was trustworthy."

"I didn't say in *all* things."

Sandra Madden

Coop groaned. He couldn't seem to win with this woman. "There's the hotel," he said, pointing to the only two-story building on the street. He refused to discuss matrimony again. Despite what Matilda Rose believed, he'd be hog-tied before he married Phoebe Applebee or anyone else.

"First thing I'm gonna do is have a long hot bath," she declared with more spirit than he'd heard in several days. "And then I'm gonna buy me some boots."

Grateful to have arrived at last and in one piece, Coop pulled the wagon to a stop in front of the town stables. His mouth still ached, his thigh felt sore, his ankle itched, and his pride was battered.

"I'm heading directly for the telegraph office after we hire our rooms. Headquarters expected me in San Francisco five days ago. It would be mighty disappointing to lose that James job." He jumped down from the wagon and held his arms out to her.

"Forgive me for sayin' so, but you can't go off chasin' bandits once you're married to Phoebe Pearl."

"Matil—"

She fell lightly against him. The brief contact sparked a curling heat in his midsection that left Coop slightly stunned and momentarily speechless.

Matilda Rose stepped back out of his arms quickly, making a great show of brushing the dust from her shirt and trousers. He noticed her hands trembled as she swept away the remains of the trail.

"But I am not going to marry Phoebe Pearl," he growled, recovering himself.

"When we—"

"And I'm not arguing about this again. You know, you might try sweet-talking me sometime instead of or-

Heaven Sent

dering me around like I was a new ranch hand on your daddy's spread."

"Sweet-talk?"

"Like women do. Men respond better to honey than castor oil."

She shrugged.

He made arrangements to board the horses and house the wagon before they walked to the hotel. It was full. Not even one room in the lone hotel was available. Looking decidedly glum, Matilda Rose chewed on her lower lip until the hotel clerk suggested Mrs. Gill's boardinghouse. They hurried back down the main street.

"I only have one room left," the exceedingly plump Mrs. Gill told them. "Everybody is in town to celebrate the Fourth of July."

"One room will do," Matilda Rose said. "We're married. Carl and Maggie Smith."

A light breeze could have knocked Coop over. The petite woman at his side had a quick mind and a lively imagination. His wife! Matilda Rose Davis?

His hands shook as he handed Mrs. Gill the money for one night's lodging. He couldn't breathe. No air was making its way into his lungs.

"Ma . . . Maggie—"

"Weren't you goin' to the telegraph office, dear?"

She smiled as sweetly as an angel. And it frightened him.

Coop headed for the telegraph office, his mind reeling. He could never know what Matilda Rose Applebee would do next! Brother and sister, man and wife. In the past few weeks, they'd been everything to each other but friends and . . . lovers. And perhaps, in a way, they had become friends. But lovers?

Sandra Madden

On the way back to the boardinghouse after sending his telegram to Pinkerton's West Coast headquarters, he passed the general store and came to an abrupt stop.

He stared at the beautiful blue dress in the center of the small window. It looked to be his "wife's" size, small and sweetly feminine.

Tonight might be his only opportunity to see Matilda Rose in a dress. They were only a day or two away from their destination. He'd make the dress a gift and ask her to wear the silk-and-lace confection to dinner.

A delicate bell tinkled as he opened the door to the dressmaker's shop. The tall, gaunt proprietress, dressed in black, smiled tentatively. Her salt-and-pepper hair had been pulled severely back into a bun in the nape of her neck and her hazel eyes protruded slightly.

Coop removed his hat and pulled the toothpick from his still tender mouth. He shifted from one foot to the other, feeling as awkward as a young man at his first dance. He'd never bought a dress before.

"Howdy. I'd like to buy the dress you've got there in the window," he said in a rush.

"Is it your wife's size?"

"Oh, it isn't . . ." His voice trailed off. "If it isn't the size, it's darn close."

"She must be a tiny little thing."

"Like a doll."

"Not all of us ladies are able to retain our figures once we marry. The customer for whom the dress was intended outgrew it before I finished the hem. Treasure your lady."

"Yes, ma'am."

"It's an expensive dress," she warned, eyeing him as if she doubted he could afford the cost.

Heaven Sent

"Money is no object," he declared. In truth, if he was lucky, he'd make it to San Francisco with a dollar left in his pocket. Carrot-Top's holdup had left a dent in his ready finances. "Wrap it up."

The woman smiled, a cold twitch of her mouth. "Will your wife be needing any undergarments to wear with her new dress?"

"Unmentionables?" He felt himself flush.

"Yes."

Coop pointed to the box. "Put whatever you think she might need right there in the box. Can't hurt to have new . . ." He cleared his throat. ". . . unmentionables."

Eager to show Matilda Rose the beautiful blue dress, Coop strode into their room at the boardinghouse without knocking first. Feeling fit to burst, he carried the box from the dressmaker's shop triumphantly before him.

"Cooper T.!" Matilda Rose wailed at the sight of him. Eyes as wide as they could possibly go, she sputtered indignantly, sliding deeper into the big shiny copper tub of bubbles.

"Oh . . . sorry." He stared. He didn't feel sorry at all. Mesmerized, he couldn't take his eyes off the woman in the copper bubble-filled tub. Essence of rose filled the warm room. He forgot to breathe.

Her eyes fired daggers. But Coop prided himself on his thick hide. He just grinned, completely captivated.

In beguiling disarray, her mass of sun-streaked chestnut curls had been pinned to the top of her head. Long wispy tendrils spilled from her combs to frame her face and adhere to her long elegant neck. Sun bronzed and breathtaking, her skin glowed.

Sandra Madden

Bubbles danced on her bare shoulders and the chain around her neck. He followed the path of the chain to where it disappeared down into the soft valley between her breasts. Billy's ring, he figured. He'd give the Appaloosas and every bottle of Dr. Van Kurem's tonic to kiss the spot where Bowed-Legs's ring nestled.

"Don't you have any manners? Is there nothin' under your hat but hair?" she railed. Her eyes, dark as a stormy sea, flashed on his. "Go! Go away."

But he couldn't. She was a feast for his eyes. Coop struggled with an overwhelming ache, a compelling urge to scoop Matilda Rose from the tub. Desire shot through him as he fought the need to carry her dripping body to the bed, dry her tenderly, inch by inch, and then make love to her through the night.

He held out the box. "I brought you something."

"Leave it," she said, breathing hard. "Leave it on the bed."

How could he leave when he wanted her like he'd never wanted another woman? Placing the box carefully on the bed, as if it would break, Coop removed the top. He pulled out the dress and held it up for her to see.

"I thought you might like a dress to wear for dinner . . . since we're in town and it's a celebration."

Her spitfire eyes softened; her mouth fell open.

Streaks of fading sunlight filtered through the lace curtain at the window. A horse whinnied in the distance. A dog barked. But soon silence enveloped the room so completely, he could hear the sound of his breathing.

"What do you think, Matilda Rose?"

Her eyes gleamed and grew misty. "I think . . ." Her voice seemed to catch in her throat. She looked up at

Heaven Sent

him and then back at the dress. "Nobody has ever given me such a beautiful . . . gift. A dress," she said in a hushed, marveling tone.

"You'll wear it, then?"

"Oh my, yes, Cooper T., My, my, my. I'll be spraddled out real fine." She met his gaze, regarding him steadily, silently, for several long moments. Finally, with a wistful smile she added softly, "You might not recognize me."

His heart knocked against his chest and his stomach did a nervous little dance. He couldn't tear his eyes from hers. For the moment his spirited little gun-toting companion appeared as vulnerable and sweet as an innocent child. At last he was glimpsing the real Matilda Rose Applebee. All Coop could think to do was to protect her unguarded feelings.

"Don't worry about that. I'd recognize you anywhere, anytime . . . precious."

His feeble attempt to lighten the serious atmosphere was immediately rewarded with a splendid, blinding smile, and lavender-blue eyes shining like a star-filled sky. "Thank you, Cooper T."

Unable to speak with his heart lodged in his windpipe, Coop shrugged and inhaled his first deep, normal breath since entering the room.

"Do you understand about my little fabrication?"

"You mean the lie about us being man and wife?"

"Yes, though it's not necessary to put it quite that way."

"No?"

"No. We needed a room, somewhere to really rest. I'd been lookin' forward to sleepin' in a bed tonight. I was feelin' desperate, Cooper T. But if talk got started about a single lady travelin' through town and sharin' a room with a drummer—"

"Detective."

She rolled her eyes in exasperation without losing the rhythm of her explanation. "Such talk might well reach my daddy's ears and lead to problems. We're not that far away from the Silver Star now. You don't mind being my husband for just one night, do you?"

Not if a husband's privileges went along in the bargain, Coop thought. But he knew without asking they didn't.

"Hell, no," he replied resolutely. "Not for a night."

"Thank you. You're provin' yourself more a gentleman than I ever reckoned."

Damned if she wasn't sweet-talking him! Smiling, he nodded, unconvinced Matilda Rose really believed what she was saying. "Character will always win out. You can't hide it."

"Can't hide arrogance either, it appears."

So much for her sweet talk.

"Well, I am a gentleman and, as further proof, I'd like to be taking you to the dance later tonight. Seems we've arrived in time for the shindig and most of the other festivities."

She gave him a halfhearted smile. "I don't dance. I don't know how."

"I'll show you. It's real easy."

"I don't know . . ."

She wavered. He could tell by the tone of her voice.

"If we go," he pressed, "there's a chance we might run into the circuit rider."

"Do you think so? Do you think Horace Hawkins will be there?"

"Can't promise. But I wouldn't be surprised."

Heaven Sent

"Then we'll go."

"Matilda Rose . . ."

"Yes?" She lifted her eyes to his, beautiful lavender-blue pools of light, softer and brighter than he had ever seen them.

Coop's insides felt like soft candy left in the summer sun, all warm and melted. "Has anyone ever told you how beautiful you are?"

He left the room without waiting for an answer.

Beautiful? Cooper T. had called her beautiful. No one had ever accused Matty of being beautiful before. But later, standing before the looking glass, wearing her new blue silk dress, she felt beautiful. She was almost as pretty as Phoebe. The light blue shade of her gown put her in mind of a clear spring sky. The color complemented her eyes and the golden bronze of her skin.

Small mother-of-pearl buttons ran down the front of the princess-style gown. Exquisite white lace trimmed the cap sleeves and low neckline. A daring glimpse of her breasts rose above the tight bodice. But she didn't care. Neither did she care that she had no jewels to wear. Billy's gold nugget ring on a chain looked odd with the delicate dress, so she removed it for the evening.

The beautiful blue gown was enough. It made her feel different. Lighter, as if her feet didn't quite touch the ground. Lovelier, like the heroine in a fairy tale.

She'd cleaned her strumpet slippers and swept her hair back, held on either side by simple combs. Her heart beat a bit faster, her pulse thumped a bit stronger. She looked like a woman . . . feminine and fine.

But why had the drummer done this? Beautiful, he'd said.

Sandra Madden

Matty whirled away from the mirror, angry with herself for making more of his comment than she should. The fast-talking peddler simply wanted to win her over. He obviously would do anything to avoid marrying Phoebe, including plying Matty with gifts.

But for this one evening, would it hurt to pretend he'd meant what he said? For one evening did she dare to forget Phoebe's plight? Could she relax and pretend Cooper T. was courting her, Matilda Rose Applebee?

She might never have another opportunity to make-believe in this manner.

Lifting her eyes to heaven, she whispered her question. "What do you think, Billy?"

Before her old angel friend could send her a sign, she heard a soft rap at the door. Cooper T. waited on the other side.

Chapter Eight

When Matilda Rose Applebee opened the door, Coop marveled at the vision before him, gawking like a mail-order cowboy catching his first look at the sun setting over the mountains. It had been years since he'd seen a sight quite so inspiring.

The change in Matilda Rose struck him dumb. Something akin to warm molasses spread through Coop's body. While he stood immobilized, the sweet stuff poured through him; through his gut, his arms, his legs . . . even his head. His mind was about as muddled as it ever had been.

He greeted her quietly, politely. "Good evening, precious."

"Evening, Cooper T."

He regarded her in rapt fascination. The blue of her silk dress made her lavender-blue eyes look bigger, and bluer. They shone like precious stones. Her full lips, moist and rosy, were parted in a sassy smile. As if she'd expected his stunned admiration, and delighted in it.

Long, sun-streaked chestnut curls cascaded from the back of her head, spilling over her shoulders, drawing Coop's gaze down to a delectable display of satin cleavage. The dainty lace trim could not conceal a tantalizing glimpse of full, lush breasts straining against the low-cut bodice.

Billy Bowed-Legs's ring was nowhere in sight. Was it possible the heavenly cowhand's influence was on the wane?

Coop's palms grew warm with desire, desire he thought he'd successfully suppressed with a cold bath minutes earlier. But here it was again, the insistent need deep inside him to caress and press his lips against Matilda Rose's magnificent, virginal breasts. He closed his eyes, silently counting boxcars in his mind. Boxcars full of train robbers he'd caught single-handedly. At last he'd composed himself.

"Is something wrong, Cooper T.? Are you feeling sickly?"

"No. Not at all." Eyes wide open, he scratched the back of his neck, partly from habit but most of all for lack of knowing the right thing to say or do. Why did he suddenly feel so uncomfortable with her? Why did his hands ache to span her small waist? Until this moment, he'd only suspected, hadn't really known her figure had more curves than a mountain trail. "It . . . it's you."

"Me?"

"Matilda Rose, you'll be the loveliest woman in the dining room this evening." His voice sounded raspy, strained.

Apparently pleased by his compliment, she bestowed

Heaven Sent

a smile as wide as the Rio Grande. The warmth of it made him feel weak all over.

"And look at you," she said, looking him over from head to toe in a slow, appreciative perusal. "All cleaned and pressed and freshly shaven in your fancy suit and string tie. Where'd you come by that satin vest?"

"Well, now, I did dig deep in the wagon for these Sunday-best duds," he admitted with a grin.

She reached out and brushed his cheek with the back of her hand. Streaks of heat shot down his spine.

"Bay rum," he murmured inanely.

"All the ladies will be lookin' your way."

At the moment, only one woman's attention mattered. And if she liked what she saw in him tonight that was all a man could want.

Giving Matilda Rose the blue dress was the best thing Coop had ever done—possibly in his entire life. He offered his arm. "Shall we go?"

By the time they reached the hotel and entered its grand dining room, he had recovered. In less than an hour, the woman on his arm had undergone an astonishing metamorphosis from spunky cowgirl to captivating princess. Although he'd seen enough of Matilda Rose in the tub this afternoon to confirm his suspicions, the blue dress erased all doubt. Her ranch-hand garb disguised a perfect body. A body men would duel to win, die to possess.

A hush fell as Matilda Rose walked before him into the paneled, velvet-draped dining room. Heads turned and conversation stopped. Both men and women paused to watch the young beauty pass.

Coop's chest swelled up like a crazy fool, proud to

Sandra Madden

be with the prettiest girl in the place. It was the damnedest thing. He wouldn't be here if she hadn't put a gun to his nose.

"I'm walking like Phoebe now," she whispered, glancing back at him, amusement glimmering in her eyes.

"Well, that's a fetching little wiggle your sister has," he replied with a grin, following in the sweet wake of essence of rose.

"Thank you." She gave him a saucy smile, tossed her head, and lifted her chin.

"Didn't know you had it in you." He chuckled. She actually seemed to be enjoying her new persona.

"I—" She stopped in the center of the room and turned slowly to Coop. "What are these folks looking at?" she whispered in a worried tone.

"Me. My striking good looks."

She giggled.

"I know you don't believe me, Matilda Rose, but some women find me attractive."

Her smile faded and she studied him for a long time, standing there in the center of the dining room. Her serious expression gave him a case of the willies. "I do believe you, Cooper T.," she said at last. "Why else would my sister be carryin' your child? She found you attractive and you seduced her."

Blowing out a deep sigh of exasperation, he shook his head. "No. I did not seduce your sister. Someday you'll believe me; you'll know the truth."

She rolled her eyes in response.

"Let's put our differences aside for the night. I'm begging you, Matilda Rose."

She studied him again, searching his eyes with an intensity that caused Coop to hold his breath. Fortu-

126

Heaven Sent

nately, she came to a decision before he expired. "I think a truce is in order for one night."

Tension drained from his body as they arrived at their table.

The hotel dining room featured wide polished plank floors and a thick-beamed ceiling. Candles blazed throughout the room, from sconces, chandeliers, and at every linen-covered table.

A variety of aromas vied for Matty's favor; baking apples, roast turkey, and sizzling pan-fried steak wafted through the intimate room.

Cooper T. held her chair. Happy to have reached the table and to no longer be on public view, she quickly sat. "Is my dress on backwards?"

"No. Why do you ask?"

"I've never had so many eyes on me in my life!"

"Maybe you have never looked as . . . lovely as you do tonight."

Her eyes locked on his. "Lovely?"

"Yes."

"It is a beautiful dress," she admitted, lowering her eyes to smooth the soft silk skirt.

"It's not just the dress. It's the woman." He cocked his head and frowned, as if he was deep in thought. "And perhaps you should wiggle a bit more on a regular basis. Your new way of walking may have something to do with the extra attention."

Matty couldn't help but laugh. Cooper T. possessed a quick wit, as well as a ready . . . disarming . . . grin.

Moments ago, when she'd opened the door of her room to join him for dinner, she'd puzzled at his reaction to her. She'd held her breath as his eyes, twinkling like green crystal, swept her body. His scrutiny struck her as more intense, more disturbing than earlier in the afternoon, when he'd walked in on her bath.

By the time he lifted his gaze once more to Matty's eyes, goosebumps covered her arms and her heart pounded inexplicably, as if she'd been riding Spirit hard and fast.

Cooper T.'s compelling features could transfix a man-hater tonight. His neat black suit and burgundy, satin-striped vest were almost as handsome as the man himself, and did nothing to hide his riveting physique. The warm surge Matty experienced as she made her purely objective observation seemed to settle in the mysteriously womanly region just below her belly. Undaunted, she continued.

The crisp white linen shirt the would-be Pinkerton wore contrasted quite attractively with his rugged tanned visage. Even the narrow string tie fastened in a knot at his neck was eye-pleasing. The small sigh that escaped her had nothing to do with the fact that there was no denying the drummer presented a downright devastating figure all slicked up.

"Shall we order?" he asked, bringing her back to the present, to the bemused quirk of his lips. Lips that had drunk from hers.

Her mouth went dry. "Yes, I'm famished."

Matty savored the first decent meal she'd had in almost two weeks. She relished each bite of moist turkey, mashed potatoes, hot bread, and apple pie.

After eating the last crumb of his pie, Cooper leaned back and patted his stomach in the way of a man deeply contented.

In addition to being devilishly handsome, he gave off some kind of powerful masculinity, Matty decided, more powerful than the tonic he sold.

He grinned at her, a heart-stirring twist of his lips

Heaven Sent

that set her insides a rockin'. "Are you ready to go dancing now, Matilda Rose?"

"After another cup of coffee," she demurred. Matty wasn't eager to demonstrate her lack of skill on the dance floor, and she'd determined to put off the moment as long as possible. Besides, she enjoyed the languid feeling of a full stomach, the comfort of her chair . . . and Cooper T.'s company.

After he married her sister, Matty would still be able to enjoy the drummer's twinklin' eyes and teasing smile . . . occasionally. She would still be sparring with him in after-dinner conversation now and again, she told herself.

"May I ask a personal question, Matilda Rose?"

"We've been out on the trail together for days. There's not much more personal than that. So I reckon you can ask."

"You've been all worried about your sister. But what about you? When are you going to get yourself hitched?"

"Me? Married?" Matty hadn't given much thought to marriage. No one within courting range of the Silver Star had ever shown any interest in her. Conversely, no neighboring cowboys had piqued her interest. Her standards were high. Besides, she wasn't about to get her heart broken.

"Don't tell me you haven't once thought about it."

She raised her chin. "Maybe once."

"When you walked into the dining room heads turned. I'm the envy of every male here tonight."

"Envy? You're just sayin' . . . saying that." Matty had been making an effort to use better English. Much as she hated to admit it, Cooper T. had a point. She shouldn't be talking like a bull wacker.

Sandra Madden

"You can have any man in the place right now. Just stand up and point." He pushed his chair back, as if he would stand up and point for her.

"Sit down!" she hissed under her breath. Her cheeks were hot with embarrassment. The turn of the conversation made her exceedingly uncomfortable.

Chuckling, Cooper T. settled himself. "Just for conversation, tell me what kind of man you'd marry."

"I'm not interested in getting married. There's too much to do on the ranch. What makes you think I have time for romancing?"

Cooper T.'s only reply was an annoying enigmatic smile as he raised a skeptical brow. She realized with a sinking stomach that he wasn't going to allow her to evade the subject. She might as well just bluff it out.

"Mind you, if I did want to marry," Matty continued after drawing a deep breath, "I'd be lookin' for a good-hearted man. A cowboy who'd love the Silver Star as much as I do. And he'd be true to me always. No tenderfoot dude's ever gonna win my heart. He's got to be brave and smart and . . . and a man of high moral fiber," she added with a meaningful gaze.

"Certainly." He nodded apparently in agreement with her requirements. "You deserve a saint."

"A man like Billy Bowed-Legs."

"Old and decrepit?"

"No!" Even though she knew Cooper T. was teasing, he still managed to rile her. "But when I . . . if I fall in love, age and looks won't have anything to do with it."

"Love? You want all those qualities in a man and you want to be in love with him too?"

Realizing her error, she chewed on her bottom lip. "Maybe love isn't a good idea. My daddy loved Mama something awful. And then she ran off with a no-

Heaven Sent

account actor. Daddy mooned around for months, his heart broken. He never really got over her leaving."

"Did you?"

The question shot through Matty like a lance. Pain rushed from her heart in a burning stream. She swallowed hard before she lashed out at Cooper. "You are the nosiest, rudest man! Probably comes from drinkin' too much of your own snake oil."

"No." He shook his head. His usual playful smile had been replaced with a hapless little grin. "I'm a detective.

Detectives ask questions. It's a habit. I didn't mean to be nosy . . . or hurt you."

"It's a bad habit," she bristled, clutching the edges of the table. "Asking questions that don't concern you."

Cooper T. leaned forward and covered her hand with his. "Don't be afraid to love, Matilda Rose. When you love someone, like you loved your ma, and they leave you . . . well, it's hard. But there are lots of people you'll meet, just like Billy Bowed-Legs, who will want to love you. Let them. Let them love you."

"My mama didn't leave me—"

"Have you heard from her?" he asked gently.

"No." A wellspring of hot tears gathered behind her eyes. Blinking them back, she lay siege. "Something bad must have happened to keep Mama from contacting us. If you're such a hotshot detective, why don't you just discover her whereabouts? Find out why she didn't send us word."

"Maybe I'll do that. Maybe we can put an end to your grieving."

"I'm not grieving."

"We'll start by getting over to that shindig and having us a good time."

Sandra Madden

Across the candlelit table he cast a wry, crooked smile that melted her anger. A simple turn of his lips chased away the sorrow that had suddenly surfaced. His wicked smile caused her heart to quiver.

"If Horace Hawkins isn't there, I'm leaving."

Thirty minutes later, Coop ushered Matty into a new barn that had obviously just been built for the livery stable. One end of the barn opened to an outdoor dance floor, and from a raised platform a group of fiddlers, guitarists, and one piano player provided the music for the dance.

The smell of fresh-cut wood and hay filled the barn. Fourth of July banners were strung from the rafters, and straight-back chairs lined the walls. A long, lace-covered table held heaping platters of cookies, along with cold pitchers of punch and lemonade.

"I don't see the circuit rider," Matilda Rose declared with obvious disappointment after a neck-straining search.

"It's early yet. Just keep your eyes open and dance," Coop said, gathering her into his arms. He'd been looking for a reason, an excuse to do this, all day. No. If he was truthful, he'd wanted to hold Matilda Rose since he'd first kissed her.

"I can't dance," she fretted, looking down at her feet.

"There's nothing to it; just sway with me. Follow my lead."

"I've never danced before."

"You're wearing a dancer's slippers," he pointed out, coaxing. "Listen to the music, the beat."

"A strumpet's slippers, you mean."

"Don't be ornery, Matilda Rose, it's not becoming."

Heaven Sent

"Let's go outside. There aren't so many people dancin' out there yet."

Relenting, he took her hand and led her out. Under a golden moon and a mass of silver stars, Coop gathered Matilda Rose into his arms again. She fit under his chin, the top of her head stopping at his shoulder. The most beautiful girl at the dance felt as light as silver dust in his embrace. He folded her childlike hand in his and drew her closer, feeling her breasts against his chest, feeling his heart thunder.

"How . . . how am I doing?" she asked.

"You were born to dance." She'd stepped on his foot, but with the protection provided by his boots and her light weight, he hardly felt a thing.

"It's . . . it's not too hard." She sounded nervous.

"Any woman who can break a horse can waltz."

"Might come to like it." She sounded uncertain.

"You're a natural," he murmured. "We'll dance all night."

"I don't think so!"

But Coop could hold her in his arms all night. And he'd dance 'til dawn if that was what it took to keep her there. He inhaled deeply. "Essence of rose?"

"You know it is," she replied quietly.

"I like it."

"You're sweet-talkin' me so I'll let you go. I know what you're doin'."

"I'm not sweet-talking. I'm sincere."

"Sweet-talkin' won't do you any good. I can't let you go," she continued as if she hadn't heard him. "Phoebe and her baby need a husband and father."

"And any man will do?"

"No. Only you. You're the one."

"No, I am not," Coop protested, irritated that this

Sandra Madden

phantom sister called Phoebe kept coming between them. "I thought for this one night we weren't going to wrassle with your sister's predicament. When are you going to believe you've got the wrong man?"

"When Phoebe Pearl tells me so."

"And then you'll let me be on my way?"

"If she tells me you're the wrong man, you can leave to go ride your trains. You've told me more'n once you can't settle in one place. No one's gonna hold you back. If you're the wrong man."

"And I am, but—" The sudden tap on his shoulder served to further irritate Coop. They'd drifted back into the barn and were no longer alone. "What?" he blurted.

A young blond man stood at his side. "Excuse me, but I'd like to dance with the lady. May I?"

"No. Aw . . . Matilda Rose?"

She smiled at the strapping short-haired youth. "I'd be pleased to dance with you, sir."

In minutes Matilda Rose became the belle of the ball. She changed dance partners so frequently, it made Coop's head spin. He watched as she laughed with each new partner. Her eyes glittered with delight as she swooped around the floor in her beautiful blue dress . . . and her strumpet slippers.

Men, young and old, handsome and plain, lined up to dance with the woman he'd brought to the dance. The enchanting woman he ached to hold.

Smiling gaily, Matilda Rose waved to him over the shoulder of her current partner. A young dark, curly-haired man who seemed to make her laugh excessively. Coop listlessly waved back. She had little social experience; she didn't know the first thing about how to handle all these admiring young men. Shoot. Matilda Rose could find a missing calf easier than she could tell

Heaven Sent

a lie from a man prepared to steal her virtue.

The prickly fingers of irritation scratched at his spine, swirled in his stomach. He'd best be taking her back to the hotel. She'd be happy to go. Matilda Rose hadn't wanted to come to this shindig in the first place. And it looked to him like she'd forgotten she'd only come to find Horace Hawkins.

He approached her as soon as the music ended. She thanked her dance partner and turned to Coop with a brilliant smile.

"Oh, Cooper T., thank goodness you're here. I am winded! May we go get some punch and rest a bit?"

"I thought we'd go back to the hotel."

She frowned up at him. "The dance isn't over yet."

"We have to make an early start, Matilda Rose. I'm due in San Francisco sometime this year."

"But Horace Hawkins hasn't arrived. I can't go back to the Silver Star without Billy's horse. Feller is as much a part of my legacy from Billy as your wagon is from Dr. Van Kurem." She raised her eyes to the heavens, which annoyed Coop beyond all reason.

"Has it occurred to you, you might be looking in the wrong direction for Billy?" he demanded, pointing to the ground. "Mr. Bowed-Legs might be down there."

"Cooper T.! What is wrong with you? I do believe you're angry enough to bite the sights off a six-shooter."

"I am not angry. I am exercising good judgment and common sense."

"Now? We're supposed to be having a good time. That's what you said you wanted to do."

"That was before. This is now."

"But I'm having such fun. I love to dance! I wish I had known before." Her eyes gleamed with delight, melting his resolve. "Thanks to you I know it now."

Sandra Madden

"Good," he replied sternly, averting his gaze to the space over her shoulder. "I'm happy I've introduced you to something you enjoy. Let's go."

"Do you know I've learned to waltz and to polka tonight?"

"I'm . . . I'm glad for you."

"My partners have all been so sweet and patient. Each taught me something new."

"I'll just bet they have. But it's time to leave. You'll thank me in the morning." He caught her elbow. "Let's go, Matilda Rose. Now."

"One more dance."

"No."

"Please?" She wrapped her arms around his neck. Surprise immobilized him. "Listen, Cooper T. Isn't that a beautiful tune?"

The band played the haunting melody "Lorena."

"Well, yes, but—"

"Please, please dance with me." Her remarkable eyes beseeched him, her soft body brushed against his.

"I . . . I guess one more dance wouldn't hurt."

Beaming, she stepped back and placed her hand in his. He pulled her against him, so close not a blade of grass could be slipped between his body and hers. She offered no protest.

"You're the best dancer of all," she said, gazing up into his eyes, a beguiling smile on her lips.

Moist, pink lips, full and sweet. Lips he yearned to kiss. "Matilda Rose, be careful or you'll bewitch me," he warned.

She laughed, a light lilting laugh, as if he'd said something terribly amusing.

As they danced slowly, silently, the tantalizing movements of her body pressed to his, propelled Coop's

Heaven Sent

heart into an irregular rhythm. The smoky simmer of desire curled through his core, shot to his fingertips. Like some demented soul, he continued to torture himself with a woman he could not have.

Enveloped in essence of rose, he held her tightly as she swayed against him. Her thighs, her breasts brushed against his body, stirring new, alarming... wonderful sensations that skipped and sizzled inside him.

When the music ended, his lips grazed the top of her head, stealing a taste of her sweet silky hair.

Matilda Rose stepped back, her lips parted in a dazzling smile, her eyes sparkling as they met his. She had no idea how he felt, how much he wanted her.

"Thank you, Cooper T."

"Thank you," he responded hoarsely. "Now let's get out of here. It's warm enough to roast buffalo."

Coop hadn't taken two steps when the lead fiddler stepped up and shouted to the crowd in a distinctively Spanish accent.

"*Señoras, señoritas,* and *caballeros*... eet's zee time we've all been awaiting. Zee beeg event of our Fourth of Hul-ie fiesta. Look up to zee sky and see zee fireworks!"

"Cooper T., please let's stay."

He nodded, unable to say no. Her eyes widened in anticipation. At the first burst of fireworks, she turned away from him, lifting her gaze to the sky, squealing in delight.

The pops and booms felt familiar to Coop. The firework explosions sounded like his heart of late.

Matilda Rose *aaahed* with the crowd. "Oh, Cooper T., I've never seen so many fireworks! See how they light up the night. How magnificent."

Sandra Madden

"Extraordinary," he agreed. Like the fireworks, the belle of the Fourth of July Ball also lit up the night. Coop had no idea how the fireworks looked. He couldn't take his eyes off Matilda Rose. And he couldn't stop the ache, the longing within him.

The fireworks ended to enthusiastic applause, loud hoots, and piercing whistles from the appreciative crowd. Within seconds the musicians were engaged in another rousing tune.

"Are you ready to go now?" Coop asked.

"Yes." She smiled softly and slipped her arm through his.

Why did she keep touching him tonight of all nights, when even the most innocent touch drove him wild?

Just outside the barn, Coop stopped short. Matilda Rose gasped. Horace Hawkins stood three feet away.

Chapter Nine

"Dancing and drinking will lead you straight to the devil, my friends," the circuit rider warned in ominous tones.

He preached from a platform of old boxes erected directly in the path of those leaving the dance. Just in front of the platform lay a felt hat upside down in the dirt. It begged a body to toss in a coin before passing. Coop figured Horace had already collected two dollars or more.

"Now, isn't that just the pot calling the kettle black?" Matilda Rose's eyes flashed as she dug her fists into her hips.

"What about horse stealing?" Cooper T. shouted.

"Any man who steals another man's horse will burn for all eternity. Same as a cattle rustler." Hawkins peered into the crowd in the dark alley, one hand shading his eyes as if it was midday and the sun was blinding him. "Who asked such a foolish question? Step forward and show yourself."

Coop strode through the crowd, pulling Matilda Rose along beside him. "Remember us? The people who picked you up on the trail? The folks who fed and gave you shelter? The folks whose horse you rode out on at dawn?"

"The horse you stole while we were sleeping!" Matilda Rose added in full mettle.

The hairy preacher stiffened, as if severely offended. Lifting his head, he stroked his bushy beard with the dignity of a scholar. Ignoring Matilda Rose, he responded to Coop. "I did not steal your horse. I took it in payment for a tooth extraction."

"I don't recollect you asking for a fee," Coop drawled.

"You were delirious, young man. How could you remember anything? I warrant you don't. As I recall, you lost a great deal of blood after I pulled your tooth. Have *you* forgotten, Davis? I saved your life."

"The hell you did!"

Horace pointed an accusing finger. "Blasphemy, heathen!"

The crowd looked from one man to the other during the exchange, but judging from the expressions, Coop rather thought they sided with the circuit rider. Who would suspect a preacher of being a horse thief?

Once again, Matilda Rose jumped into the foray. "If it's payment you want, you'll get it. You might have asked instead of just takin'. Now give me back Billy's horse," she demanded, her face flushed pink with anger.

"He's gone."

"Gone!" she repeated.

Heaven Sent

"Strayed away. As I wish you would." Horace spread his arms out to his makeshift flock, bestowing a saintly, martyred smile. "I'm here spreading the word, hoping to make enough to stake me to another horse so I can ride out where no other preacher goes and bring the word of our Maker to those in the wilderness who go hungry for moral strength."

But Matilda Rose wasn't having any of it. "Tarnation, Horace. How could you lose Feller?"

Coop took her elbow. "Come with me, precious."

She resisted as he hustled her down the alley, away from what could swiftly become a prickly situation. She kept looking over her shoulder as Hawkins continued his preaching. But the sermon took a new direction that Coop and Matilda Rose couldn't fail to hear as the circuit rider boomed his message.

"Brothers and sisters, you've just witnessed a chilling example. The devil has possession of those young folks. Don't let Satan into your life. Beware of his many faces."

"I'm not leavin' town without Billy's horse," Matilda Rose bit out. "Feller didn't stray. He's hidden somewhere. I know it."

"I'm guessing you're right, and if he is I'll find him," Coop assured her, attempting to calm his companion. "Remember . . . I'm a Pinkerton."

"With no identification, nothin' that says so," she scoffed.

His heart sank. He'd lost the sweet beautiful lady he'd danced with minutes ago. Matilda Rose, rancher and stubborn tomboy, had returned, full of spit and vinegar. Any ideas he might have had of seducing the vixen evaporated as he hurried her along to the boardinghouse.

141

Sandra Madden

"I telegraphed ahead. Replacement credentials will be waiting for me in San Francisco."

"As if that helps here and now. *If* you really are what you claim," she argued, wrenching out of his grip. "Which I doubt."

"As you so frequently point out."

Coop had done more than wire about his credentials and latest estimated arrival at headquarters. He'd requested a document of validation especially for Matilda Rose. Further, he'd asked for information regarding a missing person: Mary Louise Applebee, last seen leaving Santa Barbara with an actor, name unknown.

"You told my sister you were a drummer."

"Of course I did. That's my cover," he growled under his breath. The disappointment he felt in losing his enchanting dance partner edged close to anger. With each step his impatience with Matilda Rose's unyielding stubbornness grew.

"That's what you say," she mumbled.

"I will find Feller as soon as you are safely in your room." He paused for impact. "Trust me."

She stopped in her tracks. "Trust you?"

Frowning, he nodded. What was so difficult for her to understand? "Yes. Trust me," he repeated tersely.

"When pigs fly."

"Be reasonable."

She met his gaze. The lavender light in her eyes blazed with determination. "I'm goin' with you."

With a rustle of skirts, she spun on her heel and marched toward the stables.

Coop seized her arm. "Matilda Rose, the cowboys on the street have been celebrating all day. They're liquored up, and the sight of a pretty girl is going to put

Heaven Sent

you in danger. I can't fight off a gang of rowdy cowboys single-handed."

She was quiet for a moment, obviously mulling over his words. "Do you really think you can find Feller?" she asked with a trace of uncertainty. "Will you know her when you see her?"

"Yes."

"She comes when I whistle. Billy taught her to do that."

"I understand she means a lot to you. At dawn's first light I'll find her and we'll take off for the Silver Star."

"What's wrong with now? Why can't you go after her now?"

"Because Horace will have some of his flock standing guard, expecting us to go after her now."

"Oh."

Coop breathed a sigh of relief at her soft acceptance. When they reached the boardinghouse, he walked her up the steps to the porch. "Good night, Matilda Rose."

She raised questioning eyes to his. "Where are you goin'?"

He wasn't made of gun metal. For the latter half of the evening, he'd held her in his arms as they'd danced. He'd felt the simmering heat deep within him building as his body brushed against hers in teasing torment. For hours, Coop had inhaled essence of rose, and been mesmerized by eyes that sparkled like lavender-blue stars. He'd listened to the light silver sound of her laughter, and it had filled his heart with music.

Although the mood had been broken, Coop knew it wouldn't take much to ignite his desire. He couldn't spend the night alone with Matilda Rose in one small bedroom and guarantee her safety. From him. Gazing down at her upturned eyes, petite figure, and sweet, full lips, he drew a deep breath to collect himself. He needed to exert every ounce of willpower at his command. Even as he summoned the strength, his eyes drifted slowly down to the creamy valley of her cleavage. His heart slammed against his chest.

"I'm going out for a cigar, a whiskey, and a hand or two of poker with the boys."

"You don't mean it," she said softly, sounding slightly dazed.

"And later, so as not to disturb you, I'll sleep in the wagon."

"You're going to leave me here alone?"

"Believe me, precious, you're safer here alone than you would be if I stayed."

She shot him a puzzled look before she frowned and, amazingly enough, gave in to him without an argument. "I don't understand . . . but good night, Cooper T."

He tweaked her nose. "Be ready to leave at dawn."

But at dawn, Matty sat behind bars. She brooded in a small, ugly jail cell. A prisoner being treated the same as a common criminal. Each time Marshal Pennington looked over at her he shook his head. She found his attitude annoying. And she was mortified.

Her beautiful blue dress had been packed away and she was back in buckskins, which appeared a bit odd with her strumpet slippers. Her plans to buy storebought boots this morning had hit a snag.

Matty rose before dawn, expecting she'd run into Cooper T. searching for Feller. She thought to join him, since Billy's horse knew her and would come easily. But instead, purely by accident, setting out by the back door, she found Feller tied up behind Mrs. Gill's boardinghouse. She'd discovered the horse in less than five

Heaven Sent

minutes. Obviously, Horace had chosen to stay in the same place, ironic but convenient.

Matty decided to take Feller to the stable where Spirit, Traveler, the Appaloosas, and the medicine wagon were lodged. After untying the horse she whistled, expecting Feller to follow her. Instead Feller neighed. Loudly.

"Tarnation!"

Unfortunately, Horace Hawkins heard. Just as Matty made it to the street with Feller, the circuit rider was up and running. Dressed only in his worn gray long underwear, the hairy preacher chased down the center of the street behind her squawking, "Horse thief! Stop the horse thief!"

She'd tried to hush him and talk some sense into the man, but he'd grabbed her. Surprisingly, Horace Hawkins possessed more strength than most circuit riders, and he dragged her to the marshal's office. There, to Matty's utter amazement, the marshal chose to believe the lying rider rather than her.

Within a matter of minutes, Hawkins left with Billy's horse and Matty was locked up. Pleading had done no good.

"Do I look like a horse thief?"

"Belle Starr doesn't look like no bank robber neither."

Pennington refused to listen to her. He just pulled at his long gray mustache and shook his head.

"When Cooper T. gets here, he'll straighten this all out," she told the bullheaded lawman for the fifth time.

"My deputy's gone after him."

At least the marshal had agreed to send for Cooper. But she'd had to argue long and hard before he gave in. "Feller is my horse. My friend Billy Bowed-Legs told me to take care of her if anythin' ever happened to him. Horace Hawkins stole Feller."

"Preachers don't steal."

"He admitted taking the horse in front of a dozen witnesses last night." Matty left out the part where he'd claimed the horse in payment for the tooth extraction. She didn't want to confuse the marshal with falsehoods. Cooper T. could explain that later. "And then your Bible-packing varmint lied again and claimed Feller strayed away."

"Can you produce any of these witnesses?"

She hung her head. "No."

"Then it's the circuit rider's word against yours. And preachers don't lie."

"Neither do I!"

Matty drew a breath, preparing to launch into a tirade about how the circuit rider had used and abused them. How he was pulling the wool over the marshal's eyes, how the preacher had hair sprouting from his ears.

But the door opened, and in ambled Cooper T. Matty had never been so happy to see a man in her life. She leaped to her feet.

His clear green eyes swept the small jail as if he owned it. Strength and power shimmered from him like the highest, most magnificent mountain. A muscle constricted in the strong set of his jaw. He was no ordinary drummer; she knew it in her heart. He might even be a Pinkerton detective, as he kept insisting.

Matty couldn't take her eyes off his towering figure and she reckoned it was the excitement causing her heart to jump and thump hard against her chest. Cooper T. had come to her rescue. In minutes she would be free.

Heaven Sent

"Well, what do we have here?" he asked, sauntering over to Matty's cell.

She clasped her fingers around the bars. "A misunderstanding. That's what it is. Tell the marshal about Feller."

"She stole a horse," Marshal Pennington grumbled.

Cooper T. twirled the toothpick in his mouth. "Can we have a few minutes alone, Marshal?"

"Reckon."

"Can't we talk later, once I'm out of here?"

"No. We're going to talk now, Matilda Rose. I thought we made a pact that I was going to take care of our business with the Reverend Hawkins."

"Yes, and I was just trying to help you. Feller knows me. I didn't expect to find her behind the boardinghouse as I was leaving. How was I to know Hawkins was staying at Mrs. Gill's too?"

"That's not the point." Cooper T. spoke slowly and deliberately. "Sometimes you have to trust other people."

Cooper T. was angry. She could see it in his eyes, the icy green glitter. She heard it in his voice, the quiet monotone. She'd never seen him angry before.

"Please don't, don't be . . . upset with me," Matty stammered. "I trust you . . . as much as I can."

"That's not enough. I've tried to show you the man I am, and that's not the man your sister claims to know. Is it?"

"Well . . ."

He clutched the bars of her cell, looking down at her, biting the words out. "Do you know that since the day we met you've shown nothing but a headstrong, stubborn streak that would have driven a normal man plum loco? But I've been patient. Until now."

Sandra Madden

"Wha . . . what do you mean?"

"You won't give a man an inch."

"I meant to go lookin' for you as soon as I had Feller safe in the stable."

His eyes were cold as they locked on hers. He shook his head wearily. "I'm tired of talking to the wind. You don't listen. And now you've landed yourself in jail. Well, maybe that's where you belong."

"Cooper T.!" Matty couldn't believe what she heard. Tears welled in her eyes; her hands trembled.

"Don't go crying on me now. It's too late." He turned on his heel and strode to the door. "It's the end of the trail for us, precious. I'm going where I belong. I'm heading to San Francisco."

"You're not going to leave me here?"

He stopped at the door. "I've had all I can take."

"I was just tryin' to help."

"That's your problem. Sometimes you have to let well enough alone and let other people do the fixing."

"I will. I promise. I won't try to help you—"

"Next time a man says he's going to do something for you, exercise a little faith. Let him do it."

"I'm . . . I'm sorry."

"It's too late for apologies, Matilda Rose. Since the day you aimed that rifle at my head it's—"

"I did it for Phoebe Pearl—"

He heaved a heavy sigh. "This is good-bye."

"No!" Hot tears she couldn't blink back streamed down Matty's cheeks. Her pulse pounded with fear. "You can't leave me!"

"But I can. In the future, I'd advise you to listen to your partners every once in awhile and stop acting like you were the only person with a care."

"Please, please, don't leave me here, Cooper T."

Heaven Sent

"I'll have the marshal send word to your daddy to come and get you. In the meantime you can cool your heels and think about where your headstrong nature has landed you this time."

The door banged shut behind him.

Matty fell to the bunk. What was she going to do without him? What was going to happen to her now? Her heart squeezed up inside her like a concertina, and the pain in her chest took her breath away.

She'd been abandoned. Again.

A sense of despair washed over Matty in rolling, suffocating waves. She'd experienced these same feelings a long time ago. When she discovered her mother had left.

At the sound of the door opening, hope lost minutes ago blossomed in a surge of excitement. He'd come back for her. She knew Cooper T. couldn't leave her there!

Hastily brushing the tears from her cheeks, Matty looked up.

Marshal Pennington swaggered through the door. He shot her a sour look before sinking into his chair and plopping his feet up on the desk. "Meggie will be bringin' us some breakfast soon."

"I don't care about breakfast. Please don't let them get away!"

"Don't let who get away?"

"Horace Hawkins and Cooper T. Davis."

"I was hoping Davis would take you off my hands. Bail's not that high." He sulked.

Matty raised her chin in a vain attempt to save what little pride she had left. "Evidently, he's in a hurry."

"If I were in his boots . . . I would be too."

"He stole my sister's . . . heart."

"A man don't git hanged for that. He gits hanged for stealin' horses and cattle."

Incensed to be so wronged, Matty jumped up. "I only took back what was mine."

"You don't have any proof that horse belongs to you."

"Cooper T. Davis knows. Didn't he tell you?"

"You expect me to take the word of a man you've got wrapped around your little finger?"

"If he's so wrapped, why did he leave me here?"

"He's got important business."

"More important than leavin' me and his responsibilities?"

"Lady, I can't say as I blame him. Leavin' a woman like you must have its rewards."

"What do you mean, a woman like me?"

"You're a thief, Matilda Rose. A horse thief."

"No!"

"Never had a woman in my jail before."

"Then let me go," she pleaded, casting what she hoped was a pathetic gaze.

"I can't. You broke the law. Hawkins wants you here until you pay for your sins and repent. And Davis says you're not to travel on by yourself. He left instructions. I'm sendin' my third deputy, Leland, up to your daddy's ranch. Leland doesn't git much work. We'll wait for your daddy to come get you."

The pit of Matty's stomach gave way. "That will take days."

"Give you time to think about the consequences of horse stealin'. Be grateful you're not goin' to a hangin' party as the guest of honor."

It was no use. The marshal was a mule-headed man who believed Horace Hawkins over her, and he'd

Heaven Sent

plainly been intimidated by Cooper T. Her daddy would have her hide for disgracing him.

Where was her guardian angel now, when she most needed him? Wasn't Billy Bowed-Legs looking after her anymore?

Matty had never felt so helpless. Unwanted woman's tears flowed again. It was all she could do not to sob outright. Throwing herself on the bunk, she rolled to face the wall. She'd rather die than let the marshal see her cry.

When the door opened again, she did not look around. Despair had killed her curiosity. If it was the breakfast the marshal expected, Matty knew her churning stomach couldn't hold a bite of food. Life had never been this bleak. She'd really done it this time, made a mess of things.

Cooper T. had fled. Phoebe would be shamed for life. Uriah Applebee would disown her; her daddy had threatened before.

"Billy Bowed-Legs," she whispered, "I was only tryin' to get Feller back. I didn't mean to make Cooper T. mad, or shame you and Daddy. Phoebe will be upset with me too. Havin' a jailbird for a sister isn't likely socially acceptable. Can't you help me, just one more time?"

"Matilda Rose."

Chapter Ten

Her name. Spoken so softly, Matty thought she might be hearing things. Life had taken such a bad turn in the last few hours, she wouldn't be surprised to find herself hallucinating and hearing voices.

Billy Bowed-Legs sometimes called her by her full name. Usually when he was displeased. Might be acting as her guardian angel was beginning to disagree with him. A fresh stream of tears spilled down her cheeks.

"Matilda Rose."

Breakfast had been delivered. That was it. The marshal was tryin' to tell her he was ready to open the cell and deliver the stale bread and gruel—which was the only food she'd heard jail prisoners were served. But at least the door would be open for a few seconds. Tarnation!

Suddenly afire, Matty's mind raced with possibilities. Could she make a break for it? She was smaller than the marshal, but she probably was a lot faster. If she

Heaven Sent

could make it to a horse she could hightail it. . . .

What was she thinking? From jailbird to jail break? She sniffled loudly.

"Matilda Rose, have you gone to the last roundup?"

Cooper T.! She couldn't believe her ears!

"Damnation, are you dead in there?"

Swiping her tears away with the back of her hand, Matty rolled over. Cooper T.!

She almost fell over herself getting up.

He filled the center of the room, a towering figure in black. His rigid stance was at once magnificent and ominously somber.

One glance told her that he was still angry. His narrowed eyes were the color of dark jade. His mouth turned down and his lips were pressed together in a thin, terse line. A shiver skipped down Matty's spine. His bristles were up, all right. No doubt he was in a horn-tossing mood.

Afraid to let hope claim her, to dare think he might have returned to spring her from this humiliating incarceration, she slowly strolled to the cell door. Her pulse beat wildly.

Straightening her shoulders and tilting her chin, she looked him straight in the eye. "Howdy, Cooper T."

His eyes narrowed even more until all she could see was a glimpse of frosty green gleaming between two fixed slits. His jaw set tighter than a bowstring.

"Are you ready to ride?"

She lifted her chin higher. "I believe I am."

"No conniption fits, no arguing, no sassing me?"

"My lips are sealed." Once out of jail, she would never talk to the double-crossing drummer varmint ever again. She was furious. How dare he leave her in a small, dirty cell believing he wasn't coming back?

Sandra Madden

He coolly turned away from her. "Marshal Pennington, I'm going to take Matilda Rose home to her daddy. I made her that promise a few weeks back, and I'm a man of my word."

"Glad to have her gone. Saltiest woman I ever met. But I just can't let her walk out of here."

Cooper T. popped a fresh toothpick into his mouth. "I understand."

"The horse stays."

"Feller is Billy Bowed Legs's horse—" Matty protested.

"Matilda Rose."

"But . . . but I guess Hawkins needs her more."

"One more thing."

Cooper T. hiked a brow. "What's that?"

"Restitution. Bail."

Matty knew Cooper T. didn't have any more money. He'd used what he'd had left from the robbery to buy her the beautiful blue dress. "I'll have my daddy send some, soon as I get back to the ranch."

"What if he don't?" the marshal asked.

"He will." She would use her own savings.

The stoic lawman objected. "Can't take your word."

"You can trust me," Matty assured him, slightly appalled that he didn't believe her. The man was treating her like some hardened desperado.

"I'll leave my wagon as collateral," Cooper T. said. "The patent medicine wagon."

Matty gasped.

"The wagon and the Appaloosas," Pennington countered.

"Do I have your word the team will be stabled and taken care of until I return?" the drummer bargained in a steely voice.

154

Heaven Sent

"You do." To seal the agreement, the marshal shook Cooper T.'s hand before crossing to unlock Matty's cell. "And I don't want to see you in this town again, young woman. Horse thieves aren't welcome in the City of Angels."

She sailed from the cell past the marshal, head held high. "I did not steal. I simply took back what was mine and—"

"Did you not just make a deal with me?" Cooper T. interrupted, grinding out the question between his teeth.

Lowering her eyes, she nodded.

"Good day, Marshal." With a hard hand on her shoulder, Cooper T. guided Matty from the jail. "We'll make arrangements to get to Santa Barbara by steamer. It will be faster."

Fast wasn't swift enough. She couldn't wait to get home and away from the man who strode so purposefully at her side. She doubted she would ever leave the peace and safety of the Silver Star spread again.

"But first—" Matty stopped on the wooden walk and pointed at her feet. "I need some ready-made boots."

His frown was dark and deep. "You don't mean to steal them, do you?"

"Cooper T., I am wounded."

He rolled his eyes.

Coop stood at the rail of the *Shady Lady* smoking a cigar. Staring into the foggy darkness, he listened to the giant steamer make its way along the coast. The whoosh of the water, the blast of the foghorn. The night was cool. Matilda Rose was cool. She hadn't spoken to him since they boarded the steamer bound for Santa Barbara that afternoon.

Sandra Madden

He'd been more riled than he'd ever remembered when summoned to the hoosegow to claim Matilda Rose; angrier than a wet cat and primed to lock horns. The crazy, featherheaded, pistol-packing spitfire had agreed to let him fetch Feller, then turned right around and snatched the horse herself. After all this time she still couldn't bring herself to trust him.

He didn't need any more of her trouble. She could grow old in jail for all he cared.

Coop had reached the edge of town before he knew he couldn't leave Matilda Rose alone and locked up. He'd be haunted by those misty eyes peering from between the cell bars for the rest of his life. He'd never be able to forget the tears streaming down her pale cheeks.

The steamer carried only a few other passengers. Earlier in the evening, dinner had been served at the captain's table. Coop and Matilda Rose conversed with the others, but not with one another. So far, it had been a silent journey. He'd never known her to be quiet for nearly this long.

Hearing a movement at the far end of the rail, he glanced over from the corner of his eye.

Matilda Rose appeared to be contemplating the choppy black seawater below. From the time he'd escorted her from the marshal's office, she'd lacked the spark, the spirit he'd come to know. Complacent, seemingly cowed, she said nothing and avoided eye contact with him. Suddenly, an alarming thought struck.

"Don't jump!" he yelled.

Her head snapped toward him.

"It's not that bad," he assured her, tossing his cigar into the water to free his hands. He moved slowly toward her, speaking softly and calmly. "You're almost

Heaven Sent

home now and this . . . this incredible journey will be behind you."

For a moment she regarded him silently, frowning. And then she exploded.

"Are you daft, Cooper T.?" Her eyes blazed angrily as she stomped her newly booted foot—and winced. "Do you think throwing myself to a watery grave is the only way I can be rid of you?"

Brought up short, he stopped. "Of course not."

"Wish I had my mouth organ," she muttered, turning her gaze back to the sea. "Could use a tune about now. I'm gonna go get it."

"Wait."

"Why?"

Because he had a feeling he wouldn't see her again until morning if she left now.

"Do you really want to be rid of me?" he asked, aggrieved more than he wanted to be or cared to let her know.

"Oh, I reckon I can stand the sight of you 'til we reach the Silver Star," she allowed wearily, turning back to the sea. "But I can't say I'm pleased you left me to rot in jail like a common criminal."

"I didn't. I came back for you."

"But you chose to leave me first. They might have lynched me."

"Not likely." He leaned on the rail beside her, staring into the darkness, inhaling the heavy scent of salt and the light, sweet essence of rose. "I'm sorry we had to give up Feller to spring you this morning. But breaking you out of jail might have offended my fellow Pinkertons."

She nodded.

Sandra Madden

"Matilda Rose, I'd appreciate it if you would talk to me. I don't like the silent treatment."

She continued to stare over the rail into the night. "I didn't think you wanted me to talk."

"That's not what I said. I don't want to argue anymore."

She didn't respond immediately. In the heavy silence, Coop wondered why he even bothered. Why should he be the one to seek a truce? After a full minute, she turned to him, locking her enormous eyes on his. "Why did you come back for me?"

He didn't rightly know how to answer. From minute to minute he changed his mind. What did bring him back? Had it been her pitiful expression from behind bars? Fear that Marshal Pennington might not treat her right? Her haunting eyes? Her sensuous mouth?

"I gave my word to deliver you safely to the gates of the Silver Star," he said more gruffly than he intended.

"You had the perfect opportunity to get away, from me and from Phoebe. You were free. I didn't expect to ever see you again."

"Well, now, I was riled and lost my temper. It happens." To hide his embarrassment, his uncertainty, Coop looked off to the rising moon and shoved his fingers through his hair. "A man can only be pushed so far. You've got to learn to back off and let a man be a man."

"But you're losing time. If you had kept on going, you would have been well on your way to San Francisco."

"Yes, but I made the mistake of looking back."

She grinned. "Big mistake."

"I sent another telegram explaining the delay."

Heaven Sent

"You gave up your wagon, your legacy, for me," she whispered with a bowed head.

"Didn't give up a thing," he protested, although it almost killed him to leave the wagon in the City of Angels. "I'll be back within two months' time with the money. It's like I'm boarding the wagon for a spell, that's all."

"You puzzle me, Cooper T. Just when I think I have you all sorted out in my mind, you do something to surprise me."

He gave her a lopsided smile and shrugged. "You know, it's said that surprise is the spice of life."

A blast from the foghorn jolted them into nervous laughter. Someone down belowdeck played a violin; the rising water slapped against the steamer. Matilda Rose smiled up at him and Coop felt his heart melt.

"Cooper T., you have a way of turning things around."

"Well, now, I'm hoping our . . . association can prove helpful to you. You're a pretty little thing, precious. And you know I'm telling you the truth. Last night, in your blue dress, you saw heads turn. You looked like a great lady, all feminine and sweet smiles. If you gave him half a chance, a man could be downright captivated by your charms." Not to mention her eyes and lips and breasts and hips, all lush and ripe. "There's no sense looking or acting like a man all the time."

"If I want to convince my daddy to let me run the ranch, he has to know I can be tough."

"Your daddy knows that it's what's up here that counts," Coop said, tapping his temple. "And I figure he knows how smart you are by now."

"It doesn't do for a woman to be smart. And she has

to be strong in ranching. I'm just doing what I need to do."

"What about a husband and babies? Don't you want a family?"

She turned away, leaning against the rail. "Someday. Maybe. What about you?"

Coop shook his head. "Never thought much about a family. Told you, I like the excitement of being on the move. Chasing after the crooks. Before long train robbers will weep when they hear my name. They'll turn themselves in, just you wait and see." He paused as a chestnut lock of Matilda Rose's hair blew onto his cheek in a silky caress. "Besides, I don't remember what it feels like to be settled."

"Don't you remember your folks?"

"Vaguely. We started out from Ohio, traveling west. My pa dreamed of having a farm. He was a big man, a farmer."

"What happened?"

"Not long after we reached Sacramento, they both came down with fever. My pa died first. Two days later my ma was gone."

"Oh, Cooper . . ."

"It happened quick."

"I'm so sorry," she said, laying a hand gently on his arm.

His stomach jackknifed. "I figure I was the most miserable boy in the world for a stretch."

"You were so young," she whispered.

Coop heard the crooning ache in her voice, looked down to see her lavender-blue eyes brimming with compassion. His throat grew thick.

"Yeah." He drew a deep breath and once again fastened his eyes on the black horizon. Why was he telling

Join the Historical Romance Book Club and GET 4 FREE* BOOKS NOW!

A $23.96 Value!

Yes! I want to subscribe to the Historical Romance Book Club.

Please send me my **4 FREE* BOOKS.** I have enclosed $2.00 for shipping/handling. Each month I'll receive the four newest Historical Romance selections to preview for 10 days. If I decide to keep them, I will pay the Special Members Only discounted price of just $4.24 each, a total of $16.96, plus $2.00 shipping/handling ($23.55 US in Canada). This is a **SAVINGS OF AT LEAST $5.00** off the bookstore price. There is no minimum number of books I must buy, and I may cancel the program at any time. In any case, the **4 FREE* BOOKS** are mine to keep.

*In Canada, add $5.00 shipping/handling per order for the first shipment. For all future shipments to Canada, the cost of membership is $23.55 US, which includes shipping and handling. (All payments must be made in US dollars.)

NAME: _____
ADDRESS: _____
CITY: _____ STATE: _____
COUNTRY: _____ ZIP: _____
TELEPHONE: _____
E-MAIL: _____
SIGNATURE: _____

If under 18, Parent or Guardian must sign. Terms, prices, and conditions subject to change. Subscription subject to acceptance. Dorchester Publishing reserves the right to reject any order or cancel any subscription.

The Best in Historical Romance!
Get Four Books Totally FREE*!

A $23.96 Value! FREE!

PLEASE RUSH MY FOUR FREE BOOKS TO ME RIGHT AWAY!

Enclose this card with $2.00 in an envelope and send to:

Historical Romance Book Club
20 Academy Street
Norwalk, CT 06850-4032

Heaven Sent

her all this? He never talked about that dark time. A man didn't talk about his grief. "Anyhow, I buried them there in Sacramento and hitched a ride south with one of the other wagons. The McDermotts had five kids and didn't really want another mouth to feed, but I worked as hard as I could for them until they left me off in San Francisco. Pretty much have played a lone hand since then."

"What about Angus? When did he find you?"

Coop knew he should put an end to Matilda Rose's quiet questions, but strangely enough it felt good to talk.

"About six months later in San Francisco. Now and again, I was forced to steal in order to eat. Angus caught me in the back of his wagon one day, trying to get away with a couple of bottles of tonic." He shot her a wry smile. "The old Scot put me to work right then."

"You had a difficult time."

"Some would say. But when I ran into Angus, my luck changed. He took me in, fed me, taught me a trade, and educated me. Angus was an educated man and made sure I studied at least four hours a day. I have a lot to be thankful for."

She squeezed his arm. "You were a brave little boy. It must have hurt real bad to lose your ma and pa. And yet you went on."

It had. But Coop had never allowed himself to cry. A man held his grief, held the pain close to his heart. Pain he never burdened another body with, or shared with another soul. Until now.

No one had ever encouraged him to talk about these things, showed him they cared . . . or understood. He gazed at the woman standing beside him with some surprise. It was Matilda Rose Applebee who cared, whose eyes shone with admiration.

He nodded. "It always hurts to lose people you love."

"It makes you afraid to love again," she said in a voice barely audible.

"You're right about that."

He heard her take in a deep breath, and then her tone changed to a brisk, cheery lilt. "But then you learn to fill the empty spaces with other things."

"Like ranching?"

"And running?" Challenge gleamed in her eyes like a sizzling bolt of blue lightning. "Always running from town to town on the trail of the bad guys?"

He jumped on that. "Then you believe me about being a Pinkerton?"

"No." She grinned. "I was just supposin'. It's a big old leap from drummer to detective."

"Well, now, it wasn't a direct leap. First I went east to see what I might be missing."

"Did you like big city life?"

"Didn't make it to New York City, where I intended. I only got as far as Ohio. Before I knew it, I was wearing a Union uniform."

"Tarnation," she huffed, "Fate has not been kind to you Cooper T."

"Can't say I enjoyed the experience," he said, rubbing the back of his neck. "But I worked my way up to a lieutenant and did some peacekeeping after the war ended."

"Which led to the Pinkerton Agency?"

Just as natural as can be, the girl in men's clothes had learned it all. He'd told her his life story without even thinking twice. Coop didn't know whether to be alarmed or to marvel at her talents. She possessed more

Heaven Sent

than a glance would indicate, and right now she knew more about his history than any other living soul.

"I had all the weapons skills, and Alan Pinkerton was looking for men so he could expand the agency west."

"So you came back as a Pinkerton."

"Couldn't sell tonic, couldn't sit in a building all day, couldn't stay in one town. I had no money to stake out land for a ranch or farm. But I had a good mind, a good shooting eye, and a strong fist. The Pinkerton Agency offered me a decent wage and a heap of adventure."

"Up until you got shot in the thigh and met up with me."

"Getting shot was nothing." He grinned. "I've been wounded a few times before."

Her eyes deepened to indigo and the dark brows creased in a deep frown. "Meeting up with me was worse?"

"Matilda Rose, I must admit, you're the most exasperating woman I ever did know."

Her head went up, her body stiffened, and she spoke into the wind. "Don't worry. You won't find Phoebe exasperating. She's the kind of woman a man likes. No sass, all sugar. My sister is as accommodatin' as bread pudding. Excessively biddable." Turning back to Coop, she flashed a brilliant smile. "Ready or not, you're about to embark on a family life. And . . . and I'm sure you'll be very happy together."

"I am not marrying your sister. You might better get that through your head before we reach the Silver Star."

But she ignored him; clutching the rail, gazing into the pitch black sea. "Tomorrow. I'll be home at last. And all the difficulties of this horrid journey will be behind us."

Sandra Madden

"This horrid journey wasn't my idea," he mumbled.

She let out a sigh that seemed to Coop more wistful than one of relief. "No. And you, as a . . . reluctant traveler—"

"Hostage."

"I'll confess you have been a gentleman and exceedingly cooperative—more than I expected. And now, in just a matter of hours, you and Phoebe will be reunited."

When the *Shady Lady* tied up for the night at the dock in San Fernando, Matty spent the night bunking in a small cubicle, wondering what life-threatening malady she'd caught in Los Angles. Although she wasn't running a fever, her body felt heavy and lethargic. She'd lost her appetite and for no good reason felt as irritable as a snake in a sack.

In contrast, Cooper T. had a new spring to his step. He hadn't stopped smiling since spotting Santa Barbara from the steamer. A smile so powerful and devastating it would soften the most hardhearted woman.

Pushing her feet forward, she followed Cooper T. off the steamer. While she should have been whooping for joy to be so close to home, she felt on the verge of tears.

Matty hoped she'd contracted only a mild case of whatever it was ailing her.

"You're almost home now, precious. Wait for me here and I'll get the horses."

She nodded listlessly. Traveler and Spirit had made the trip on the livestock deck.

"Are you all right?" he asked, puzzling at her.

"I'm happier than I've been for weeks," she told him, forcing a smile and batting back tears.

He frowned. "I can see that."

Heaven Sent

"Hurry and fetch the horses, Cooper T. I can't wait to feel Silver Star earth under my boots."

"Right." But he didn't move. His eyes narrowed. Cocking his head to one side, he asked, "By the way, Matilda Rose, where did you get the money to buy those ready-made boots?"

She couldn't help feeling smug. Unable to stifle her grin, she told him. "I sold the rest of Dr. Van Kurem's tonic to Mrs. Gill at the boardinghouse."

Throwing his head back, Cooper T. roared with laughter.

"Go on now and get the horses," she said, laughing with him. "We'll be at the ranch in just a few hours. You're about to embark on a new adventure. Family life."

Chapter Eleven

It was late afternoon when Matty and Cooper T. reached the high whitewashed gates of the Silver Star Ranch. Riding through the impressive gates never failed to give Matty goosebumps. She pulled Spirit to a stop.

Although Cooper T. wasn't aware of it, they had been on Applebee property for an hour. The route to her home had taken them over rolling lush green hills and through thick copses of pine, oak, and sycamore, fields of wild yellow daisies and crimson red poppies. They'd waded Traveler and Spirit across wide streams and narrow brooks that wound through the ranch.

"Welcome to the Silver Star, Cooper T." Matty grinned proudly.

He scanned the land from their hillside vantage point. "Looks to be a mighty big spread."

"One thousand acres of fine cattle grazing land," she told him. Her love for the ranch swelled inside her. It

Heaven Sent

felt so good to be back. Her odd malaise seemed a thing of the past. Turning her face into the soft breeze, she surveyed the familiar ground. Grinning with pleasure, she inhaled the distinctive fragrance of rich soil.

She was home on the Silver Star.

"Isn't it beautiful, Cooper T.?"

He nodded solemnly. "Yes, it is. Can't say as I've ever seen a spread quite like it."

"The house is up on the next ridge."

His stony expression was inscrutable as his eyes locked on hers. "I only promised to bring you to the gates of the Silver Star, Matilda Rose."

"It's almost dark," she protested. "You can't travel any farther today."

He shook his head.

"I'm not going to tie you down or force you to marry Phoebe tonight at gunpoint. I . . . I promise." At the moment, she would promise him anything.

"You're not planning to lock me up in the barn, are you?" he asked with a droll twist of his lips.

"No. What good would it do? I've got a feeling you're experienced at escapin' from just about anywhere."

"You've come to know me well."

"Besides, when you meet Phoebe you may just change your mind about leaving." And if he didn't, Matty reckoned her daddy could convince Cooper T. to make an honest woman of Phoebe.

"Not likely."

"The house is just another mile beyond the gates."

He shot her a crooked smile. "Our last mile together?"

A hard, tight pain tore at her heart.

"I reckon," she said as soon as she figured she could speak. With a slight movement of her knee, Matty signaled Spirit to move on. She didn't want Cooper T. to see the tears that had suddenly sprung to her eyes. She didn't know where they'd come from or why.

This was the time she'd been looking forward to since she'd taken Cooper T. Finally, she had the drummer where she wanted him.

Cooper T.'s horse walked slowly beside hers. "Matilda Rose . . ."

"Yes?"

"Although we've encountered some . . . ah, problems on this journey together, I want you to know that . . ."

"Yes?"

"More often than not, you made a good companion." His tone softened. "You've got spirit, Matilda Rose. And courage. And intelligence."

Cooper T.'s unexpected kind words caused a burning heat to settle on her cheeks and her throat to feel as if a whole pound of rock candy was stuck there. Not daring to look at him because of the strange trembly way she felt inside, she focused straight ahead, on Spirit's ears.

"Those are the nicest . . . the finest compliments anyone has ever paid me," she rasped. "Thank you, Cooper T."

"You deserve a lot of nice things to be said to you . . . to happen to you."

"And I believe you ought to be savin' this kind of talk for Phoebe."

"I don't speak of my feelings to strangers . . . like your sister."

Matty twisted in the saddle to fasten a frown on the quiet-talking man at her side. "Are you denyin' that you know Phoebe?"

Heaven Sent

"No. We met. But one dance doesn't make a close friendship."

"One dance," she scoffed. "Must have been some dance!"

Cooper T. groaned.

But it could have been only one dance that led to Phoebe's delicate condition. Dancing in Cooper T.'s arms could weaken the strongest-willed of women. Matty knew from experience.

She'd ached to be back in the drummer's arms since the Independence Day dance in the City of Angels. She'd yearned for his kiss since the first touch of his lips on hers.

At the moment, during their last few minutes alone together, it was taking a powerful exercise of will to resist throwing herself at him, to remember this was her sister's man. Matty had no right to even think of Cooper T., let alone be hankering for his kiss, his caress.

If Billy Bowed-Legs was up there where he could read her thoughts, she'd be one lucky cowgirl not to be struck by lightning, or swallowed up in quicksand before this ride was over. Coveting her sister's man was downright shameful, not to mention sinful.

Silently, she vowed to put the good-looking drummer—or detective—out of her mind from this moment on.

"There are a few things we need to get straight before we reach the ranch, Cooper T." Matty had other pressing concerns.

"What would those be, precious?"

"We can't tell my daddy you bailed me out of jail with your wagon. Daddy wouldn't be happy if he knew I'd been in jail," she said, understating the truth a mite.

169

Sandra Madden

"Your secret is safe with me," he replied with a playful wink that triggered warm shivers all over her body.

"I'll pay you back from my own savings. There's more than enough to cover my bail and get your wagon back."

"Matilda Rose, I can't return to Los Angeles right away. If I don't get to San Francisco, I won't have a job. The marshal will hold my wagon when he gets verification I work for the Pinkerton organization. Tomorrow I'll take the steamer on to San Francisco and be at headquarters by nightfall."

Matty nodded, unwilling to argue the point. If it made Cooper T. happy to believe he was leaving tomorrow, she'd let him. He'd brought her home safely, as he promised he would. He had been true to his word all along. She had to give him that much.

The closer they came to the ranch house, the faster her heart beat, the quicker her pulse drummed. She'd been awfully homesick. Someone who'd spent his entire life moving from town to town like Cooper T. couldn't possibly understand.

"Are we there yet?" he asked.

"Look!"

She pointed down the winding road, now shaded on either side with majestic oak trees. A sprawling adobe tile-roofed ranch house sat high on the ridge straight ahead.

Coop could see not only the main ranch house but many of the outlying buildings as well. He couldn't help but be impressed by the expansive Silver Star Ranch, a small kingdom unto itself. Silently he scanned the large stable, what appeared to be a maze of corrals, two bunkhouses, and a long, low barn surrounding the

Heaven Sent

main house. Lush rolling vineyards extended eastward as far as the eye could see.

Coop understood why Matilda Rose believed she lived in paradise. The idyllic setting presented a picture of peace, family, comfort . . . and success.

"What do you think?" she asked, nudging her horse on.

"I see a lot of white fence. But if man or beast had to be corralled, this might surely be as good a place as any," he allowed, keeping pace.

"In a few minutes we'll be walkin' through the door." Her voice bubbled with excitement, her eyes sparkled with joy.

Coop had never seen her so radiant . . . so beautiful. He doubted there was a man alive who could inspire the same glow. She outshone the sun.

He had a worrisome thought. "Precious, aren't you afraid your daddy's gonna whip you?"

"No, he'll be too glad to see me. At least at first. Billy and I planned to be back a lot sooner than this." She chewed on her lower lip as she slowed down her horse. Glancing over at Coop, her brow collapsed in a troubled frown. "It's going to be difficult explaining about Billy Bowed-Legs. Daddy and Billy were made of the same leather. They were as close as brothers."

"Billy's time had come. There was nothing you could have done to save him."

" 'Cept not takin' him along with me. He could have gone peaceful, here at the ranch."

"No way for an old rawhider to go."

"I'll turn over his saddlebag to Daddy," she replied on a sigh. "But what will I say about Feller?"

"Billy's horse got stolen. Period."

Sandra Madden

"If I ever run into Horace Hawkins again, the piker better start prayin'."

He grinned. "Matilda Rose, it's not ladylike to hold a grudge. Now, let's get on with it. But remember, I'm only staying the night. Tomorrow I leave for San Francisco."

He'd been with her too long as it was. Much too long.

Coop realized he was in trouble when he found himself waiting for her first bright smile in the morning, the sound of her laughter. Days ago, he'd known there was a problem when what began as a passing glance at her full rosy lips became a study . . . a study that stirred a need in him. His belly tightened, and his mouth went dry.

It was past time for him to go.

When they reached the house, Matilda Rose jumped from Spirit and dashed up the steps to the veranda before she stopped and looked back. Luminous eyes met his. Obviously impatient to cross the threshold, she shifted from one foot to the other. This new energy and heart-stopping glow had nothing to do with him.

"Come on, Cooper T., this is no time to dawdle."

He grinned. Matilda Rose would be issuing orders until she earned her wings and joined Billy Bowed-Legs in buckaroo heaven. "Yes, ma'am."

As she took his hand and led him into the house, Coop clamped his jaw and gritted his teeth. An unaccustomed nervousness gnawed at his stomach. He was made of stouter stuff than this, yet his nerve endings prickled as if he were about to face a grizzly. But a mile or so ago, he'd resigned himself to meet Matilda Rose's father and sister—and prepared for the worst.

The adobe house was dark, cool, and quiet. Most California settlers chose adobe because of its ability to

Heaven Sent

keep a home cool in the summer and warm in the winter. The fragrance from a basket of large oranges in the foyer mingled with the aroma of frying chicken. He drew a deep breath.

"Lupe!" Matilda Rose called. "Lupe, where are you?"

When there was no answer, she turned to him. "Probably in the kitchen. Come." She tugged at his hand, and he followed like a sheep. A sheep to slaughter.

Chills ran down his spine. During his three years as a Pinkerton detective, Coop had found himself in many dangerous situations. But this was the first time, he felt the same physical symptoms of fear in a purely social one. His palms had grown clammy cold. Silently, he rebuked himself for not having the foresight to fortify his body with a bit of Van Kurem tonic.

"*Señorita!*" A short, round Mexican woman opened her arms at the sight of Matilda Rose, who dropped his hand to embrace her.

"It's so good to see you again, Lupe."

"We have been so worried, *señorita. Su padre es loco* without you." The woman named Lupe wagged a disapproving finger at Matilda Rose. "You have been naughty, *niña*."

"I had no choice. I'm sorry. Will you forgive me?"

Before his eyes, Coop watched Matilda wheedle and wield the considerable charm he'd only caught glimpses of during their journey together.

"*Sí, señorita.*" With forgiveness came a fierce hug from the plump housekeeper.

When Matilda Rose stepped back, she turned her twinkling eyes on him. "Lupe, this is Cooper T. Davis, a friend . . . of Phoebe's."

She gave a small bow and a broad smile, revealing

Sandra Madden

an oversized front-and-center gold tooth. "Welcome, *señor.*"

"Cooper T. will be staying for dinner. Actually, he'll be staying for . . . a few days."

She gave Coop a wink.

He forced a smile.

"*Sí, señorita,* we will make up a room for your friend."

"Phoebe's friend."

"Oh, *sí.*"

"Where's Daddy?"

"*Señor* Applebee is in his study. He just came home."

"And Phoebe?"

"She is at Miss Polly's quilting bee."

"See how domestic my sister is, Cooper T.? Phoebe quilts. She knows how to make a home a home."

"Funny, but I've never missed having a quilt," he replied drolly.

"Never mind," she said, blithely ignoring his jibe. "Phoebe will be home soon. Let's . . . let's go meet Daddy."

He followed her down a long corridor, floored as the rest of the house was with large, cool terra-cotta tiles. Shooting Coop a nervous smile, Matilda Rose knocked on a heavy oak door.

"What is it?" came the gruff response.

"Daddy . . . I'm home."

"Matilda!"

It was a lion's roar. She was leading Coop into a lion's den.

"I think we can go in now," she whispered.

He drew a deep breath, preparing to deal with his share of her father's wrath. Coop had been traveling alone with the rancher's daughter for days. What if Ap-

Heaven Sent

plebee insisted he marry her? Marry Matilda Rose, not her sister.

Coop rubbed the back of his neck nervously, reproaching himself for not considering this particular ramification before now. But for the past few days all he could think about was delivering Matilda Rose safely home and getting to San Francisco in good time—despite the endless obstacles.

Matilda Rose threw back her shoulders and entered the room with her head held high and a tremulous smile on her sweet lips.

A white-haired man with a bulbous nose stood behind a massive hand-carved desk. His startling bush of hair wrapped round his head like a wiry swath of untreated cotton. Applebee looked a bit like sketches of journalist Samuel Clemens that Coop had seen.

"Where in Sam Hill have you been, girl?" he thundered.

"Daddy, I left word—"

"And who are you?"

"Cooper Davis," Coop answered quickly, struck by the older man's riveting appearance.

Although average in height and weight, Applebee's dark, weather-beaten hide gave evidence of a life on the range. His dark complexion intensified the sharp, crackling blue eyes he turned on Coop.

"Uriah Applebee." The older man extended his hand, giving Coop a firm, almost painful grip. A swift appraising gaze accompanied his handshake. The brusque introduction abruptly ended with a command. With a flick of his wrist, he motioned to the two wing-backed chairs in front of his desk. "Sit down."

Coop sat. Matilda Rose flew to her father's side and

threw her arms around him. "I'm so glad to be home! I missed you so much, Daddy!"

For a fleeting moment, Applebee appeared to return his daughter's embrace. The old man's eyes closed as if he might have been offering silent thanks. And then he set his daughter back from him. "You're a sight for sore eyes, girl. Now sit down."

Matilda Rose sat in the chair next to Coop's.

"Well, girl, I'm waitin'."

"While I was in Los Angeles, I ran into Cooper T. here. He's a friend of—"

"Is that so?" The older man's scowl grew deeper. "You traveled with this fellow from Los Angeles to the Silver Star?"

"Yes, sir."

Well, she'd admitted half the truth, Coop thought as he leaned forward in his chair and spoke in her behalf. "I came with Matilda Rose to make sure she got home safely."

"Why would you be doin' a fool thing like travelin' alone?" Uriah barked at his daughter. "Where's Billy? Your note said you were travelin' with Bowed-Legs."

"I was. I did." Matilda Rose's big eyes grew misty. Coop's instinct was to reach out and hold her hand, give her support, but he held back. Uriah Applebee might misinterpret such a gesture. The old man's gaze didn't miss a thing.

"Well . . . where is he?"

"Billy . . . Billy died, Daddy."

Uriah's white brows knit together until they were all one piece. He pressed his lips tightly and shook his head slowly. The grandfather clock in the corner ticked loudly.

"How'd it happen?"

Heaven Sent

"He was sleepin'—"

"No better way to go. But the old-timer was entitled to a warm corner for a spell."

"He didn't appear to suffer," Coop put in. "Looked as if his heart might have given out."

Uriah nodded. "I reckon Billy's time was comin'," he said at last. "Goin' to be a loss around here. I'll miss the old coot."

"If I'd known he was sick I never would have—"

"Billy belonged out on the trail," Uriah interrupted his daughter sternly. "Reckon he wouldn't have been happy to make the big jump from the bunkhouse."

"Cooper T. helped me bury Billy and say a few words over his grave."

Uriah shot a penetrating gaze at Coop before lowering his head. He seemingly contemplated the papers on his desk for several seconds before he spoke. "Old Billy lived a long and good life."

Matilda Rose raised her eyes. "He's up there watching over us."

Uriah lifted his gaze to his daughter somewhat skeptically, in Coop's opinion.

"Cooper T. has agreed to stay with us a few days, Daddy."

"Actually, I can only stay the night."

"He's been shot in the leg and had a tooth pulled. He needs to rest up."

"I'm on my way to San Francisco and way behind schedule. Got to leave at daybreak."

"Cooper—"

"Young lady, go tell Lupe to put another plate on the table and fix a room while I talk to your young man alone."

"He's not my young—"

Sandra Madden

Uriah pointed toward the door. "Go, girl."

"Yes, Daddy."

When the door closed behind Matilda Rose, the elder Applebee slumped down into his desk chair and gazed at Coop over steepled fingers.

"I've been waitin' for you a long time, boy."

Coop stiffened. "I beg your pardon?"

"Never thought I'd get that girl married off."

His heart stopped. "Sir?"

"Matty is not feminine in her ways. She's not a flirtatious woman. A man must look beyond what she pretends."

Coop choked.

Uriah pulled a bottle of whiskey from his desk drawer and poured two shots. He slid one over to Coop.

"I could see by the look in your eye you're taken with my girl. And rightly so. Despite her . . . er, particularities, Matty carries a good head on her shoulders."

Coop swallowed the whiskey in one gulp.

"A smart cowboy can easily see the quality in my girl."

"She's . . . unique," Coop admitted, carefully. "I've come to admire Matilda Rose, but—"

"That's good, young man, because you've been alone with her on the trail for quite a spell. With all good intentions, you've nevertheless put my daughter in a damned compromisin' position."

"No one who knows Matilda Rose would dare even dream that she and I—"

"What happened and what didn't, don't matter. My daughter's reputation is . . . dubious at best. Her clothes, her manner of speakin' have caused talk in the

Heaven Sent

past. Now this?" He raised his magnificent snowy brows. "You'll marry Matty."

"Impossible—as much as I would like to make Matilda Rose my bride." Coop stood up, ready to make his getaway. His knees wobbled more than he cared. "Unfortunately, I have to be in San Francisco. My job is at stake. My future."

"Your future is here. A sizable dowery comes with Matty, Mr. Davis. A stake in the biggest ranch in this part of California."

"Well, now, I don't mean to sound ungrateful, but I'm not a rancher."

"Matty will teach you everything you need to know."

"I did not. . . . harm your daughter. She'll back me up on that," Coop argued, back-stepping toward the door. "Someday Matilda Rose will meet a man who will appreciate her. One who knows how to run a ranch as good as she—"

Uriah jumped out of his chair, scowling. "Mister, I can't wait forever. I need to get on with it. I've got another daughter just pantin' to be married, and it can't happen until Matty's hitched."

"Perhaps your younger daughter—"

Matilda Rose's father headed round the desk, stopping only inches from Coop. The old man proceeded to inspect him as he might a stud stallion. "You're a young, healthy man. Can't see anything readily objectionable about you. You'll make a fine husband."

"But, Matilda Rose deserves someone who—"

"Matty can consider herself fortunate."

Further argument with the strong-willed man seemed senseless at the moment. Coop gave it up. He would be on his way to San Francisco in the morning. "Yes, sir."

Uriah Applebee expected him to marry Matilda Rose; Matilda Rose expected him to marry her sister Phoebe. Ordinarily he would have found the situation amusing. This afternoon, he considered his predicament all-fired annoying.

While the idea of a wife and family appealed to him sometime in the future, that time was for a far-off someday when he was too beat up and tired to chase criminals across the land, too weary to ride the rails and catch train robbers in the act.

"I'll see you at dinner in about an hour, Davis. We'll continue this discussion then. Matty will want to make plans."

The aroma of fried chicken wafted through the house. Matty's stomach gurgled. After bathing and changing into clean trousers and a light blue shirt, she strolled out to the veranda to await Phoebe's return.

She could hardly wait to see her sister's face when she broke the news that the drummer had returned to marry her and be a father to their child. No matter that Matty's stomach constricted into a tight little knot as she paced the porch. She had managed to bring the man back. Phoebe and her baby would have a husband and a father.

During her journey with Cooper T., Matty had discovered many redeeming qualities about the drummer—in addition to his good looks. She could only hope Phoebe would appreciate him and be the best wife possible.

"Dinner sure smells good."

Matty turned to see Cooper T. in the doorway. He made a compelling figure in the dusk, filling the door frame. Her heart skipped, her insides warmed.

Heaven Sent

"Lupe is the best cook in the world," she replied, and added quickly, "Besides Phoebe."

He sauntered out to stand beside her at the rail. "Nice view you have here."

"Only the most beautiful in the world." Directly to the east a meadow filled with a brilliant rainbow of wildflowers rolled down into a valley where high green grass waved in the gentle breeze.

"You may be right," he replied quietly.

Cooper T. had cleaned up too. He smelled of soap, and his own good scent that she'd come to recognize. A scent that made her blood flow hot.

Matty wandered aimlessly down the veranda, away from the tall handsome man she'd come to depend upon so often during the last few weeks. She walked away from the heat and deep masculinity of him that charged the air and seeped beneath her skin.

"I'm . . . I'm waiting for Phoebe. She should be home any minute now. She usually doesn't stay at quilting this long. But I reckon the ladies' lose track of time now and again."

"Reckon they do. Have you ever made a quilt?"

She gave him a rueful smile. "No, I'd just stick myself and bleed all over it."

"How do you know? Have you tried?"

"No. I'd rather be here watching the sunset over the ranch."

"It's peaceful."

"What did you and Daddy talk about?" she asked.

"He thinks I should marry you."

"Me?" she gasped. She could feel her cheeks flush. The blood rushed through her veins.

"Your father believes I have compromised your reputation by traveling with you alone."

181

"But did you explain we weren't . . ." Her voice fell off before she could utter the word: *intimate.*

"Yes."

"Did you tell him I wasn't interested in you?"

"You're not?" he teased, with a twist of his lips.

"Cooper T.! This is serious."

"Sorry."

But she could tell he wasn't sorry. "Did you explain to Daddy that you weren't interested in me?"

"No. It slipped my mind."

"What!" She knew he was teasing her again, but Cooper T. appeared strangely troubled, which alarmed Matty more than she could say. His light green eyes had darkened to a deep jade as they met hers. "Cooper T., we have to do something! We have to make Daddy believe you are wildly in love with Phoebe so he won't object to your marrying her."

"Your father seems to think you should marry first."

"Under the circumstances, that's nonsense."

"It's traditional for the eldest to marry first."

She spun away from him, her mind reeling, her stomach tossing. "But I'm never going to marry. There's no reason to hold Phoebe back. I'll speak to him after supper. I'll make him understand."

"Here comes a rider."

Matty turned back as Cooper T. dipped his head toward the road leading up to the ranch house. "Would that be Phoebe?"

"I don't know." Matty followed Cooper T.'s gaze to the silhouette of a rider. Whoever it was, they were driving the horse hard.

"I hope it is. I've been looking forward to this moment for weeks now."

Heaven Sent

"What moment?" Matty asked, preoccupied with the horse and rider rapidly approaching.

"When she tells you that you have the wrong man."

"Cooper T., it's not Phoebe. She never rides that fast. Besides, she uses a wagon most times."

Matty moved down the stairs toward the rider, curious, but her mind still locked on the thought. Cooper T., the wrong man? Not the man who fathered Phoebe's child? What if it were so?

If she did have the wrong man for Phoebe, was Cooper T. the right man for her? Were her feelings such that she could obey her father's wishes and marry the drummer? If she was forced? To save her reputation? She'd never worried about her reputation before.

No. No, she could never marry a man who didn't love her, who wouldn't stay and work beside her on the Silver Star. A man who would always be hankering to leave the ranch she loved.

Cooper T. followed her down the stairs. He stood behind her as the rider approached, sheltering her as a tall sycamore might. Sheltering her with the strength and force he emitted. She could hardly breathe.

The rider slowed, bringing his horse to a stop. He appeared to be a Mexican ranch hand, but Matty didn't recognize him.

He thrust an envelope at her, and before she could ask his name, turned his horse and galloped off.

Her fingers trembled at she tore at the envelope. Her eyes fixed on the dirty sheet of paper. As she read the brief message, her knees turned to mush. The blood seemed to drain from her body. All of a sudden Matty felt cold all over.

"What does it say?" Cooper T. asked, reaching out to steady her.

"It says my sister has been kidnapped."

183

Chapter Twelve

"Do you know of any reason why someone would take your daughter?" Coop asked, scrutinizing the crudely written message for the third time.

After the first reading, he and a very pale Matilda Rose had rushed to Uriah's study to break the news. The old man had erupted with fury, shouting, stalking his study and punching the air. He'd threatened death and worse to the kidnappers. "Hangin's too good for the damned varmints."

Matilda Rose attempted to calm him. "It's good to air the lungs, Daddy. Let it go."

But even after the elder Applebee had quieted somewhat, Coop could feel the rage simmering inside the man, spilling into the room to settle thickly in the air like suffocating dust. One oil lamp burned on Applebee's desk. As dusk deepened into night, the single globe did not shed enough light to chase away the fear and gloom.

Heaven Sent

"Nope. I don't know why anyone would take Phoebe." Slouched in the old, cracked leather chair behind his desk, Uriah frowned and swept a hand through his cloud of wiry white hair. "Phoebe's a quiet one . . . fragile, if you take my meaning. She'd never hurt a gnat, let alone a man, woman, or child. No, my little Phoebe would never do anything to put a body off."

Coop read between the lines. While Phoebe had no faults, Matilda Rose was another matter.

"My sister may be scared of her own shadow, but everyone loves her. Phoebe is sweet as sugar. She has no enemies."

All the charming, sparky spirit seemed to have drained from Matilda Rose. Her eyes, reflecting her anxiety, had darkened to a troubled indigo. While pacing the room she gnawed on her lower lip.

His experience in kidnap cases made him pessimistic. And he didn't like being unable to honestly ease her concern or soothe her fears. It felt as if all his nerve endings were opened and chafing against one another. He didn't understand the feeling, didn't like it. Coop's impulse to gather the agonized sprite into his arms and comfort her added to his exasperation.

The sooner he was on his way to San Francisco, the better. In the meantime, until the morning, Coop resolved to do whatever he could to help find Phoebe.

Without her, he could not prove his innocence, could not win a confession that he had not seduced her. Matty would never know she had the wrong man.

Sometimes, though not often, the "kidnapped" person staged his or her own disappearance. Coop had known cases where an angry wife had used the ploy as an act of manipulation.

Sandra Madden

"Do you recognize the handwriting?" he asked, passing the note back to Uriah.

Uriah gave the note only a fleeting glance. "I told you before . . . nope."

"Look again," Coop urged. "You might be missing something."

"I never miss a thing," the older man snapped, his blue eyes piercing and bright.

"Of course not. Right. If you could tell me a little about Phoebe, it might be helpful. Has your daughter behaved in any way unusual during the past few weeks?"

"Ouch!"

"Matilda Rose?"

"I bit my lip. Sorry."

"Hadn't noticed Phoebe actin' any different. Nope."

"Has she seemed distracted? Lost her appetite? Appeared angry or especially irritable?"

"Nope! Nope! Nope!"

"What are you driving at, Cooper T.?" Matilda Rose's body tensed. Her eyes flashed an unmistakable warning.

"Maybe Phoebe had been threatened by someone," he suggested. "Maybe she's spurned a suitor that you didn't realize existed."

"My daughters don't keep secrets from me," Uriah growled.

Coop turned to Matilda Rose, who had fixed her gaze on an overhead beam, as innocent as an angel.

He let out a sigh. "Of course not."

"Just who do you think you are with all these questions?"

"Cooper T. claims to be a . . . Pinkerton," Matilda Rose answered.

Heaven Sent

Uriah's gaze narrowed on him. "Where you from, Davis?"

"I'm headquartered in San Francisco right now. Although I'm expecting a transfer within the month. I'll be riding the railroads out of Kansas."

"Do you have any papers to prove you're who you say you are?"

"There's a telegram on its way, sir."

"Likely story." The elder Applebee *harumphfed* in Matilda Rose's favorite expression of contempt.

Nonetheless, Coop persisted. "Do you have any enemies, Mr. Applebee?"

"Sure I do." Uriah again pulled a bottle of whiskey from the bottom drawer of his desk. He waved Coop and his daughter to sit in the chairs facing him. "You don't think I became the biggest rancher in these parts without making enemies?"

"Well, now, I guess not, sir."

"Care for a drink?"

"No, thanks." He sat back in his chair, noting Matilda Rose perched on the edge of her seat, obviously unable to relax. "How many enemies do you figure you have, Mr. Applebee?"

"You can call me Uriah, son. No need to be misterin' me. Expect you city boys learn high-falutin' manners in San Francisco."

"Yes, sir." Coop chose to ignore the slight of being referred to as a "city boy."

"How's a city boy going to find a snake in the grass out here in cattle country anyway?"

"In his job as a Pinkerton detective, Cooper T. covers the entire state of California, Daddy. He knows cattle country just as well as he does the city."

Matilda Rose defending him? Casting a sideways

187

glance, Coop raised a questioning eyebrow.

She blinked and gave him a bright, heartening smile.

"Well, we'll see," Uriah responded gruffly, straightening himself in his chair.

Yet another Applebee he had to prove himself to, Coop thought with resignation. "Enemies, sir?" he prodded.

"Well . . . there's Jerky, the trail cook. Fired him about a month ago for drinkin' out in the cookhouse. Stealin' my wine, he was."

"Daddy, Jerky couldn't plot a kidnapping. He could barely find his way off the ranch."

"Reckon you're right about that."

"Who else?" Coop coaxed. This was one kidnapping case he'd like to solve. He didn't feel right about leaving Matilda Rose in the middle of a mess. But he only had hours to find Phoebe before he'd have to be on his way.

"What about the water, Daddy? Things have been bad since the drought. Could it be about the water?"

"It's only been bad because Thomas Tyler had the damned audacity to take our water. Dammed up the river so's more than half the outflow ended up on his property."

"Wait a minute," Coop interrupted. "Who's Thomas Tyler?"

"Our neighbor," Matilda Rose replied, shooting her father an accusing glance. "And a good friend of Daddy's."

"Until he took what was mine."

"But, Daddy—"

"Sam Hill, girl, it's the damn principle. No man takes what's mine. It's one thing to ask and another to take. A hangin' party's too good for that old piece of buzzard bait."

Heaven Sent

"But Mr. Tyler did ask. I know you had discussions with him and Zak about the water rights. I know you did."

"Matty—"

"Hold on," Coop interrupted again. "Who's Zak?"

"Thomas's son," Matilda Rose replied.

Frowning, Coop rubbed the back of his neck. "Let me get this straight. You've had trouble with your neighbors over water rights for going on several years now?"

"I told Zak if he married Matty—"

"What?!" Matilda Rose wailed in shock.

A deathly silence fell over the room. No one breathed, no one moved, no one spoke.

Coop watched her body stiffen, her lips tighten. One hand went to cover her stomach, as if she'd been kicked in the belly. Her eyes darkened to a deep purple.

She raised her chin, speaking slowly and deliberately. "Did you try to trade water rights for me, Daddy? Did you try to force Zak to marry me?"

"Hell, honey, we could have increased our herd and grain land with a merger. I was suggestin' he could marry the prettiest little girl in the county and have the water rights his pa wanted so much, in return for a few acres."

"Daddy!"

Uriah reared back in his chair. "What's so wrong with that? Thomas would have plenty of water. You'd have a husband. I'd have more land. Everyone would have been happy."

"Apparently not Zak!" she steamed.

"You can't run this ranch by yourself, no matter what you think, girl," Uriah barked. "You need a partner, a husband—"

Sandra Madden

Matilda Rose bolted from her chair and began to pace the room. "How am I ever going to look Zak in the eye again?"

"You're not!" the old man declared, slamming the desk with his fist. "We're havin' nothin' more to do with the Tylers."

"But what if your neighbors are holding Phoebe? Are the Tylers that desperate for water rights?"

"Yes!" Matilda Rose answered.

"No!" Her father replied.

Cooper T. scratched the back of his head. "It appears we need to ask your neighbors some questions."

"If Zak Tyler's responsible for this, I'm gonna shoot him down like a dog," Uriah vowed. "He's a belly-crawlin' snake who doesn't deserve to live a day longer. Your poor sister's probably gonna die of fright. Phoebe hasn't got your . . . your . . ."

"Gumption," Coop offered.

Matilda Rose glowered at him for a long, withering moment, before turning back to her father. "You brought this on yourself for being stubborn and mule-headed and—"

"Don't you sass your father, young lady. It's manners like those that have forced me to look for your mate in a—"

"Hold on, hold on." Taking the role of peacemaker, Coop stepped between the angry father and daughter. "You're both all wrought up with worry over Phoebe, so don't go saying things to each other that you don't mean. First thing in the morning, we'll go over to the Tyler ranch and get this straightened out."

"Now. We have to go now, Daddy."

Uriah threw his arms in the air. "And risk having a

Heaven Sent

horse fall in the dark or something happenin' to you ridin' the range at night?"

"I'm willing to take any risk for Phoebe. Think how frightened she must be."

At that, Uriah appeared to waver. Coop held up the crumpled, dirty piece of paper. "This note says she's safe. It says there will be further instructions in the morning. If you're right about your neighbors, Thomas and Zak aren't going to hurt Phoebe."

"Makes sense," Uriah agreed. "Sorry as I am for Phoebe, for my baby, Davis is right, Matty."

"Matilda Rose, I know how you feel." Coop stood and ambled toward her. She had raised Phoebe, been like a mother to her sister when she was still just a girl herself. Hell, she'd come after Coop with a gun, believing he'd wronged her beloved sister. For all the tough cowboy front she put up, the girl with the lavender-blue eyes had a heart as soft as pudding.

She put up her hands as if to ward him off. Raised misty eyes to his as she shook her head forlornly. "You can't possibly know."

"This is the right thing to do," he insisted softly. "We'll bring Phoebe home safe and sound first thing tomorrow."

She simply stared at him. In her large, troubled eyes he read her frustration, felt her reluctance to trust him. Finally, with an imperceptible nod of her head, she acquiesced. "I reckon."

"The best thing we all can do is get a good night's sleep and be ready to pay a visit in the morning," Coop declared with a certainty designed to convince both of the anxious Applebees everything would be all right. He still couldn't believe Matilda Rose had deferred to him. "Your daughter—your sister—is going to be back

191

Sandra Madden

here eating dinner at the Silver Star tomorrow night."

And he would be on his way to San Francisco.

Coop gave father and daughter a bracing smile as each mulled over his words and struggled to regain their composure.

Uriah poured himself another shot of whiskey. "Go along; I've got thinkin' to do."

Matty had no idea how she could sleep while Phoebe was being held prisoner, even if it was only Zak Tyler holding her sister hostage. She was certain she couldn't eat.

"Come with me," she said, flicking her wrist in the direction she wished Cooper T. to follow.

She led him to the west wing of the house and opened the door to a guest bedroom directly opposite hers.

"Lupe made up this room for you."

"It looks mighty comfortable," he said, gazing at the bed.

The clean, neat room featured a huge, hand-carved oak bed covered with a thick down quilt comforter, a writing desk, an armoire, a washstand, and two windows draped with satin. Steam rose from a copper tub in the middle of the room.

"A bath. Looks as if you've thought of everything."

"Lupe always does," Matty corrected him primly. "She'll bring you a dinner tray shortly. If there's anything else you need, I'm across the hall; just knock."

"Don't worry about me. I'll be fine. And don't you worry, Matilda Rose. We'll bring Phoebe home soon."

"This wouldn't have happened, she wouldn't have been taken away if . . ." Her voice trailed off as her eyes filled with tears. "My father can't even marry me off for water!"

Heaven Sent

"Precious, did it ever occur to you this Zak Tyler is a fool?"

She blinked back the hot tears, unwilling for Cooper T. to see her cry. Whatever he was, he'd proved himself a gentleman several times over.

"No," she answered curtly, afraid to say more and risk dissolving into a river of tears. A show of such womanly weakness would just add to her earlier humiliation. "Zak Tyler is no fool."

"I'll bet the man has a simple mind and the face of a bull," Cooper T. ventured, giving her a wry, teasing grin.

Matty thought of Zak's wide-set brown eyes and broad, high forehead. One minute ago she had been on the verge of tears; now she allowed herself a small sheepish smile. "You might win that bet."

He nodded knowingly, and jerked his head toward the bed. "I'm looking forward to sleeping in a real bed tonight."

"You go on and get a good night's rest, Cooper T. I— I just hope . . . I hope you are a real Pinkerton detective."

"Phoebe's going to be back here with you tomorrow," he assured her again with a soft twist of his lips. Unexpectedly, he reached out and tenderly stroked her cheek with the back of his hand. "Soon you'll be smiling again, Matilda Rose. Your eyes will be shining again."

Her cheek grew warm at his touch, tingling. Matty backed away quickly so that he wouldn't hear the sudden loud thudding of her heart. "Good . . . good night, Cooper T."

His eyes met hers for a long moment. She felt as if

Sandra Madden

he wanted to say more, knew that she herself wanted to say more, but couldn't.

Matty desperately wanted to believe the tall handsome drummer, to believe he was an experienced detective who could find Phoebe and return her safely. And more than all else, she wanted to know that he hadn't put her sister in the family way. But she couldn't indulge in wishful thinking. This wasn't the time to think of anything other than Phoebe's imminent release and return.

Like it or not, immediately following her beautiful sister's homecoming, Cooper T. would become Phoebe's husband.

"Good night, Matilda Rose."

Matty turned quickly and heard his door close softly as she crossed the corridor to her own room.

She slowly undressed and bathed, her mind a confused tumble of thoughts. Shifting emotions played with her mood. Anxiety gave way to confidence all would be solved in the morning. Confidence gave way to doubt, doubt gave way to longing and a strange emptiness in the pit of her stomach.

Her bedroom retreat had been decorated by Phoebe, giving it a decidedly feminine flair. The imported French furnishings included a looking glass, a skirted dressing table, a sizable bed, an armoire, a writing table, and a chaise. Shades of soft blue and butter yellow accented the room.

"To complement the blue in your eyes, Matty dear," Phoebe had explained.

Her sister had sewn the beautiful quilted comforter covering the bed. She'd also made the filmy curtains that fell over both windows, allowing the cool evening

Heaven Sent

breeze to pass through. The walls were adorned with watercolors—painted by Phoebe.

Matty heard her father's heavy steps in the hall as he passed on the way to his room. She heard his door open and close.

Too upset to sleep, Matty wandered her room in her long, fine, white linen shift and dressing gown. In the privacy of her room she dressed as anyone of her sex and age would. Sleeping did not require a tough exterior.

Pacing aimlessly, she touched the items closest to her. For a brief moment, she held an old rag doll given to her long ago by her mother. She drew a finger across a row of leather-bound books on a wall of bookshelves. She picked up a smooth pebble from the dressing table. The pebble had been from the pile Billy Bowed-Legs presented to her the first time he'd taught her to skip stones over the back pond. She lifted the blue-tinted bottle of perfume called Passion Flower, a birthday gift from Phoebe that she'd never worn.

"It's from Paris and will make you smell less like a horse, Matty. Please just try it."

Now, halfheartedly, she dabbed a drop of the perfume on her wrist and at the pulse of her neck.

Although Matty had successfully avoided the truth for a very long time, she was forced to face facts in the still, dimly lit room. Obviously, she was a disappointment to her sister as well as her father. Phoebe wanted a sister who shared her interests in quilting and homemaking and fashions. Her father wanted a daughter men would want to marry . . . to cherish. She had failed as both sister and daughter.

But if she could save her sister, perhaps Phoebe and her father would think better of her. And perhaps there was a clue to Phoebe's whereabouts in her room!

With new excitement and hope rushing through her Matty slipped quietly from her room and into her sister's bedroom right next door. Phoebe's scent, at once exotic and sweet, filled the pink and white room with the fragrance of wildflowers and spices. Every object was in its place. No crooked stack of books or foreign objects like pebbles or road-runner feathers would be found in Phoebe's room. Silver brushes and combs, a row of perfume bottles, powders, and hair combs marched in perfect order along Phoebe's dressing table.

A round needlepoint form lay on the table beside Phoebe's dusky pink satin chaise. The work in progress was a cardinal bound to cover a dining room chair.

Matty opened the armoire. Silk and satin, taffeta and fine linen dresses filled the space. Lace and flounces, ribbons, and ruffles adorned each garment. Kid slippers in varying shades were neatly aligned at the bottom of the armoire. There were no boots here.

And no clues.

Next, Matty went to the writing desk. A Bible sat atop the desk, the only reading material in Phoebe's room. Matty opened the drawer, feeling guilty for invading her sister's privacy but telling herself it was a necessary step. A fabric-covered book, quill pen, and inkwell sat inside. Matty withdrew the book and opened it.

PHOEBE PEARL APPLEBEE'S JOURNAL.

Matty had no idea her sister kept a journal! There had to be clues in here.

She started her reading near the middle of the thick book. It was a March entry.

I declare John is the most handsome man in these

Heaven Sent

parts. When he smiles at me, my knees grow weak. I lack for breath.

John? Did Phoebe mean John Burrows, the minister's son? John was attractive, but he had no muscle, no character beyond a rather simpering smile.

The next entry concerned a row Phoebe had had with her father over money, and the one that followed began with a harangue against Matty.

I do wish Matty would end her tomboy stage and find a man who will make her feel like a woman. The way my John makes me feel. My heart flutters so rapidly, I feel I will fall into a swoon. The vapors come near to claiming me when he seeks my eyes from across the church pews. He is on a love mission, he says. To fill the world with love. But he cautions me to keep our feelings secret for a time. His father would not approve of any entanglements before John finishes his schooling. My beloved intends to follow in his father's footsteps and to study at seminary in the east.

Phoebe and John Burrows! My, oh my, my, my. She never would have guessed.

Two entries later, following a long dissertation on the gossip attending a church social, Matty read a passage that made her heart ache.

Why can't I convince Matty to act and dress like a woman so that someone will fall in love with her and marry her? Father says I cannot marry until she does. Which is so unfair. She hides her best qualities. She talks like our foreman and follows Billy Bowed-Legs. She rides astride, wearing smelly chaps. Oh, I do love her, but what man will ever want my sister? Matty scares men.

John will be leaving soon. I want to leave with him as his wife. I will be a wonderful minister's wife.

Poor Phoebe. Matty had held her back, never guessing, or paying much attention to, how her sister felt. At the same time, Phoebe's ramblings cut deep. She felt Matty was unfit to be loved by any man. Her own sister felt that way.

The pain in her chest took Matty's breath away. But why should she be surprised? Less than an hour before she'd learned her father had attempted to barter her to Zak Tyler. He'd been willing to make a match, a trade—as if she were a prized breeding mare.

Although she knew he loved her, her father's words had stung. And by the time he'd caught himself, he'd said enough. It couldn't have hurt more if he'd slapped her. Mortification had washed over Matty, leaving her body numb. And Cooper T. had heard it, stood witness to her humiliation.

But she couldn't dwell on that now. Matty skipped several pages forward in Phoebe's journal. One page contained a single sentence.

I know how it feels to be loved by a man in every sense.

What in tarnation did that mean? Matty had a bad feeling. She skipped ahead again to a point six weeks later.

I feel terribly unwell. John talks of leaving soon. I have begged him to stay longer, but he only re-

Heaven Sent

gards me sadly and says his calling awaits him. We must sacrifice for the greater good.

Matty's astonishment mounted. Why had she not noticed her sister's infatuation or more . . . involvement, with the minister's son? Because she was too busy with the ranch, of course.

It has been eight weeks since John departed and I have received only one letter from him. A small line promising he would write soon. But there has been no other letter, and I fear my heart will break. It is difficult to hide my melancholy from Father and Matty. Thankfully, they are occupied with the ranch.

Phoebe Pearl suffered from a broken heart and Matty hadn't even realized it? What a featherhead she'd been! The next entry was written two weeks later.

It has been ten weeks since John and I were separated and I have not heard anything further from him. I fear for his life and mean to speak to his mother and father at church next Sunday. I am with child. What was just a suspicion a week ago has become a certainty. He must come back.

Oh, her poor sister! Why hadn't Phoebe confided in Matty?
Matty will never understand. I do not think she likes men, except to be as much like one of them as possible.
Tarnation! That just wasn't true. She just hadn't met a real man . . . not until she met Cooper T. Cooper T.! Phoebe hadn't written a word in the journal about the

drummer . . . detective. He'd been completely missing from Phoebe's diary.

> The Reverend and Mrs. Burrows told me that John was fine and living in Pittsburgh near the seminary. He'd recently become engaged to a girl he'd met there. My heart is breaking. What am I to do? Who will understand? Tonight is my birthday party, and while I must smile, I may perish from grief.

That was the night Cooper T. came by and danced with Phoebe Pearl while Matty watched from a distance. She remembered it well. And it was not more than ten days later that Phoebe told Matty the tall, handsome stranger had put her in a delicate condition.

> Dear God, what am I to do now? I told Matty it was the good-looking drummer who seduced me. How was I to know my headstrong sister would go after the man? This morning I found a note saying she intended to bring him back and force him to marry me! Lord help us all. She is so hot-headed, so controlling. She always thinks she knows best and rushes to take matters into her own hands. I just pray she returns alive. In the meantime I will find someone to marry quickly. Bert is sweet on me, and Malcolm too.

Cooper T. was an innocent man. Her sister had indeed lied—and apparently wasn't quite as fragile as she pretended.

Clasping the journal to her breast, Matty raised her eyes heavenward. "Oh, Billy Bowed-Legs . . . what have I done? And how can I fix it?"

Chapter Thirteen

Matty owed Cooper T. an apology. A big one. Even before reading Phoebe's journal she hadn't expected to sleep tonight. She was certain of it now. Not only was she worried about her little sister, but her conscience weighed heavily. She'd wronged an innocent man. She'd refused to believe him because her sister never lied. At least, not up until six weeks ago.

It felt as if all the fires in Hades burned in the pit of Matty's stomach. Based on Phoebe's deception, she had done Cooper T. a grave injustice. She'd forced him to travel hundreds of miles out of his way during which he'd been trapped, robbed, and compelled to sacrifice the wagon he loved—his legacy from Angus Van Kurem. She swallowed hard.

As much as she hated eating crow, she might just as well apologize to Cooper T. now and be done with it.

Matty opened her door, started across the hall, and stopped. From the corner of her eye she caught the flash of a white shirttail slipping out the back door.

The low-down drummer planned on hightailing it! After all that fine talk about engaging his crack Pinkerton skills to help find Phoebe, he was leaving without a good-bye. Not so much as an adios. Well, she'd just see about that. Although she couldn't altogether blame him for wanting to vamoose, Matty gave chase.

Cooper T. headed toward the stables in his easy, loping manner. He cast a long shadow under the light of the full, golden moon. His hair curled at the nape of his neck in shaggy little-boy fashion. What an odd thing to tug at her heartstrings! His wide shoulders appeared broad enough to carry the weight of the world—or any problems a woman might have.

Trailing behind him, admiring the physique she'd almost come to take for granted on the long journey home, Matty's heart beat double time. She wasn't sure if it was fear he might turn and discover her, or anger that he was leaving, following his rover's heart.

Her throat tightened.

Cooper T. lit a lantern and entered the stables. Matty slipped in to hover in the darkest corner. Being careful to avoid the pail and buckets in her path, she ducked behind a broad beam.

The tang of medicinal ointment and fresh hay defined the dark stables. A mix Matty found oddly pleasant.

"Hey there, boy." Grinning broadly, Cooper T. opened Traveler's stall. "Look what I've got for you." He pulled a small sack of sugar from his shirt pocket.

Matty's gaze fixed on Cooper T.'s chest. His unbuttoned shirt revealed a strip of crisp chest hair, muscled chest, and flat, corded stomach. Her throat went dry.

Since reading Phoebe's journal, Matty regarded Cooper T. with deeper interest. If that was possible. She

Heaven Sent

watched, transfixed, as his big hands rubbed the horse affectionately.

"How do you like these fancy digs, Traveler?" he asked. "Do you remember the Silver Star from when we passed through before?"

Matty hated herself for eavesdropping, but she couldn't move. Her feet were rooted to the spot. Cooper T. had every right to leave the Silver Star any time he chose. He'd warned her from the first that he would not, could not, stay.

"It's a pretty big spread and we didn't stay long. Just passing through on the trail of that bigamist dude. Funny, but I barely remember Phoebe. There's a fuzzy picture in my head of a vapid, eye-batting blond flirt. Don't think I met Uriah at all. And I know I didn't meet Matilda Rose. I surely would have remembered her."

Matty grimaced. She'd made his life so all-fired miserable, Cooper T. had just declared he would never forget her.

"Couldn't sleep," Cooper T. told his horse. "Had to move. I'm as restless as a hungry coyote for no good reason I can think of. Had to talk to someone. They say a man's horse is his best friend."

Matty knew she should really go away. There seemed no sense in lingering. It didn't sound as if the Pinkerton was fixing to leave right away. She shouldn't be listening to a man she reckoned was about to share his innermost thoughts with his horse. Overhearing was one thing; eavesdropping another. But her feet remained planted to the spot.

"Matilda Rose has gone and got under my skin. I know, I know," he added, as if the gelding had responded to the simple statement that caused Matty's heart to leap into her throat. "Damned if I know how it happened. We should be on our way to San Francisco, but I can't leave the little firecracker all distraught about her fabricating sister.

"I'd be seeing those eyes for the rest of my life. Sad eyes. All big and blue and misty, making my insides mush, making me feel guilty. No matter how far away from here we got, she'd be in my mind." He tapped his temple. "I'd always see those eyes accusing me of deserting her when she needed me. Not that she'd ever mention she needed me."

She had gone and got under his skin! That's what Cooper T. told his horse. And the way he said it, it sounded like a good thing. Needed him? He needed to be needed?

Matty needed to take a breath. She'd been motionless, breathless, since Cooper T. first started conversing with Traveler. But her chest felt way too tight to breathe. If she wasn't careful, she'd be hyperventilating and giving herself away. Any second something inside was bound to snap.

"Damned if I need her, either. She's been trouble from the start, complicating my life like some prickly tumbleweed blowing by my side." He chuckled softly. "I've never known what to expect since the day I met Matilda Rose. Being with her is a little like never knowing what's beyond the next bend in the road."

If she'd been nothing but trouble to him, which she admitted ruefully to herself was true, why had he laughed? Why had his tone softened?

"That little woman has made me laugh, made me angry, even made me want her."

He'd wanted her!

"You didn't see her in the blue dress. But let me tell you. Little Matilda Rose has a waist a man could circle

Heaven Sent

with one hand, and hips that promise . . ." His voice drifted off. "No sense talking about this. I've got more lip than a muley cow tonight. Tomorrow we'll find Phoebe Applebee and we'll be on our way, old boy. Life will get back to normal again."

It sounded as if Cooper T. had finished talking to his horse. Not wishing to be caught, Matty spun around to dash out of the stables. Instead she stumbled over the tin pail packed with grooming implements. As she fell, the pail toppled against another one, creating a terrible, telltale din.

"Tarnation," she murmured beneath her breath.

"Precious."

She looked up.

"Why am I not surprised?"

"There's a good reason why I'm . . . I'm here."

The sight of Matilda Rose on the ground surrounded by yards of filmy white fabric took his breath away. If a man didn't know better, he might mistake her for an angel in her snowy dressing gown. Rosy, full lips parted expectantly, and her lavender-blue eyes contemplated him in wide-eyed apprehension.

"What good reason would that be?" he asked thickly.

Her chest heaved, drawing his gaze to the deep, creamy cleavage rising above a broad band of white lace. Coop could almost hear her mind racing, but his eyes were on her hair. A mass of shining curls tumbled about her gleaming shoulders. For an instant, he considered falling to his knees beside her and taking her into his arms.

"I . . . I couldn't sleep," she stammered. "I'm worried."

"I can understand that. So you came out to the stables to take a ride in your nightgown."

Sandra Madden

"No."

"You followed me."

"Y . . . yes." She lowered her head. "I thought you were going to leave."

She wasn't too far off the mark. He planned to be on his way before dusk of the following day. Coop figured it would take most of the next morning to negotiate a truce between the Applebees and the Tylers. Especially if the Tylers were as stubborn as the Applebees. With luck, Phoebe would be returned unharmed long before dusk.

Earlier in the afternoon, when Uriah bluntly announced that he wasn't able to arrange a marriage between Matilda Rose and Zak Tyler, even for much-needed water rights, Coop had caught her expression. Her eyes reflected a heart-wrenching combination of astonishment and pain. He'd fought the desire then to gather her in his arms and comfort her with kisses and caresses.

Kisses she did not want. Caresses she would refuse.

And now he struggled with an even stronger desire. He wanted her more than she would ever know. His body ached for her. But the truth was, she loved this ranch more than she could ever love a man.

"I'm not leaving until Phoebe's back here confessing the truth." Coop extended his hand and pulled Matilda Rose to her feet.

"She has."

"She has? What do you mean?" She made no move to remove her hand from his. A hand that felt small, soft, and warm in his.

"I went to her room tonight, looking for . . . for anything that might tell us where she was being held."

Heaven Sent

"And . . . ?"

"I found her journal. And I read enough to know that it wasn't you. You're not responsible for my sister's . . . delicate condition."

"What have I been trying to tell you, Matilda Rose?"

"I . . . I'm sorry. I'm sorry for taking you at gunpoint and . . . and forcing you to come back here with me."

"It's been quite an adventure."

"And I hope you won't be too late getting to San Francisco. You don't have to stay and be involved in any more of my problems. I . . . I really wouldn't blame you for leaving right this minute."

"Precious, I told you I'd get Phoebe back for you and I will."

"And then . . . you'll go."

"And then I have to go."

But he was here now. And he'd told his horse there was at least one time when he'd wanted her.

And she wanted him. The drummer. The Pinkerton. The man who filled most of her waking thoughts. Weeks of denial washed over her, releasing her. Only moments ago she had felt the exhilaration rising from the page in Phoebe's journal where she had written: *Now I know how it feels to be loved like a woman.*

Matty longed to feel that same joy. This might be her only opportunity. She looked up at Cooper T. His eyes met hers, and in their depths she saw the same desire she felt.

She stood perfectly still as his hands framed her face, as he searched her eyes. And finally he brought his mouth down on hers.

He kissed her with an almost feverish hunger. It was a kiss filled with promise that seemed to go on forever,

Sandra Madden

that erased all thought from her mind and made her weak all over. Her heart knocked against her chest. Her pulse raced. Her lips tingled.

When at last he lifted his head, Matty feared she would faint. Her whole body felt like warm pudding.

"The devil made me do it." One corner of his mouth turned up, his eyes twinkled mischievously, and he leveled a devastating crooked grin straight at her. "So shoot me."

His smile made a direct hit on her heart. "No. Come with me," she rasped, holding out her hand.

"Where?"

"I promise, no ugly surprises."

Cooper T. took her hand. Grabbing the lantern with the other, she led him from the stables down the slope toward the vineyards. Her heart pounded with expectation, anticipation. She hoped he couldn't hear the sound of a schoolgirl's excitement. She was a woman now. Or soon would be.

By the light of the moon and a mass of silver stars, Matty guided him through rows of thick vines, enveloped in the distinctive fragrance of ripe grapes and dewy grass.

"The Silver Star even has its own vineyard," Cooper T. noted softly.

"Folks have been makin' their own wine for years around these parts. Our land is fertile, our grapes are big and juicy, and we make mighty fine wine."

"I know. I had some with my dinner."

She stopped and plucked a clump of grapes from a vine. "Open wide."

Cooper T. opened his mouth obediently, and Matty popped a large, moist grape between his lips. He grinned. "Mmmmm."

Heaven Sent

A drop of dark red grape juice stained Cooper T.'s lips. For a moment, she struggled with a desperate urge to lick the juice from his lips.

She swallowed hard and forced her thoughts back to the subject. "Daddy is strictly a cattleman. Otherwise, we'd expand the vineyards and be selling our wine."

He nodded thoughtfully and ran the tip of his tongue over his lips.

With the slightest quiver of her lips, Matty smiled and continued down the dirt path, sweet chills skipping down her spine.

At the bottom of the vineyard, by a small winding creek, sat a thatched-roof cottage.

The caretaker's cottage hadn't been lived in for years. When they were little girls, Matty and Phoebe had used the one-room dwelling to play house. Since her teens, Matty had used the rustic dwelling as a refuge.

"Who lives here?" Cooper T. asked.

"No one, any more. When I need to be alone I come here." With trembling fingers, she opened the door. The only furnishings remaining were a table and four creaky pine chairs. A rocking chair padded by two of Phoebe's first attempts at quilt making sat beside a natural rock fireplace. Several cooking implements hung on pegs.

"It's cozy," he said, after scanning the cottage quickly.

"Durin' the winter afternoons I read by the fire. I rock and read like an old woman."

He nodded, looking around with a curious expression.

She closed the door, closing off the world. "Sometimes I've been known to sneak off for a nap . . . up there in the loft."

Sandra Madden

Only Billy Bowed-Legs had known where to find her. She'd never told another soul, not even Phoebe, about where she went when she needed to be alone, to think or to dream.

"This is your special place." Cooper T. spoke in a hushed tone. As if, without being told, he knew what it meant that she was sharing her hideaway with him.

"I . . . I make sure the hay is always fresh."

"Well, now, this is a nice place you've got, but why did you bring me here?"

"I . . . I have somethin' to give you,"

What she really wanted was to be alone with him. How could she say it? *I want to know how it feels to be loved like a woman.*

Matty crossed to the crudely constructed ladder that led to the loft.

"Where are you going?"

"Up here. You can come up."

Giving a shrug, he followed.

Hay packed the sloping loft, but two quilts were neatly folded where they couldn't be seen from the ground. She sank to the hay and lifted the quilts. In the bottom patched quilt Matty had cut a pocket in one of the patches. She withdrew a handful of bills and stood up.

"I think this will cover it," she said, pressing the bills into his hand.

"What is this?"

"My bail. That should be enough to get your drummer's wagon back from the marshal."

"Matilda Rose—"

"Please. It was my doing. It's only right. I'd never sleep easy again if I knew you'd lost your wagon because of me."

Heaven Sent

"I guess there's no sense arguing with you, is there?"

She shook her head. "No. You've done a lot for me, Cooper T., including giving me the most beautiful dress I ever owned."

"You'll wear it again someday, won't you?"

"On a special occasion."

"Good." He looked around, seeming awkward, or nervous. "The next time I'm riding through this way again, and I can't find you out on the range, this is where I'll come."

"Do you think you'll ever be back this way?"

"Hard to say, Matilda Rose."

"This may be our last night together."

He nodded.

Matty batted her eyes.

"Something wrong?" Cooper T. asked, frowning. "Something in your eye?"

She shook her head. "No."

Why hadn't she paid better attention when Phoebe flirted? Phoebe knew all the secrets, but Matty badly needed guidance in the art of seducing a man. And now she had no time to learn. All the nights she'd spent alone on the trail with Cooper T. came down to this one night, this one last chance.

"We'd better go," he said in a raspy voice. "I don't completely trust myself alone with you."

"Why?"

"Because when you look at me with those big eyes, I get weak. When I look at your lips, I want to kiss them."

"I want you to kiss them too," she whispered.

"Oh, good God." With a groan, Cooper T. swept her into his arms.

Chapter Fourteen

Matty could feel her knees go weak as Cooper T. held her tightly against the hard warm wall of his body. He held her fast, as if he would never let her go. Still, it wasn't enough. Matty circled her arms around his neck, closed her eyes, tilted her chin, and pursed her lips.

Waiting. Waiting in silent, heart-thudding anticipation.

When he brought his mouth down hard on hers, sparks of fire exploded through her veins. The surging flames licked at her lips, her heart, her thighs. The tips of her fingers, the soles of her feet all tingled, as if suddenly awakened after a long sleep.

Cooper T. kissed Matty with such intensity she felt dizzy, wobbling on her legs like a newborn lamb. For a fleeting moment, she feared she would swoon in his arms and it would all be over before it began. The wondrous light-headed sensation spiraled down through her body, stirring endless waves of warmth.

Heaven Sent

One minute his lips were demanding and hungry. In the next tender, teasing hers with a soft grazing touch, drawing her lower lip gently between his teeth.

Ripples of pleasure skipped down her spine. And when she parted her lips to express her delight, his tongue invaded her mouth. Swept up in new sensations, Matty surrendered herself to the moment as Cooper T. explored the soft inner recesses, entangling her tongue.

She'd had no idea! All this time she'd been secure in the belief that riding the Silver Star range was the most thrilling experience man or woman could ever have. The beauty of the hills, the smell of the rain, the brilliant blue sky moved her like nothing else. Until this moment.

Matty savored the tangy grape taste of him, drew his tongue deeper into her mouth. She inhaled the lusty leather and masculine scent of him and wanted more.

But what? What more? Certainly there must be more.

His hands slowly skimmed her body. Through the thin fabric of her dressing gown, it felt as if his fingertips were on fire as he traced each curve. His thumbs brushed over her breasts and her nipples tightened at his touch.

Oh, my. My, my, my.

She wasn't prepared for the sudden cold when Cooper T. lifted his lips from hers and stepped back. In the dim light he appeared stunned. His eyes had deepened to jade, glazed like a man in a trance. His breath came in ragged gulps.

"I'm sorry, Matilda Rose. I didn't mean for it . . ."

"Don't talk now, Cooper T." Her gaze fixed on the

Sandra Madden

sensual glimpse of his chest revealed beneath the open shirt. "This is no time for talk."

"Oh, I think it is," he rasped.

She moved closer to him, splaying her hands on his chest, touching him as she'd wanted to touch him for so long. At last she felt the strength and power there. Just beneath her fingers. The heat. The crisp mat of dark curls. The hard pounding of his heart. She sucked in a thin breath. Her pulse quickened.

Cooper T. groaned again. His eyes squeezed shut, as if he were in pain.

"Am I hurting you?" she whispered.

"Oh, no, no," he murmured. "Hell's fire, woman, you're not hurting me."

"You feel so good . . . like warm steel. I want to touch you all over," Matty confessed in quiet awe.

"Matilda Rose, there is . . . there is only so much a man can stand," he replied just as quietly.

"Then lie with me."

"What?"

"The quilts are spread."

"Your father would have my hide."

"He'll never know," she promised. A hot, honey liquid swirled through her. "Don't you want me even just a little?"

"I want you a lot. A lot," he repeated in a husky tone.

"Show me. Show me how much, Cooper T.," she coaxed. With her gaze locked on his, Matty fell to her knees on the bed of quilts.

He looked down at her. An agonized frown marked his brow. At last he shook his head. "What I want and what is right are two different things."

She raised her hand to him, meaning to tug him down to her side on the quilts.

Heaven Sent

He squeezed her hand. "It's a man's job to seduce the woman, Matilda Rose."

"Of course, Cooper T." She smiled up at him. "I have it backwards again. Is that bad?"

"No. Not necessarily." He couldn't resist. He was only human, and her soft, beguiling smile triggered a heat in his loins that almost knocked him off his feet. Lost in the deep lavender pools of her eyes, Coop fell to his knees opposite the crazy, captivating cowgirl. He dipped his head to drink from her lips one more time. That was all he intended. One brief kiss and he would toss her over his shoulder and carry her down the ladder. He'd return her to her room, to her bed, lips swollen from his kisses maybe, but otherwise untouched. Many moonlit nights on the trail, he'd overcome the temptation to make her his. He could do it now.

But the minty taste of her, the scent of roses, filled his senses and he could not pull away. His arms went around her. Crushing her small beautiful body to him, Coop smothered her with kisses he'd kept too long to himself.

Her breasts strained against his chest and ignited a fire in him that exploded out of control. He wanted her more than he'd ever wanted a woman in his life. He'd wanted her the first afternoon in the wagon, and ever after that. In the cabin, in the stream, in Bridget's Irish Emporium and Mrs. Gill's boardinghouse. And now that she was in his arms, willingly, expectantly, nothing could stop him from loving her, nothing in heaven or on earth.

The rustle and scrape against the window from the branch of a nearby sycamore were the only sounds that could be heard inside the small cottage, unless Matty

Sandra Madden

counted her thundering heartbeats, the heavy gasping as she tried to catch her breath.

"Can you hear it?" she rasped.

"What?"

"My heart." She placed his hand over her heart.

He did the same with hers, and she felt the hammering of Cooper T.'s heart beneath her fingertips. She could barely breathe.

Within seconds, Cooper T. had lowered his palm to cup her breast.

"Oh . . ." Matty's sigh of pleasure trailed to a breathless gasp. The tip of her nipple tingled and tightened as his thumb brushed slowly, sensuously, back and forth. Filled to aching with unbearable sweetness, her breasts swelled beneath his touch.

And then his lips covered Matty's, more insistent than before. She melted against him, longing to take him into her, into her heart. The ache between her thighs grew stronger, more demanding.

Demanding what?

Her knees buckled and she swayed.

Cooper T. steadied her and tenderly eased her down to the bed of quilts. His eyes locked on hers as he lay beside her. Driven by a need she did not quite understand, Matty pushed off his shirt. Her hands lingered on his thickly corded biceps. She stared.

He was magnificent. His muscular figure and lean angles boasted of a virility most men only dreamed of. Mesmerized, she couldn't drag her eyes away.

After this night Matty would never lie with another man. She knew no other man could ever compare. She knew she would never love another man as much as she loved Cooper T.

Love? But she couldn't provide the excitement he

Heaven Sent

needed. He couldn't love her for more than this one night. A night she would make the most of.

Framing her face in his hands, the drummer imposter looked deeply into her eyes, as if he was searching for an answer. Matty reckoned he found it when once more his mouth tasted hers. After a time he pulled back. His green eyes glimmered with deep golden flames of desire. Matty trembled. The strength of his desire unleashed a fiery storm within her.

"Matilda Rose, if you don't stop me now, I'll not be able to stop. Do you understand?"

"Don't stop," she purred.

Tremors of delight ricocheted through her body as Cooper T.'s lips devoured hers again, quickly skipping to taste her eyes, her nose, her cheeks. Muscles loose with liquid heat, she abandoned herself as he forged a fiery trail to the sensitive hollow of her throat.

The unremitting, bittersweet ache within her demanded release. Just when she thought she would certainly die, Cooper T. raised his mouth to cover her ear.

"I want to see you, Matilda Rose," he whispered thickly, "see and feel every lovely inch of you."

Heart thundering and giddy with anticipation, Matty pushed herself up to a sitting position. She shrugged off her dressing gown. He carefully removed her embroidered shift, peeling the fine linen garment slowly over her head.

Naked before him, as she had been with no other man, Matty raised her head proudly. His gaze raked her body until she felt ablaze, burning as hot and strong with passion as a midnight torch.

Cooper T.'s eyes shimmered with admiration. His lips curved softly in a rapt smile. The smile of a captivated man. Hurriedly, he tore away his trousers and tossed them aside.

Matty gazed at his strong splendid body.

Quietly, lovingly, he enfolded her in his arms once again, and suddenly she was lost in a flurry of deep kisses and hungry caresses. Giving up her inhibitions, she surrendered completely to the man who had melted her heart and made her soul sing.

A small groan of delight escaped Matty as Cooper T.'s mouth moved to her breast. Tarnation, she'd never dreamed such bliss existed!

My, oh my. My, my, my.

He suckled gently at her breast while his fingertips tenderly stroked circles of fire on her belly.

My, oh my, my, my.

"I want you, Matilda Rose." His raspy whisper was thick with desire. "I need you now."

Matty knew no man would ever want her in quite this way. And she was just as certain she would never want a man the way she wanted Cooper T.

"Then what are you waitin' on, Cooper T.?" she asked breathlessly.

The music and rhythm of a once-in-a-lifetime love pounded fiercely through Matty's veins as he parted her thighs.

My, my, my. What was coming next? She couldn't breathe, couldn't think. She could only feel the heat of his flesh, his hardness, his lust.

Cooper T. entered her with great gentleness. Matty felt a rush of joy as she became one with him, drawing him into the deep, soft warmth of her very core.

The swift, searing loss of her virginity gave her no pain. Instead, warm tears of happiness trickled down

Heaven Sent

her cheeks as Cooper T. swept Matty into the rhythm of a new dance.

Wrapped in Cooper T.'s arms she soared higher and higher toward an unknown light, a secret paradise, a canopy of silver stars. Just as she reached out to pluck one brightly shining star from the heavens, Matty's heart and soul shattered in a blinding fiery release.

Seconds later, before she could breathe again, Cooper T. shouted her name and filled her with his love.

Spent and languid, secure in the Pinkerton's arms, Matty slowly became aware of their hastily contrived bed of quilts, the smell of fresh hay everywhere around them.

And much, much later, still holding her, Cooper T. softly asked a question that hadn't even occurred to her. "What if . . . if after I'm gone, you find yourself in a . . . delicate condition?"

She grinned. Nothing could spoil her happiness. She knew what it felt to be loved like a woman. "Why, I'll be comin' after you with my Winchester, Cooper T."

Just before dawn, Coop took Matilda Rose back to the main house. He didn't toss her over his shoulders, but carried her carefully cradled in his arms.

Her head rested lightly on his shoulder. A soft smile teased her lips, and her dark lashes curled innocently against creamy cheeks.

Coop's heart swelled to near bursting, and the simmering heat inside him ignited into a wild flame all over again. He wondered if Matilda Rose knew what she'd done to him.

He wasn't quite sure, himself. He'd never felt so weak in the knees before. The only thing he knew for certain was that if Uriah Applebee discovered Coop

Sandra Madden

slipping in the back door at five o'clock in the morning with his daughter, the wily rancher would have him standing before a preacher before midday, taking vows.

He wouldn't blame the old man. Matilda Rose had been a virgin. She'd given Coop a gift that couldn't be replaced. The knowledge made him tremble as he looked down at her. She was a complicated creature. A woman capable of shooting the cork off a bottle at twenty paces, and exciting a man beyond endurance with her luscious, loving body.

The sleeping beauty in his arms came fully awake when Coop settled her under the covers of her bed.

"Cooper T.?"

"Go back to sleep," he whispered. "It's almost time for us to go fetch Phoebe home."

Her eyes squeezed shut as her brows knit in a tight frown. "Oh, I'm a terrible sister," she groaned. "I completely forgot about poor Phoebe Pearl."

"My fault," he assured her quickly. "I distracted you."

Her sleepy eyes, glazed with hours of lovemaking, fixed on his. She reached up and took his hand. "I wanted our night to go on forever."

"I . . . I didn't want it to end either," he confessed softly.

In truth, he was more than ready and willing to make love to her again, here and now. Her eyes held him to the spot, beautiful pools of shining light. His heart thundered within his chest. Her hand tightened around his. His pulse raced off out of control. How much could one man take?

Only immediate escape could save him. "I have to go now."

Lowering her eyes, she released his hand.

Heaven Sent

Coop took one step back and stopped. "Nothing's changed, Matilda Rose," he said quietly, gently. "You understand that."

She raised her eyes to his and smiled. "Of course. Nothing's changed."

But it had. Coop knew well enough it had. Nothing was, or would ever be, the same for him.

When he'd buried himself in her soft welcoming warmth, he'd known total joy, a completeness he'd never felt before. A hardheaded bit of a woman, a spitfire he'd feared at one time he might have to throw to the wolves, had undone him. The little lady with lavender-blue eyes had given him the greatest happiness he'd ever known.

The small orphan boy who still crouched within his soul marveled at the deep and lasting connection he'd made tonight. No matter where his work took him, a part of Matilda Rose would always be with Coop.

But he couldn't stay and he couldn't ask her to leave the ranch she loved. Disheveled and flushed, she was the loveliest creature he'd ever seen. Her face was still pink from making love, her steady lavender-blue gaze a wellspring of tenderness.

"I'll be on my way this afternoon," he said.

"But Phoebe—"

"Phoebe will be back by dinner." He'd turned and started for the door when she replied in a hushed, playful tone.

"And Jesse James will be in real big trouble."

Forcing a smile, he quipped in return, "I'll send you his spurs."

She shot him a wide, beguiling smile.

Strange that she didn't appear worried that their

night together might have resulted in the same circumstances Phoebe found herself in.

He might hate himself in the full light of morning, but he hadn't been able to resist her tonight. Matilda Rose had made it impossible for Coop to deny the reckless ache smoldering inside him. He'd kept a respectful distance between them all these weeks . . . wanting her all the while.

He stood in the middle of the room, unwilling to leave. "Matilda Rose . . ."

"Go, Cooper T. Daddy will be knocking at our doors soon."

"You know, ah . . ." Coop left off in midsentence. He hated groping for words like a schoolboy. He normally didn't have a problem speaking his mind. "Something, I just remembered something that . . . kind of slipped my mind."

"Yes?"

"Your daddy thinks, he thinks we should get married. You and me."

Matilda Rose bolted up in her bed. "He said that?"

Rubbing his neck, Coop nodded his head. "Said after traveling alone on the trail I'd compromised your reputation."

A small, wry smile formed at the corners of her mouth.

"Don't worry. You won't have to marry me. I'll explain everything."

"How?" He wanted to know. Suddenly it seemed important to know how she intended to explain him away.

"Daddy knows I'm not the kind to stand at the gate every day watching to see if my man is coming home. Or wondering if he's alive or dead somewhere in a

Heaven Sent

shoot-out. Daddy's tried to get me married off to several others before you."

"But the others never—"

"Never roused my curiosity like you did." She gave a casual toss of her silky chestnut curls. "And that's all there is to that."

An awful feeling stirred low in his gut. "I satisfied your curiosity."

She gave him a blinding, rapturous smile before exclaiming, "Yes, indeed."

The gun-slinging spitfire had used him! And now she was tossing him aside like last week's stew. He strode to the door. "You are . . . you are a most agitating woman!"

Bristling with anger, Coop almost slammed the door behind him but caught it in the nick of time.

Not more than thirty minutes later, the smell of fresh coffee permeated Matty's room. She drew a deep breath, dreamy . . . happy . . . and yes, satisfied. More than satisfied, satiated. Content spilled through her body in warm honeyed waves. She would let nothing destroy the sweet sensations.

Although she hadn't wanted to hurt his pride, Matty had purposefully misled Cooper T. She knew by now he was an honorable man. If Daddy pushed the matter, Cooper T. would marry her for all the wrong reasons. He would stay because he'd made love to her and taken her virginity.

But he didn't love her. He loved the excitement, the adventure that came with being a Pinkerton. Matty refused to marry and live with a man who didn't love her. She couldn't tether a man who had wanderlust in his soul.

If Cooper T. stayed on at the Silver Star, he'd be an

unhappy man. Eventually he would resent her and lose all the wonderful quirks and qualities she admired in him. The crooked smile that set her on fire. His deep chuckle and twinkling eyes. His quick mind and constant humor.

One day he might even lose his great powerful body. The lusty virility that warmed her in private places with only the briefest glance might evaporate.

She perched on the edge of the bed and raised her eyes toward the ceiling. "Dear Billy, if I've done wrong, put in a good word for me. If it's a sin to love someone who's movin' on, I'm guilty. I had to do it. He's the most man I ever did meet." She wiped a tear that had mysteriously appeared on her cheek. "Tarnation! I'm going to miss Cooper T."

At first she thought she heard the flapping of angel wings, and then she realized someone knocked at her door.

"*Señorita* Matty, your *padre* is ready. I bring coffee."

Wondering if she looked different now that she knew how it felt to be loved like a woman, Matty rose and went to the door. If she did look any different, perhaps nearsighted Lupe wouldn't notice.

It was time to put aside thoughts of Cooper T. The time had come to rescue poor fearful Phoebe.

"I have spent the entire night in a cold dark place. I demand to be taken home now. You have taken this far enough, Zak Tyler. Too far."

Zak looked around the entrance to the mine shaft. Yeah, it was dark, and cold. But he'd fixed it up with blankets and candles as best he could. He'd carried in buckets of fresh creek water and kept a fire going.

He knew well enough that Phoebe Applebee was a

Heaven Sent

first-class lady and wasn't used to living in the outdoors. Still, there were compensations. "Didn't you enjoy the full moon last night, Miss Phoebe?"

"No! I can see a full moon any time I want from the comfort of my front porch!" She stomped a tiny foot and pointed a finger at him. "Furthermore, I did not enjoy sleeping on the ground. I am not used to sleeping on the ground."

"I gave you my best bedroll," he reminded her. "Besides, it's worth sleepin' on the ground to see a sight like that moon."

"When did you become a nature lover?" she demanded haughtily.

He shoved his hands into his pockets. "Been one all my life, I reckon."

"Well, I confess that side of your nature comes as a surprise to me, but it's no matter," she snipped, narrowing her round blue eyes on him. Before he drew his next breath, she'd dug her fists into her hips and was marching straight at him, wearing a wicked scowl on her face. "You must let me go this instant! I shall not warn you again."

Zak folded his arms and straightened his body so he stood well over a foot taller than his prisoner. She could make his heart beat faster than it should, but she couldn't intimidate him. "You'll be home soon enough. I do regret this inconvenience, Miss Phoebe, but your daddy's been actin' just plain stubborn and unneighborly."

"In your opinion," she sniffed.

"He's been givin' me and my pa a hard time for no good reason—in just about everybody's opinion."

"What's between you and my daddy has nothing to do with me. Can't you see that?"

Sandra Madden

Her voice was starting to get all high and squeaky. Fearing he might soon be dealing with a hysterical woman, Zak lowered his. "No."

"What is the matter with you, Zak Tyler?" she shrieked. "I cannot stay here! It's dirty and—"

"Somethin' real important you got to do?"

"Yes, as a matter of fact." She raised her chin, tilting her nose up in the air, as if she smelled something bad.

He hadn't expected sweet Phoebe to give him trouble like she had. Almost from the start. He'd expected to be reviving her from the vapors every other hour. Instead, to his surprise, Zak had discovered that beneath her dainty exterior, Phoebe was almost as testy as her older sister. He'd known them both all his life. They were as different from one another as sweet pudding and sour pickles.

"And what would that important business be? You've already been to your quiltin' bee."

"Bert is coming to court me this afternoon."

"What!" Zak reeled back in shock. She might just as well have said she was expecting a visit from President Andrew Johnson himself. "Bert Brown?"

She lifted her chin higher and nodded.

"Have you lost your senses, Miss Phoebe? What, if you don't mind me askin', do you see in him?"

"Indeed I do mind." She folded her arms beneath her breasts and turned away.

"Sorry, but—"

"Sorry!" She whirled around, marching angrily on Zak once again. "For your information, all of a man's attributes are not found in his features."

"If that's how you feel, how come you never looked at me? All this time I thought you were sweet on that preacher's son."

Heaven Sent

"That's how little you know, Zak Tyler."

Snooty little thing. Even so, he'd been in love with Phoebe Pearl Applebee ever since he could remember. But there was no telling how a woman's mind worked. His pa had warned him to give thanks for being a bachelor man, and if he knew what was good for him he'd stay that way.

Zak turned away from Phoebe and hunkered down by the sack he'd dropped next to the fire.

"I'm goin' to make somethin' to eat now. Anything special you'd like?"

"I never eat breakfast."

Doubtful, he glanced up at her. She was looking down her nose at him. A real deep anger came over him, a bone-deep determination to prove he was more man than the minister's son and Bert Brown put together.

For what? If Phoebe knew how he felt about her, she'd convince him to take her back home. She'd laugh. Maybe both. So Zak just shrugged. "You should eat, Phoebe. You're just skin and bones as it is."

She gasped and sucked her breath in, and her bosom swelled out. Zak stared at the phenomenon.

"Well, I'm sorry I don't suit you, Zak. But you won't have to put up with me for long. My daddy will come to my rescue." She lowered her voice to an ominous tone. Her threat echoed eerily in the mine shaft. "And you will pay dearly for this."

Chapter Fifteen

Coop, Uriah, and Matilda Rose approached the Tyler ranch riding three abreast across an open meadow. Even with the summer sun on the rise, the powdery white outline of last night's moon still hung in the sky, a ghostly reminder of the night before. But Coop didn't need a reminder of a night he'd never forget.

Uriah sat solidly astride his horse, his expression glum. He hadn't said a word since they'd started out.

Matilda Rose appeared in high fettle. She talked confidently of finding her sister. Her spirits seemed unreasonably buoyant. At any moment he expected her to pull out her mouth organ and start to play.

His ego badly wounded, Coop could hardly speak to her.

"It's such a glorious mornin'," she chattered, her eyes lifted to the wide-open blue sky. "I think it's a good omen, Daddy. We're going to find Phoebe."

Uriah grunted.

Heaven Sent

"The Tyler ranch is just beyond that bend, Cooper T."

He grunted.

She seemed oblivious to Coop's displeasure. Or she just plain didn't care.

Wearing dark trousers that fit snug around her hips and a light blue gingham shirt, Matilda Rose looked as fetching as most women did in silks and satins. She'd pulled back her hair but left it unbraided. A shining cascade of chestnut curls fell from beneath her dark hat to the middle of her back.

Her back, smooth as silk. Last night in the cottage loft, he'd sprinkled kisses along her spine. His lips had tasted the silk of her. His palms had caressed her full lush hips, cupped her firm buttocks.

Hell's fire! Had he lost his mind altogether? He had other things to think about.

"We might should have waited for the message with further instructions to be delivered," Matilda Rose suggested.

"No use wasting time," Uriah replied. "It's the Tylers who have her."

"You're going to give them some water now, aren't you, Daddy?"

"I'll do what I have to do to get Phoebe back. And nothing more."

Expectation rang in her voice as Matilda reached out to shake Coop's arm. "There's the spread!"

A modest ranch house was nestled on the side of the next hill just ahead of them. Constructed in the old adobe style, the rambling structure was topped with a flat roof.

Coop could make out a bunkhouse and stable, but compared to the Silver Star, this ranch appeared small

Sandra Madden

and struggling. There were no vineyards or barns filled with hay. No charming cottages tucked away.

When they reached the gate, they could see that the front door and all the windows were open to catch whatever breeze might come.

"Remember, Uriah," Coop said, "you agreed to let me do the talking. I'm negotiating this peace. Pretend as if you don't speak Tyler's language."

"I don't. I haven't known what that old buzzard's been talkin' about for more'n twenty-five years. But I'll be listenin' real close to every word you say, Davis."

"What if Tom and Zak aren't here?" Matilda Rose asked.

"Then we'll wait," Coop told her.

As they turned their horses toward the hitching post in front of the house, Uriah shouted out loud enough to wake the dead, "Tom Tyler!"

"Daddy, we're going to dismount and knock on the door. We're going to be neighborly."

"Tom Tyler!" he yelled even louder.

From inside the house came a holler. "Is that you, you jughead?"

"They're made from the same leather," Matilda Rose sighed under her breath.

"Don't respond to any insults," Coop warned the elder Applebee.

With an irritated wag of her head, Matilda Rose asserted herself. "It's Matty and Uriah, Tom. We've got a friend with us. Want you to meet Cooper T. Davis."

Tom Tyler appeared in the door, carrying a rifle. Coop figured him to be about fifty years of age. With sun-darkened skin the texture of burlap, lean, and bald, the rancher owned a stubble of silver beard, a hooked nose, and hooded brown eyes. Eyes turned Coop's way.

Heaven Sent

"Who do you be?"

"Cooper T. Davis. Just like Matilda Rose said. A friend."

"We've come to make our peace, Mr. Tyler," Matty added cheerily. "You have to talk real loud, Tom's near deaf," she added in a whispered aside to Coop.

Tyler lowered his head like a bull about to charge. "No offense, Matty, but this isn't a woman's business."

"Anything havin' to do with the Sil—"

Coop interrupted her quickly. "Where's your son, Mr. Tyler? We need to speak with Zak."

"Who?"

"Zak."

"What for?"

"Because we think it's time to sit down together and come to terms on what we're going to do about the water problem."

Tom regarded Coop skeptically. "Zak left yesterday. Said he was going to Los Angeles for supplies."

"Did he say when he'd be back?"

The old man raised one hand to his ear. "Eh?"

Coop suspected Tom Tyler of selective hearing. "When is your son coming back?"

"Said he couldn't say. Suppose he'll be back by week's end."

"What'd he do with my Phoebe?" Uriah blurted.

"Do? What are you talking about, you old fool?"

"Your four-flusher son took my Phoebe, and if you think you can play like you don't know anything about it, you're mistaken!"

"I don't know whatjer talking about. Yer jest old and slippin' in the saddle."

"Zak took Phoebe and he's holding her hostage. If you think kidnappin' my baby is the way to get things

231

done, you're the one slippin' in the saddle, Tom Tyler."

Apparently inspired by her father, Matilda Rose lifted up in her saddle to join the fray. "My sister is not accustomed to inhumane treatment of any kind!" she declared, jabbing a finger at Tom, who appeared to be having difficulty hearing her. "Phoebe is an extremely fragile . . . flower."

"Matilda Rose—"

"If you don't tell us where they are by the time I count to three, you'll never see a drop of water," the elder Applebee growled.

"Uriah—"

"I don't know anything more than what I already told you. If Phoebe's missin', maybe you'd better look elsewhere. Zak went to town, and that's all I know'd."

Uriah went for his gun. "He's lyin'. I can always tell a lyin' dog."

Tom Tyler raised his rifle.

Coop eased his horse between the two men, one poised in the doorway, the other in the saddle about to draw from his holster. "We're not going to find out anything more here right now. Let's go."

"Where?"

"We're going back to the Silver Star and wait on those instructions the kidnapper promised."

"You're just gonna give up on Tom?" Uriah barked in protest.

"He doesn't know anything. He thinks his son is in Los Angeles. Maybe Zak didn't want his father involved."

"Could be," Uriah grudgingly acknowledged. "Zak's the hothead."

"And you wanted to marry me off to him."

"Girl, you get hotheaded too."

Heaven Sent

"This is not the time nor the place to argue," Coop reminded father and daughter quickly and harshly. He was feeling mighty edgy himself. The way things were going, he wouldn't be leaving the Silver Star today. "Let's go."

Coop nudged Traveler toward the open fields. He'd counted on a fast and easy solution to finding Phoebe. But instead of things getting less complicated, they seemed to get worse.

They'd reached a stream on a ridge halfway back to the Silver Star Ranch when Coop stopped. "Let's give the horses a drink and a few minutes' rest. We're on Silver Star land, aren't we? This is your water?"

But Uriah's attention was directed down toward the canyon. "What in Sam Hill!"

"What is it, Daddy?"

"Cattle thieves rustlin' our strays! And it's a damn poor piece of timin', 'cause I just feel like killin' someone."

Uriah charged forward, spurring his muscular palamino toward the bluff lowest and closest to the meadow where the outlaws had herded the cattle. When Applebee stopped for a better look, Coop grabbed hold of his reins.

"Hold on," he warned. "Let's not rush into anything here."

"Why the Sam Hill not? It's plain as day what they're doin'. No wonder my head count's been off. No tellin' how long this has been goin' on."

Stretching forward in his saddle, Coop took a long hard look. Just below, in the grazing meadow, three cowboys worked feverishly cutting steers from the herd of strays and rebranding.

The Applebees' sea of troubles had just grown

Sandra Madden

deeper. They had enough problems to keep ten Pinkertons busy. Seemed the excitement never stopped on the Silver Star.

"Those men are takin' my cattle. Are you gonna just sit here and watch?" Uriah demanded.

"No, sir."

"What kind of Pinkerton dee—tective are you?"

"This situation obviously doesn't require any detective work. Now, what I suggest is that I go down and round up those rustlers. Meantime, you get to your ranch and bring back some men to take these varmints into town for a visit with the sheriff."

"You think you can take all three of them by yourself?"

"With my help, he can, Daddy."

"No, no." Coop shook his head adamantly. "Please don't help me. Go back to the ranch with your father where you'll be safe, Matilda Rose. I can handle this alone."

"Maybe, but I think I'd better stay right here and back you up." She patted the colt in her holster. "We've worked as a team before—"

"That was then, this is now."

"Not much difference between a crooked circuit rider and a cattle thief—"

"What the hell are you two talkin' about?"

"Daddy—"

"While my cattle are bein' cut!"

"Sorry. Cooper T., I promise you won't see me unless you run into trouble."

"Matilda Rose—"

"My daughter's right. You need a backup and . . . well, she can do that for you. I don't want those blasted rustlers gettin' away with my stock."

Heaven Sent

Coop heaved a sigh. "All right. Let's not waste anymore time arguing. Go get your men, Uriah."

With a grunt and a nod, the crusty elder Applebee rode off in a hard gallop.

Matilda Rose smiled over at Coop. "Daddy likes you."

"How can you tell?"

"I've never seen him take orders from another man before. Not even Billy Bowed-Legs. And did you hear what he said?"

"I don't think I've missed a syllable."

"Daddy admitted I'd make a good backup for you."

"He's slipping in the saddle," Coop muttered.

"What?"

"I'm glad for you, if that's what you want." He looked out over the meadow, sizing up the scene.

The serene setting seemed at odds with the situation. Buttercups bordered the land as if some artist had painted a flower fence, bright yellow against the rich green of the grazing land. Bees and mosquitos buzzed over the landscape, and orange and black butterflies flew two by two in graceful loops across the wide field. All of nature seemed to be at play in the field, including the hummingbirds darting in and out of the flowers.

"See the chaparral of pine and oak to the east, Cooper T.?" Matty leaned forward in the saddle, pointing toward the densely wooded area. "If we're not careful, these cow thieves will make a run for it. We'll never find them if they get in there."

"Think maybe I'll go down and do some talking, some bluffing, and maybe some shooting. You stay here."

This was her land, her cows, and Cooper T. was still

trying to order her about. "No. I'm not going to let them kill you."

"No one's going to kill me," he assured her with a wink and a wry grin. "Stay put."

He rode off before Matty could argue. Tarnation! He was a mule-headed man. Too used to going it alone, he was. But Cooper T. needed her help whether he knew it or not. And he would have it.

Hoping he knew what he was doing, she watched carefully as he circled around back to make it appear he came from the chaparral.

To the south, a lone cowboy stood watch over the dozen head of cattle that already had been cut from the herd. Nearby, with his horse grazing close at hand, another cow puncher built up a fire for branding.

Nerves all edgy and restless in the saddle, Matty swore if anything happened to Cooper T., she would never forgive herself. No way she would take her eyes off him until he was out of danger.

Hiding Traveler behind the trees, Coop climbed a young oak and lay out flat along a limb at the widest section of the path. He whistled softly so that only the lookout could hear him. The man turned quickly, but after a few seconds the outlaw turned back to the cattle.

"Come on, come on and find me," Coop murmured impatiently before letting out a long, low whistle.

This time the cowboy jumped in his saddle. Turning his horse around, he cocked his head. After staring for some time in the direction of the chaparral, he rode slowly toward the area where Coop lay in wait.

The heavy growth made even the edge of the chaparral quite dark. Coop gauged that while the rustler adjusted to the change in light, he could take the thief by surprise. He whistled again to lure the man to just

Heaven Sent

the right spot. His luck held. The varmint stopped just beneath the tree.

Coop jumped his target, and they both fell to the ground in a flurry of fists and flailing legs. Nothing connected until Coop managed to get the man beneath him and land one solid blow with his fist. He knocked the rustler out.

"One down," he rasped, out of breath.

Before tying and gagging the snake in the grass, Coop exchanged shirts and hats with him. When he went out to join the herd, the others might not notice for a spell.

He wasn't that lucky. The second rustler, a heavyset threat, walked toward him almost as soon as he'd emerged from the spot he'd hidden the first.

"Where'd you go?" the rustler called.

Coop waved him back. "Took a leak."

"You didn't signal."

Knowing his voice was bound to give him away, Coop simply shrugged. The second cow thief had come close enough for Coop to recognize him. It was Clyde, the bandit who'd taken Matilda Rose's boots. And sure as Hell, Clyde would be recognizing Coop.

Coop knew the overweight bandit didn't move quickly. Withdrawing his Colt, he urged Traveler forward in a burst of speed that took him to Clyde's side in seconds.

"Drop your gun and get off that horse," he barked.

Clyde's eyes grew round. "Don't I know you?"

Seeing Clyde in trouble, the third rustler was bound to descend on Coop, guns blazing. With his weapon leveled on Clyde, Coop dismounted, grabbed the remaining loop of rope from his saddle horn, and advanced on the scowling thief. "Never thought I'd meet up with any of you folks again. I can't tell you what pleasure this gives me."

"I do know you!" the round rustler exclaimed, eyes and mouth equally wide with surprise.

"Yes, you do." He grinned wickedly.

Clyde's eyes narrowed. "You're the drummer."

"Glad you didn't forget me, Clyde."

"Where's your wagon, drummer?" the surly cow thief taunted. "Did you get out of the snake-oil business?"

"In a manner of speaking. Where're Josh and the rest of your friends? Did they get out of the bandit business?"

"Josh is dead, Luke's in jail, and the rest are in Mexico."

Half the men he pursued during his career as a Pinkerton could be found in Mexico, Coop thought. Damn disconcerting. Well, it would be different working the railroads.

In the split second his thoughts drifted, the prisoner bolted. It was Coop's turn to be surprised. Clyde traveled faster on foot than on horseback. But Coop managed to tackle him with a flying leap at the edge of the chaparral. They landed under an oak tree, flattening untold numbers of buttercups. A swarm of wasps angrily buzzed above them.

Coop looked up. Attached to a low branch of the old tree was the biggest wasp nest he'd ever come across. With one eye on the wasps and the other on Clyde, he retrieved his gun and pulled all two hundred and fifty pounds of rustler to his feet. His first order of business was to get away from the wasps. And then he heard the horse behind him.

Heaven Sent

"Drop that gun and raise your arms. High. I got no problem shootin' a man in the back."

"I'll just bet you don't," Coop gritted between his teeth.

"Turn around, mister."

He did as he was told, prepared to meet the rustler who'd been by the fire, heating the branding iron. More than likely the leader of the gang.

Before Coop could respond, a shot rang out. He spun toward the rustlers, ducking as he did. The head man's gun flew out of his hand as he was hit in the arm. He fell off his horse, right on top of Coop. Throwing one arm around the fallen thief's neck, Coop pushed to his feet, holding the man in front of him as a shield. Clyde stared. Uncertainty clouded his eyes.

The swarm of wasps outside the nest buzzed louder, grew larger. It was time to get out of there. "Come on," Coop barked. "Let's get out of here."

But Clyde didn't move. The bandit shield just moaned.

"Yeow!" Clyde howled, the first to be stung.

"Serves you right. You didn't think I'd come after you alone? My men are surrounding us, waiting for me to give the signal," Coop bluffed. "The shoot-to-kill signal."

But only one set of hooves galloped toward them. He turned. Matilda Rose bore down on the three men with her gun drawn.

"No!" Coop yelled. "Go back; there's a wasp nest!"

She either didn't hear him or didn't care. She kept coming, pulling Spirit up short to a stop beside Clyde. "Are you all right, Cooper T.?"

" 'Course I am, but you won't be if you don't hightail it."

Sandra Madden

But she wasn't listening. Her gaze had fixed on Clyde. "Tarnation! This is the sidewinder who stole my made-to-measure boots!"

"We're right under a wasp's nest, Matilda Rose; get out of here."

She looked toward the tree and frowned before turning back to him. "I can't leave you unarmed with two rattlesnakes."

"Please!" If anything happened to her on his account, he would never be able to live with himself. "Toss me your pistol and get out."

"Look, there's Daddy!" Matilda Rose pointed to the ridge behind him. "We've got help coming!"

"Go!" he shouted.

"Ouch!" she yelped.

Matilda Rose had been stung.

The next few minutes passed in a blur for Coop. Instead of attacking the men who had initially disturbed them, the wasps attacked the most innocent and vulnerable—Matilda Rose.

Coop knew enough to understand that even a heavy dose of Doctor Van Kurem's tonic wasn't going to help if she was seriously stung. With no time to lose, he pushed the head rustler on top of Clyde and dived for Matilda, pulling her off her horse.

All he heard was the buzzing and Matilda's muffled protests as he threw her on the ground and covered her with his body. Coop became the target of angry wasps, jabbed again and again by their sharp stingers. But he wouldn't suffer any lasting effects beyond the immediate prickly pain.

A stream ran through the chaparral. If he could get Matilda Rose to it with no further wasp stings, she might be safe.

Heaven Sent

The two rustlers cussed, danced, and swatted, diverting a goodly amount of the swarm. Coop could hear Uriah and his men galloping toward them, firing warning shots that echoed in the valley.

Scooping Matilda Rose from the ground and protecting her as best he could from the wasps, he raced head down to the stream.

He threw himself and his flailing companion into the cool clear, water. Holding her in his arms, with her face against his chest, he splashed at the irate insects until they gave up and flew away.

Coop waited a few minutes to make sure they wouldn't return. Finally, as he staggered to his feet, he realized Matilda Rose had passed out. One angry red welt ballooned near her eye, another on her neck.

Had his protective zealousness caused her to faint, or was it the poison from the wasp stings? Whichever it was, Coop knew he couldn't take any chances. He raced toward the clearing.

"What in Sam Hill?" Uriah and several of his men watched from horseback as Coop emerged from the wooded area carrying Matilda Rose in his arms.

"She's been stung by wasps," Coop hollered. "Send for a doctor."

Chapter Sixteen

Late that same afternoon, Matty looked in the mirror and saw a chipmunk. Her cheeks were swollen, her eyelids puffed up, her complexion splotchy red. "I'm hideous," she wailed.

"When have you ever cared what you looked like?" her father asked in surprise. "Be thankful you're alive and those thieves are behind bars."

"You'll have your looks back in a day or so," Dr. Collins assured her. "We'll have Lupe keep applying the clay plasters. They've drawn out most of the venom already."

Matty felt miserable inside and out. Sharp, stabbing pain combined with a feverish heat and uncomfortable bloating consumed her.

"Those critters act just like snake bite on you," Dr. Collins informed her as if she didn't know.

"I know."

Heaven Sent

"Well, then, why'd you ride into a wasps nest?" her father demanded.

"Cooper T. was in trouble."

"So you didn't pay no mind to those angry stingers?"

"Has he left yet, Daddy?"

"The Pinkerton? Where do you think he'd be goin'? Nope, he's just outside, been pacin' the hall for two hours waitin' to see you. Wants to see with his own eyes you're alive."

Her heart nearly stopped. "Oh, no! No, he can't see me like this."

"I'll tell him he can see you in the morning, though I don't know as it will do any good. The man's agitated; he's liable to break down the door."

"He is?" Matty couldn't help a small smile.

With Doc Collins right behind him, her father started to leave. "We're getting ready to ride out—"

"Where?" Matty pushed herself up in bed, bracing herself on her elbows. Her head spun. Her stomach did a bad somersault. "Has there been word about Phoebe?"

The doctor poked a finger toward her. "You get some rest, young lady. You lie back down and don't rile yourself."

"Now that you're out of the woods, we're gonna start searchin' for Phoebe. We're spreadin' out and lookin' over Tyler land inch by inch."

"I'll come with you."

"Can't do that."

Her mounting frustration made the pain and feverishness worse. "What about the instructions from the kidnapper?"

"Nothing. We didn't get diddly. Zak's holdin' out on

Sandra Madden

us. Wantin' us to suffer, I reckon. Well, he's gonna suffer. I'm goin' to skin that boy alive when I find him."

"Take a nap, Matty," the doctor ordered.

"I'll see you when I get back." After uttering his brusque promise, her father strode out the door with Dr. Collins close on his heels.

"But Daddy! Come back, I want to—" Matty stopped in midsentence as the door banged open and Cooper ambled into her bedroom.

He stopped at the foot of the bed. His green eyes regarded her intently. "Precious."

She lowered her head. "Don't look at me."

"You look fine . . . to me."

"I could use a bottle of Dr. Van Kurem's tonic long about now."

"Perhaps I can arrange it. Let me look at you." He sat on the edge of the bed. Reaching out, he cupped her chin, tilted her head. She closed her eyes. "A little swollen, but alive."

"Did you think you'd rid yourself of me at last?" she asked, quickly lowering her head again.

"Wouldn't like to think you hurt yourself to save my sorry life."

"Well, I didn't. I didn't know those wasps were there."

"I called and warned you they were."

"Guess I didn't hear you," she replied. Matty didn't know where to look, what to do. She didn't want Cooper T. to stay while she looked like this. Neither did she want him to leave.

"Thanks for your help. Although I do recall asking you to stay put."

"Reckon I'm just not good at taking orders."

"One of your father's men brought this telegram

back from town." He held up an envelope. "The sheriff had been keeping it for you."

"For me?" She took it from him. "Is this the telegram to tell me you're a bona fide Pinkerton?"

"Read it."

"It does." She smiled at the piece of paper. "It has Alan Pinkerton's address should I need any further evidence."

"Do you believe me now?"

"Yes. I believe you." She flicked her wrist toward another envelope he held. "Is that another telegram?"

"This one's for me, from headquarters."

"Oh." Her stomach rolled. This telegram, she feared, was telling him to leave the Silver Star immediately.

"This is about your mother."

"Mama?" Matty raised her gaze to his in surprise. Her heart felt as if it had stopped.

"I had inquiries made."

She couldn't speak.

He took her hand in his. A warm, strong, enveloping hand. "I'm sorry, Matilda Rose, but I have sad news. Your mama is dead."

Matty's fever gave way to chills. Her body stiffened and she gripped Cooper T.'s hand tightly.

"Do you remember the cholera epidemic last year?" he asked gently.

Unable to speak, she nodded.

"Your mama was on her way home when she fell sick."

A lump as large as the state of Texas lodged in her throat. "How . . . how do you know that?"

"She told the woman nursing her in the hospital. My colleague interviewed the nurse."

"She was coming home?" Matty repeated his state-

Sandra Madden

ment, awed and comforted at the same time by this bit of news.

"Your mama loved you, Matilda Rose."

Her heart splintered painfully. Tears she could not restrain, and made no attempt to hide, streamed hot and fast down Matty's cheeks.

"Your mama loved you and Phoebe, and she wanted to be with you again."

She nodded, feeling as if she were smothering in a deep, abiding sorrow. She swiped at the tears with the back of her hand.

"Sorry it couldn't have been better news."

"What could be better news than that? Mama was comin' home." She forced a smile through her tears. Her lips quivered. "Thank you . . . thank you, Cooper T. At last we know. We won't be looking for Mama to come riding down the road anymore."

Cooper T. leaned over and brushed his mouth tenderly against her forehead.

"Will you tell Daddy?"

"That's not my place," he answered. "It's up to you."

"I'll think on it."

"Well, now, I guess you learned something from the wasps today."

She sniffled and nodded. "Reckon I did."

He stood up slowly. "I've got to go now."

"Go where?"

"The message delivered from the kidnapper while we were gone this morning doesn't suit your father. But I'm of another mind."

"What did it say?"

" 'If you want to see Phoebe again, bring a signed, witnessed solicitor's document giving water rights to

Heaven Sent

Thomas Tyler. Leave the document under the black rock at Spring Creek by sunset today.' "

"Daddy's not goin' to give them the water rights?" She could hardly believe her father continued to be so stubborn. His belligerence fueled her anger—and her energy. "What's the matter with him? Poor Phoebe must be scared to death out there in the wilderness with no one but Zak!"

"Apparently your daddy still doesn't take to the notion of being forced to share."

"Billy Bowed-Legs could talk sense to Daddy."

"But Billy isn't here."

She raised her eyes heavenward and sighed.

"You get some rest. I'm going to stake out the Tyler ranch. Sooner or later Zak will show up, or Tom will go to him."

Matty threw back her covers. "I'm going with you."

"No. Please be sensible. Your eyes are half shut. How are you going to see? A stakeout is a watch," he pointed out. "It's long and boring, but it's the best way to catch the bad guy if you have half an idea who it is."

"Maybe if I were with you it wouldn't be so boring."

Coop couldn't help but grin. That was a fact. It was also a fact that he couldn't seem to stay angry with Matilda Rose for long. One smile wiped away old wounds.

"Nothing is boring with you," he said.

"Have you ever made love on a stakeout?"

"Matilda Rose, I am shocked!" But Coop couldn't mask his silly smile nor shake the feeling of unabashed pleasure. "No, I've never made love during a stakeout. Are you bent on using me to satisfy your curiosity again?"

"Oh, no Cooper T.!"

Sandra Madden

"Maybe wasp venom talking? The poison has made you delirious?"

"Nooooo, Cooper T."

"Then what kind of thoughts are those to be having when you're still all swollen?"

"Good ones," she assured him with a wistful sigh. "Really good ones."

"Then hold on to them." He leaned over to kiss the top of her head.

"I will," she promised.

"And get some rest, because I'm not coming back without your sister."

Coop had a bad feeling. Making good on his promise that he wouldn't return without Phoebe was going to cost him more than another day. His job was at stake more now than when this neverending journey began. He'd be lucky to reclaim his Pinkerton badge, let alone win a transfer to the railroad detail. But how could he turn his back on the situation at the Silver Star Ranch? A damsel in distress awaited rescue, and he had a kidnapper to capture. All in a day's work. Except, at the moment, the usual excitement eluded him.

Personal feelings had never hampered his work before. But as he rode off from the main ranch house, Coop felt a gnawing uneasiness deep in his gut. Matilda Rose had risked her life to save him.

He'd never experienced the kind of fear he'd felt when he first saw her swollen face back in the meadow. Pulse racing, he'd rushed with her limp body from the stream to his horse. Urging Traveler to a full gallop, he'd raced to the ranch holding Matilda Rose's unconscious form tightly against him, as if through pure force of will he could mend her.

Heaven Sent

Coop had watched her sweet face distort as the swelling increased, listened anxiously to her labored breathing. Tension coiled inside him like an overwound spring.

Even though it had all happened hours ago, the anxious moments played over and over in his mind, still raising the hairs on the back of his neck.

He'd paced the veranda, waiting for the doctor, cursing the man for taking so long to get there. He'd badgered Lupe whenever she entered or left Matilda Rose's room.

"What is that?" he'd asked.

"Raw onion, *señor*. Pull out the poison."

While he doubted the healing power of the vegetable, he supposed it was better than doing nothing. "Do you have enough? Do you need more?"

Hell, he could peel an onion or two.

She shot him an encouraging smile. "*Sí, señor*. Do not worry. It has helped in the past."

When Dr. Collins finally rode up, Uriah ushered the old physician into Matilda's bedroom. Ignored, and as nervous as a wild rabbit cornered by a wolf, Coop paced for another good hour or more outside the door. He couldn't cast off the resentment that simmered inside. He should be in there beside her. On the long trail they'd work together to fix things. Now he was shut out.

But he had no right to demand a place at her side.

And knowing she was out of danger at least enabled him to breathe normally again. Coop smiled. The sight of her all swollen but determined to ride with him to the stakeout triggered a warmth that spread through him like smooth whiskey. Gritty resolve had glittered in her extraordinary eyes. His chest tightened. Nothing seemed to bow the brave little spitfire.

Damnation! What was he thinking?

Matilda Rose was alive and would be well. He'd never been so relieved to hear any news. And that was that.

With a nudge of his heels, Coop increased Traveler's speed, putting the ranch and the beguiling Miss Applebee a safe distance behind him.

By late afternoon, he was up a tree. Literally. He'd found the best stakeout spot for surveillance of the Tyler ranch house to be the broad, rough limb of a knotty old oak on a hill above the ranch. If he got really lucky, he'd discover the Tylers were holding Phoebe, right down there on the ranch. In the barn, maybe. But so far there had been no suspicious movement.

He didn't hold out much hope that Uriah would discover anything on his land search. Traditionally, in Coop's business, stakeouts were more successful than the searching-for-a-needle-in-a-haystack-approach. But stakeouts were also often long, tedious, and lonely ventures. Although necessary, they were his least favorite part of detective work. How long, he wondered, would he have to wait for a break?

Shortly after dawn, when all was still quiet except for the shrill song of the earliest birds, Matty slipped out of the house. She'd waited just as long as she could without word. Giving Spirit free rein, she rode toward the Tyler ranch. The air already felt sultry and heavy. It promised to be one hot summer day.

Occasionally a chaparral bird scooted along the trail before her. The funny-looking birds were called roadrunners because, although they couldn't fly, they were fast afoot.

Most of her facial swelling had receded, but red splotchy traces of her encounter with the wasps remained. Since Cooper T. had already seen her looking like a full moon gone to fire, Matty brushed aside her vanity. Helping him find Phoebe was much more important.

She found Traveler first, grazing under an aged giant oak. Knowing his horse would never roam far from Cooper T., Matty searched the scrub around the small clearing. When that proved futile, she just listened, as Billy Bowed-Legs had taught her to do. And then, hearing the merest rustle of leaves, she looked up into the tree and caught a glimpse of blue shirtsleeve in the midst of green.

"Cooper T.! What are you doing up there?"

His dark, handsome face appeared between two branches. "What are you doing down there?"

She lifted the hamper she carried. "I brought you breakfast."

The grin he bestowed on her made Matty's heart skip like a pebble on a stream. "Well, that's mighty nice of you, Matilda Rose. If I didn't know better, I'd say I was beginning to grow on you."

To grow on her? He was locked in Matty's heart forever. Somehow, when she wasn't paying attention, the arrogant Pinkerton had slipped in and planted himself permanently in the center of her mind and heart. Not that he would ever know. Not that she could tell him, when he was so eager to go, to be on his way from her and the Silver Star Ranch.

"Reckon you've got to keep your strength up," she replied.

He chuckled, started to move, groaned, and then stretched very carefully. "Believe I'm too old to be sleeping in trees."

Matty's gaze fixed on Cooper T. He moved with animal grace, a muscular, sinewy elegance that just about took her breath away. His green eyes glittered like a big cat stalking his prey, alert and intense. Matty felt certain those compelling eyes could see deep into a criminal mind . . . or a vulnerable woman's soul.

She looked away as he neared the ground.

"When you're chasing after Jesse James you'll be sleeping in railroad boxcars."

"I expect a boxcar will be a sight more comfortable than the limb of this old tree."

Discussing his eventual departure, even in a lighthearted fashion, disturbed Matty more than she cared to admit. Although she prepared every day for his leaving, she feared her heart might break when the time actually came to say good-bye.

She had stored away the memory of the sweet achy feeling of each of his kisses, each caress. She would never again feel the way she had felt in Cooper T.'s arms. Because, although she often talked to Billy Bowed-Legs to see what he could do about changing Coop's mind, she didn't believe in miracles. She wasn't even absolutely sure that Billy still watched over her. It seemed to Matty a vigilant guardian angel would have prevented the wasp attack.

As she spread a blanket beneath the tree, her heart felt as if one of those big old iron railroad ties had fallen across it. Matty silently scolded herself for selfishly thinking of her own problem when her sweet, fragile sister was being held prisoner.

"Has there been any sign of Tom or Zak or Phoebe since you've been staked out?"

"No, it's been quiet," Cooper T. answered, jumping down from his perch as quietly as any Indian scout. "A stakeout is tedious business at best."

"Well, I don't think my sister is feeling like her predicament is especially tedious. 'Course, Zak wouldn't hurt Phoebe."

"Did your daddy find anything in his search yesterday afternoon?"

"No. If I were running the ranch—"

"And you will someday," he assured her with a rueful smile.

"Maybe. If I don't do anything foolish."

"You? Do something foolish?" He flashed yet another teasing, spine-tingling grin as he sidled up to her.

Matty swallowed hard. He'd stopped inches away. The surging heat of him stirred memories of their night in the cottage, and worse . . . a tantalizing smoldering deep inside her.

"You look a lot better this morning, precious. Swelling's down; your eyes, your lips . . ." His voice trailed off as he lightly brushed a fingertip along her bottom lip.

"Yes . . ." Matty confirmed his observation—on her last breath. "I'm . . . I'm right as rain."

"Right as rain," he repeated in a husky tone. His eyes locked on hers, penetrating, mesmerizing.

Matty's knees buckled like a day-old colt and she swayed against him. Feeling excessively light-headed, she couldn't tear her gaze away from the intense crystal light of Cooper T.'s eyes. Without moving, without breathing, she struggled to suppress the temptation to throw her arms around him and beg him to test her lips for signs of recovery.

But her silent prayers were answered. Cooper T. dipped his head and slowly, slowly, his mouth came down on hers.

Oh my, my, my, my, oh my.

He kissed her gently, brushing her mouth as softly as the warm summer breeze that danced around them. Matty's lips parted in answer, and Cooper T. gathered her in his arms. What began as a gentle touch deepened into a soul-searching kiss, inciting, consuming.

A fire ignited in her heart and shot through her trembling body, faster than lightning, more swiftly than wildfire. Waves of incredible warmth rippled down her spine.

Soon they were undressed, their naked flesh caressed by the summer sun. Cooper T. eased her down to the blanket, enfolding her, crushing her in his arms. He kissed her fiercely, thoroughly. Matty's mind spiraled in dizzying delight as she abandoned propriety for passion. While his tongue eagerly explored her mouth, Cooper T.'s palms cupped her bottom, pressing her against his body.

Matty's heart hammered wildly as she felt the hard proof of his passion against her, the strength of his desire.

"Precious Matilda Rose," he murmured as his lips brushed her cheeks, her chin, her eyes, and nuzzled her ear. "We can't do this. We're . . ." His voice trailed off, the words seeming to stick in his throat. He began again. "We're on stakeout."

"But if you stop, I'll die," she said breathlessly.

He groaned, responding thickly, "You leave me no choice."

Heaven Sent

In broad daylight, under a rising sun, Matty surrendered to Cooper T. once more. Aroused, alive with love, she savored every lovely, laughing, nibbling, nuzzling moment. All he gave to her, she returned in full measure. She learned to love him, hold him, treasure him.

As summer butterflies swooped and dove around them, Matty soared in a cloud of heat and light. Sultry. Sensual. And when together she and Cooper T. reached a shattering pinnacle of pleasure, her body hummed and her flesh tingled.

My, oh my.

He held her close to him for a long while. There was no need for words. Enfolded in his strong warm arms, she at last knew the meaning of happiness and contentment.

Finally, Cooper T. broke the silence in a husky, teasing timbre. "Now, what was it you brought me?"

Laughing, Matty wiggled out of his arms and reached for the basket. "Lupe packed you two fried egg sandwiches, oranges, cheese, and a fresh-baked loaf of bread."

"A breakfast fit for a king." He grinned, pulling on his trousers.

"Yes. Well, Lupe thinks of you as a king. She likes you."

He hiked an eyebrow and put on his dark blue shirt. "What are you having?"

"There's an extra orange for me."

"Doesn't she like you?"

Chuckling, Matty began to dress. When she was fully clothed again, she sank down beside him. Drawing her knees up under her chin, she gazed out at the Tyler ranch below.

Sandra Madden

Guilt bubbled up inside her. She had distracted Cooper T. from the watch. What kind of sister was she? What had he done to her that she couldn't keep her emotions under control? "I . . . I hope we didn't miss anything."

"Don't think so. Smoke just started rising from the chimney. Tom is obviously not an early riser."

"I guess not. Daddy says if he worked harder he'd have more."

"Why does he need more if he's enjoying his life?"

"I don't know." She shrugged. "Zak and Tom Tyler are good men. It shouldn't have come to this."

"Why is your daddy so unneighborly?"

"He's hardheaded. Things have to be his way."

"Must be something in the blood."

"What?"

"Nothing."

"Daddy's lived beside Tom Tyler peacefully for almost twenty-five years."

"Then I figure they'll be happy to get this behind them."

"A rancher's life is mostly peaceful, despite what you're witnessing now," Matty said, watching his big hands deftly peel the orange. Moments ago, those same hands had wakened her body and brought her to a new ecstasy. With the mere thought, she felt herself growing warm again. Clearing her throat, she swallowed hard. "I mean, this little feud, and the run-in with the rustlers, are not everyday events."

"If you say so."

"Most of the time we're workin' out on the land. No one tells us what to do next . . . or where we have to be . . . or when," she added for good measure. "We know our job and we do it."

Heaven Sent

"Well now, that's a good thing. A man's got to—or a woman—they have to feel free. I've never spent more than a few hours on a ranch before, but ranching appears to have its rewards."

"Oh, it does," she declared enthusiastically. Her pride wouldn't allow her to ask Cooper T. to stay a few more days and let her show him how rewarding life on the Silver Star could be.

"Just like being a detective has its rewards."

With a curt nod of her head and a lump of disappointment settling into her stomach, Matty turned her attention back to the Tyler ranch. "Why doesn't someone do somethin' down there!" she demanded irritably.

She could no longer deal rationally with Cooper T., his leaving, her feelings about the inevitable good-bye. And what kind of sister was she? How could she forget Phoebe's plight even for one minute?

"Well, they are doing something. Don't know what, but don't you see those two cowpunchers saddling up outside the barn?"

"But there's no sign of Tom or Zak," she protested.

"Tom's still inside the house."

"Are you sure?"

"Positive."

"Maybe Phoebe's down there too."

"Maybe," he agreed.

"I suppose she can't be too fearful if it's Zak that's holding her. She's known him all her life. We used to play together when we were younger, the three of us."

"If what you're saying is true, relax. It's a waiting game we're playing here. Likely your sister and Zak are getting along fine."

"But what if they're not?"

Chapter Seventeen

Besides being a mite cold and damp, the old mine shaft didn't allow much morning light inside. Zak hadn't counted on spending more than two days here with Phoebe. Whenever he left, he had to tie her down to an old chair, which made him feel bad. Genteel ladies like Phoebe shouldn't be treated such. Sliding her an apologetic smile, he untied her hands and feet. He removed the gag from her mouth last.

She jumped up and spun on him in one swift, and fierce, move. "Where have you been?" she cried. "How could you leave me here? What kind of blackheart are you? What sort of rude, heartless villain have you become, Zak Tyler?"

"I . . . I—"

"I'll tell you! You are what my daddy calls a sidewinding snake!" The words tumbled out of Phoebe's little bow mouth faster than Zak could sort them.

Heaven Sent

"I've been out takin' care of business. Soon as it's settled, you can leave."

Her hands curled into tight little fists at her sides as she advanced on him. The little lady was stronger, more headstrong than he—and probably everyone else—imagined. "Let me go this instant, Zak Tyler, or I'll see you at the wrong end of a rope!"

"You're beginnin' to sound like your sister," he grumbled, backing off with hands raised. "Don't be gettin' mad with me. Your daddy's to blame. He didn't answer my ransom note, didn't return the agreement. Hasn't signed it, likely. Don't know how long we're gonna be up here now."

"When my daddy is forced to do something, he just digs in his heels. You're not going to get water from him this way, so you might just as well let me go now."

"Gosh, you're real pretty, Miss Phoebe."

"What?" Her voice raised so high it squeaked.

"Usually whenever I see you, you're all neat and prim and proper, kinda like a porcelain doll . . . untouchable. But my, just look at you now."

Her blue eyes filled with tears. "I don't want to look at myself now. I've barely washed in two days. My hair hasn't been brushed in forever—"

She stopped in midsentence and took two jagged breaths. Confused, Zak watched and waited, alert for new trouble.

Oh, jeez, she'd started to bawl. He hated it when she did that. He rushed to comfort her. "Sure your dress is a mite dirty, your face is a little smudged, and your hair is undone. But you still look good enough for a man to—"

"To what?"

Tempering his enthusiasm, Zak lowered his eyes and his voice. "You're a mighty appealin' woman. How many women do you think can look appealin' after two days in a mine shaft?" He turned away and answered his own question. "Not many, of that I'm certain."

"You think I'm appealing? Looking like this?"

Drawing a deep fortifying breath, he turned. She was looking at him as if he were stark raving mad.

"Yes, Miss Phoebe I do. And if you don't mind my sayin' so, you need more of a man than fat old Bert to be your husband."

Her mouth dropped open and she squeaked again. The next thing Zak knew, she'd fallen to the chair sobbing. Deep, heavy, body-racking sobs.

"What'd I say? What'd I do?"

She continued to sob, covering her face with her hands, shaking her head back and forth.

Playing as kids in a mine shaft was one thing, living in one, another. The captivity was getting to her, that's all Zak could think. He hunkered down beside her chair hoping a little sweet talk would stop her tears. "You know, since the time we were young'uns I've been sweet on you. I used to herd cattle thinking about how I could marry you. Knew I never had a chance, 'cause you never looked my way. But I used to dream about it anyway."

Phoebe's sobs became a keening wail.

She hated him. Zak felt helpless. Panic knotted his stomach. He couldn't stand to see her cry. And he didn't know how to handle a hysterical woman. He didn't know what to do with a woman at all, if the truth were known. But was there a man who did?

"You want some water, Phoebe? Would that do it for you?"

Heaven Sent

She sniffled. "Water would help."

Zak crossed to fetch the bucket and a mug, speaking softly all the while in an effort to calm his captive down. "Suppose there's no reason for you to consider me as a suitor. I know I'm not much to look at . . . but I ain't ugly either. I've had some schoolin, and I'd like to be a daddy someday. You know, a big old family strikes me as somthin' to give a man pride. Don't have a mean temper, and I'm no dandy like Bert."

Her sobs quieted. She sniffled again.

"What are you thinkin', woman, lettin' a prissy, overweight barber court you?" he continued. "You need a real man like me."

"May I remind you that you are an outlaw? Holding me against my will is called kidnapping," she snipped, before taking a sip of water from the mug. "You have definitely broken the law."

"I reckon so, but I didn't know what else to do." Zak ran his fingers through his hair and kicked up a patch of dirt. Things weren't going according to plan. Not at all. He had to think.

"Did you mean what you said? Have you always been sweet on me?"

Phoebe's soft question echoed in the mine shaft.

"Yes, Miss Phoebe, I did mean it. Indeed. There's no one prettier or smarter than you in the whole territory."

She sat up a little straighter. "If you feel that way, why are you keeping me in this dark, damp, dirty old place? We would be much more comfortable at your ranch."

"I know it, and I'm sorry as all get out. It's nothing personal against you." Phoebe's nose was all red and swollen; her eyes too. Mildly astonished, he realized she still looked beautiful after all the weeping and wailing.

Sandra Madden

"My business with your pa called for desperate action."

"My sister—"

"A born spinster, that one. Sorry to say it, but I'd just as soon mate with a rattler. Matty scares me, and most men around these parts."

"Matty has a heart of gold, and she's not going to like this when she finds out. She'll come after you."

"Your sister's been off somewheres for weeks. Don't you think I know? She's not going to find us."

Phoebe's disheveled blond curls bobbed in a stringy mass as she lowered her head. "Wha . . . what can I do to make you let me go? I'll do anything."

Zak's first thought was downright shameful.

Coop watched Matilda Rose fold the picnic blanket. A small breeze blew a wisp of her silky chestnut hair into her face. She'd worn it long this morning, tied back by a bright red ribbon. "Thank you kindly for bringing me breakfast."

A hint of a smile played on her lips. "My pleasure."

Grinning, he helped her fold the last section of the blanket. He knew as well as she that they weren't talking about the food. Despite what she'd said earlier, Matilda Rose had made love to him as if . . . as if she meant it. But he knew better.

He walked his portion of the blanket up to her and inhaled deeply . . . essence of rose. Coop knew he'd miss her sweet fragrance.

"Thank you, Cooper T."

"You go home now and wait for word."

Her eyes blazed with indignation. "Go home and wait for word?"

"For all we know, you might still have some of that wasp venom running through your blood. Get some

Heaven Sent

rest, Matilda Rose, and watch to make sure your daddy doesn't do anything hotheaded and reckless."

"But Zak might show up, or Tom might ride out. All kinds of things might happen here. Nothing is happening at the Silver Star. You need someone to help you here."

"I've been doing this kind of work for a long time. Trust me, the best way you can help me is by going home. Knowing you're safe, that will be . . . like a gift to me."

"You're treating me just like, just as if I were a . . . a woman!"

"Exactly."

She rolled her eyes and marched off toward her horse.

He watched her mount and smiled as he strode up to her. "Appreciate it if you would thank Lupe for me. I sure did enjoy the vittles."

"Harumphf!"

"And the company."

Matilda Rose rode off without another word, leaving Coop mildly disturbed. As hotheaded and impulsive as her daddy, Matilda Rose could wind up hurt. And he didn't know how he could deal with that.

He resumed the stakeout, on the verge of sending a prayer to her guardian angel. If Billy Bowed-Legs couldn't get her home safely, no one could.

Matty traveled two miles toward the Silver Star, seething in the saddle. The feeling of being wronged gave way to resentment, indignation, and righteousness. She'd wanted to help Cooper T., be by his side until he caught Zak and . . . left for San Francisco.

Soon she would be alone with Daddy and Phoebe

again. The only people in the world who truly loved her. She and Phoebe used to play in these hills when they were young. Sometimes Zak played with them. Bandits and sheriff was his favorite game. He always played the sheriff; Matty and Phoebe were the bandits. Their hideout had been an abandoned mine shaft not far from here. Thirty years ago, gold seekers had mined the spot in vain.

"Tarnation!"

Matty pulled Spirit to a stop. Why hadn't she thought of the old mine before? Because Zak wouldn't take Phoebe there. Would he?

It wasn't far. She really should check while she was so close. If nothing else, a quick look would eliminate a possibility.

She couldn't go back for Cooper T. Someone needed to watch the Tyler ranch, and the short ride she meant to take to the mine shaft was just a lark, a look-see.

Her hair blew out behind her as Spirit galloped from the glen and up a rocky slope to an area of high chaparral. As she remembered, the mine shaft was hidden by a thick copse of pine trees.

The landscape had changed, and it had been at least a dozen years since Matty had been up here. A niggling uncertainty pricked at her belly. She hadn't brought along her Winchester, but she did have her gun belt and revolver tucked into the saddlebag.

Although usually not so persnickety, she hadn't wanted to have breakfast with Cooper T. looking like a gunslinger. She'd let her hair loose and tied it with a ribbon especially to present a more feminine picture. She still hadn't recovered from him seeing her all bitten and swollen.

Dismounting, she tied Spirit to a tall thin pine and

Heaven Sent

took out her gun belt and revolver. The entrance to the mine shaft wasn't visible from where Matty stood. She reckoned it was about fifty yards straight up the steep incline facing her.

The reason they liked the spot as children was that no one could sneak up on them. Especially parents. Tom Tyler had a way of hunting Zak down to do his chores.

"Spirit, I'm leaving you here, girl," Matty soothed, speaking into the horse's ear. "No noise, not a neigh, not a prance. Be real quiet just in case Zak's up there. He's not playin' the sheriff anymore."

After she'd tied her gun belt to her thigh, Matty stealthily made her way up the incline, darting from tree to tree. The hillside was quiet except for the chirping of birds, the pounding of her heart, and the crunch of an occasional pinecone beneath her feet.

She stopped in her tracks. Something, or someone, other than she had moved. Goosebumps raised up on Matty's arms. Had that been the snap of twigs she'd heard behind her?

The hard metal nuzzle in the small of her back confirmed her suspicion.

"Miss Matty?"

"Zak?"

He chuckled softly. "This is even better than I planned. With both of his daughters gone, Uriah has to give over the water rights."

"I-I wouldn't do this if I were you," she stammered as she felt her Colt being pulled from its holster.

"But you ain't me."

"This will just make my daddy madder than a herd of stampeding bulls," Matty predicted in a dire tone. If she could turn and look him in the eye, she might be able to back him down.

The gun in her back dug deeper.

"He'll get over it. Start walkin'."

"Phoebe better not be hurt in any way. If you did—"

"Your sister's good as gold."

"I've got an idea."

"I'll bet you do."

"Why don't you just hold me and let her go?"

"No." He pushed her shoulder, urging her uphill. "Get goin'. You're both my prisoners now."

Matty wondered how long it would be until Cooper T. discovered she hadn't gone directly back to the Silver Star.

And would he bother coming to her rescue, again?

Coop studied the layout of the Tyler ranch. Tom sat on the porch of the main house smoking a pipe. He'd sat down in his rocker right after noon and hadn't moved since. He didn't behave like a man in the middle of a kidnapping. Neither did he appear much interested in his ranch. Hired hands went about the chores of running the Tyler spread, while Tom blew smoke. Zak was nowhere to be seen.

Coop had spent many a lonely hour on stakeout, but none like this. He felt more alone than he had in years, since he was a kid. Pushing back the brim of his hat with his thumb, he scanned the road leading to the ranch, then the bunkhouse and main corral. He saw nothing out of the ordinary.

Although he wasn't much for dwelling on his feelings, he had a hunch this strange emptiness he was experiencing had something to do with Matilda Rose.

Heaven Sent

For over thirty days and nights she'd been by his side. They'd been inseparable. Only hours ago he'd made love to her, and he hadn't wanted to stop. It was only natural to feel—attached. And there was no use denying that when he'd been obligated to send her home, he'd felt downright irritated.

Here he sat. Alone. Solitary. Watching. Listening.

Tom Tyler whittled some, talked with his ranch hands some.

Chores were completed at an unhurried pace. It occurred to Coop that the efforts of a man's labor could be seen immediately in the repair of a fence, the shoeing of a string of horses, the chopping and stacking of a cord of wood. Life on a ranch could be whatever a man made of it, Coop figured by midafternoon.

The sound of horses, at least three of them, sent him scurrying back up the tree. He heard the gruff voice of Uriah Applebee even before the blustery owner of the Silver Star rode into view.

"Well, Sam Hill, he's gotta be here somewhere."

"Up here, Uriah." Coop swung down from the tree.

"What the hell are you doin' up there?" The white-haired owner of the Silver Star could have passed for a general, he sat so tall and straight in the saddle.

"I took cover. With the noise you were making, I thought it might be Zak."

"You can't ride without makin' some noise."

"Well now, Uriah, I hate to disagree with an Applebee. But I've seen a man ride nice and quiet, a time or two, around a stakeout area."

"Harumphf."

Rubbing the back of his neck, he gazed up at Uriah. "What brings you up here?"

"What do you think?" the old man scowled.

Sandra Madden

Coop didn't care for riddles, particularly on a day when he felt bedeviled. "Why don't you just tell me?"

"Matty. Where the devil is she?"

"I sent your daughter home to you after she delivered me some breakfast." A queasiness gripped the pit of Coop's stomach. "That was hours ago."

"Well, she never made it."

"Dammit." In one motion Coop took off his hat and threw it in the dirt.

Uriah tucked his chin in and growled, "Are you tryin' to tell me that Matty's missin' again?"

A dangerous mix of anger, frustration, and fear gathered in Coop's gut. "She promised me she'd go right home," he ground through his teeth.

Uriah heaved a heavy, exasperated sigh. "Do you think she got grabbed too?"

Coop shook his head and retrieved his hat from the dirt. "I don't know."

"And what do you suggest we do now, Mister Know-it-all Pinkerton detective?" the rancher demanded.

"Go back to the ranch and wait for further instructions."

"No, sir. I can't be twiddlin' my thumbs. Listenin' to you has caused me to lose not one, but two daughters. I'm gonna go down there right now and take Tom Tyler."

"You mean kidnap Tyler from his porch?"

"I do. We'll just see how that sits with Zak."

"If you don't mind my saying so, that's a damn-fool idea, Uriah." Coop slapped his hat against his thigh, then dusted the dirt off with his hand. "For one reason or another Zak Tyler is going to come home, and when he does we'll nab him. If you take Tom away, Zak might not have a reason to come back. It the man he

Heaven Sent

counts on to help is gone, why should he return to the ranch? But if his pa has been taken, he sure as hell could get plenty riled. Enough to harm one or both of your daughters."

Scowling down at the Tyler spread, Uriah sat tall in the saddle, deep in thought. "One more day, twenty-four hours of doin' it your way," he finally conceded. "That's all I'm givin' you, Davis."

"There is another way."

"What would that be?"

"Well now, you could agree to give a portion of the water rights to the Tylers and end this feud now."

"Nope. Can't do it. It's the principle of the thing," he grumbled. Shooting Coop a parting glare, he turned his horse and rode off without another word. His men followed fast behind him.

Coop stared after Uriah for a time, silently cursing the old man's stubbornness. The thought of Matilda Rose in the hands of a kidnapper made him sick. Even if the culprit was friendly neighbor Zak, as they suspected. A friendly neighbor in a water dispute couldn't be trusted.

Then again, she might have had an accident, or fallen from her horse and hurt herself.

Anxiety chewed at his nerves. He was torn. One part of him insisted he try to find Matilda Rose, the other demanded he stay where he was and wait for the break that would lead him to her.

Damn. He couldn't rest easy until he knew for certain she had not been harmed. Where the hell was that crazy, headstrong cowgirl?

Chapter Eighteen

Head held high, Matty marched into the mine shaft with the muzzle of Zak's gun in her back. The transition from bright sunlight to darkness forced her to squint until she'd accustomed her eyes to the dimly lit shaft. Hearing a muffled sound, she looked to the left of the small fire burning in the mine's entrance.

She instantly recognized the disheveled figure bound to a rickety old chair. "Phoebe!"

Without regard to the gun metal pressed against her ribs, Matty made a dash to where her sister sat, gagged by an old faded bandanna, her arms tied behind her back.

"You can untie her," Zak said.

But Matty had already begun, first yanking the bandanna from Phoebe's mouth.

"Matty!"

"I'll have your hands free in a couple of seconds.

Heaven Sent

Don't worry, Phoebe. I'm here and everything will be all right."

As she untied her sister, she entertained a dozen murderous thoughts toward Zak. She'd heard of many ways to do a man in, but a lady didn't think such thoughts, let alone act on them. And she'd been trying so hard lately to be a lady.

Freed, Phoebe jumped up and threw her arms around Matty. "I'm so glad to see you. I've been so worried about you!"

"Oh, Phoebe, it's you who has had us worried." Taking both of her sister's hands in hers, Matty stood back. "Let me look at you."

Phoebe's lips trembled and her blue eyes grew misty as she met Matty's gaze. But other than a dirty torn dress, she looked to be in good condition for a lady unused to living in a cave—which in fact the mine shaft was.

"I've missed you so much, Matty." Phoebe's sweet bow mouth curved up into the barest smile.

"Well, I'm back now, and I'm going to get you out of this mess."

"You've always tak . . . taken care of me." The catch in Phoebe's voice signaled that her emotions were getting the best of her.

"Are you gonna cry?" Zak asked suspiciously. He stood at a safe distance from Matty and Phoebe's reunion, as if he might catch some unfettered, threatening emotion. He still cradled his rifle but aimed it at the ground.

"No, I am not. No thanks to you." Phoebe bristled, slanting him a withering glance.

Sandra Madden

Her shy sister's brazen rebuke caught Matty by surprise. "Phoebe, has Zak hurt you?"

"No. No," she fretted. "He just won't let me go!"

"Tell her how I fed you beef and beans and kept you warm. Stayed up through the night to keep a fire going. You haven't lacked for one thing, Phoebe Applebee. Tell your sister. Tell Matty that."

Head inclined, hands on hips, and blue eyes blazing, Phoebe advanced on Zak. "I haven't lacked for anything? Where is the bathtub? Where is the soft bed? When have you provided proper eating utensils?"

"This isn't some fancy boardinghouse. It's a mine shaft. I've done the best I could."

"Well, it's not good enough."

Phoebe and Zak bickered like children. Slightly incredulous, Matty gave silent thanks she'd found them when she did. Her sister never talked back to anyone. Apparently, with the exception of Zak.

"Zak, I appreciate your not hurting Phoebe, but now that I've come home I think we can work out a solution to the water problem."

Her attention diverted from Zak's rigid figure, Phoebe turned back to Matty. "Just where have you been, sister?" she asked. "You left home without a word."

"I left a note."

Phoebe nodded. "You said you were going to bring back the drummer."

"And I did."

Phoebe's blue eyes grew round, her reply a whisper laced with dread. "You did?"

"Yes." Matty chewed on her lip for a moment before deciding to put her little sister to the test. "You can marry the drummer tomorrow."

Heaven Sent

"I can?" Phoebe sounded more appalled than enthusiastic.

"In less than twenty-four hours, you'll be Phoebe Pearl Davis."

"What?" Zak growled. "You got another suitor, Phoebe? That makes four. I'd lay any odds I'm a better man than any of them. And you never once looked my way."

"You weren't around to look at, Zak Tyler. You never go to church, nor to any of the ladies' guild potluck suppers. And I do believe you haven't been to a dance in town since we were ten."

"I've been workin', ridin' the range, buildin' our cattle business."

Matty stepped between the two. "Zak, are you sayin' you want to marry my sister?"

He lowered his eyes, his face flushed to a bright rosy hue. "I've always been sweet on her. If she'd have me, I'd marry her today."

"You've a fine way of showing it," Phoebe lashed out with a stomp of her foot.

Matty rolled her eyes.

Zak shifted uncomfortably from foot to foot. "This water . . . dilemma has nothin' to do with Phoebe."

"Then why did you kidnap my sister?"

"Couldn't get your daddy's attention any other way. I'm takin' over my pa's ranch soon. He's tired and ailin'. For me to increase the grazin' land I have to have water rights."

"I don't think you've thought this through," Matty said. "Is there nothin' under your hat but hair? Did you give any thought to the consequences of just up and takin' Phoebe?"

"Sure I have. Once the agreement is signed, Pa will

pay a fair price for the water. I'll be leavin' the territory for a spell—"

"Where do you think you're going?" Phoebe demanded.

"Never you mind. When your daddy has cooled off, I'll come back and run the ranch proper."

Matty shook her head. "Your plan is flawed."

"How's that?"

"You'll be lookin' through cottonwood leaves before you get the chance to leave the territory. Daddy will shoot you or hang you."

"We'll just see about that." Zak shot her an angry frown and stalked away to the entrance of the mine shaft. "Not even Uriah Applebee can take the law into his own hands."

"You're a fine one to talk about lawbreaking," Matty called after him.

"Sister," Phoebe said, taking Matty's hand and leading her to a far, dark corner. "Sister, we have to talk."

"After we escape." Matty's mind reeled with possibilities.

"No. Now," Phoebe insisted. "I can't have this on my conscious for one more minute."

"What's that?"

"I . . . I have a confession to make," Phoebe said, averting her eyes.

"You do?" Matty held her breath, hoping this was the moment her sister would clear Cooper T.'s name.

Tilting her chin to a haughty angle, Phoebe announced in a halting tone, "The . . . the drummer is not the father of my baby."

"Baby?" Zak barked. "Who's got a baby?"

Evidently, Zak possessed especially keen hearing.

Her sister's reaction was not quite as reflective.

Heaven Sent

"Ohhhh, no!" With a furtive glance their neighbor's way and a flutter of lashes, Phoebe fell into a swoon, directly into Matty's arms.

"What happened?" Zak demanded, rushing to Matty's side.

"She fainted."

"I can see that." Giving Matty a dark look, as if she were to blame, Zak scooped Phoebe into his arms and carried her to the bedroll closest to the fire. "There's water in the bucket over there."

Matty grabbed a mug and filled it with water. When she reached her sister's side, Phoebe had regained consciousness. Zak held her hand, fanning her uselessly with the other.

"I . . . I can't marry the drummer, Matty."

"Drummer? What kind of a man is that to consider?" Zak muttered. "Worse than a barber."

But Phoebe didn't appear to hear him. Her gaze was fixed on Matty. "I . . . I'm sorry for what I did. If I hadn't been feeling desperate, I wouldn't have lied. I never expected we'd see the drifter again. And I couldn't believe you would go after him."

"A drummer?" Zak repeated, shaking his head as if Phoebe had once entertained the thought of marrying a four-legged man. "Damn."

"Cooper T. Davis is not a drummer," Matty informed Phoebe and Zak coolly. "He is a professional Pinkerton detective."

"Really?" Phoebe asked in a weak, pathetic tone.

"Yes."

"And he's really here?"

"Looking for you."

"Hells fire!" Zak declared. "What's goin' on?"

Phoebe ignored him. "Can you ever . . . find it in

your heart to forgive me for one teensy lie? I truly am sorry about the drum . . . detective."

"Of course, Phoebe." Matty gave her sister a smile of assurance. "Just promise you won't lie to me again. There's no need. You can tell me anything. I'll always give you my support, no matter what."

"Sometimes . . . sister, forgive me for saying so, but you can be . . . alarming."

"I reckon . . . I reckon I have been on occasion," Matty acknowledged. But that had been before she'd found her heart. Before Cooper T. "I promise to do better."

"Will someone please explain to me what's happin' here?" Zak demanded impatiently. "I want to know what's wrong with you, Phoebe. Why'd you faint like that?"

When Phoebe just turned away, he looked to Matty. "Why'd she faint like that?"

"I . . . don't know."

"She had a sick stomach early this morning," Zak offered, as if the added information might bring forth an answer.

Phoebe sighed wearily. "Just never mind, Zak."

"I can't."

"I did not swoon because I am being held against my will in this miserable place. You needn't feel guilty about *that*." She raised her chin and looked away. "I fainted because . . . I am with child."

"Hell's fire!" Zak reared back as if he'd taken a physical blow to his middle.

"Phoebe, hush! My sister's delirious," Matty hurriedly told him. "She doesn't know what she's saying."

"Yes I do. And I've decided what I'm going to do." Phoebe turned back to Matty. "I've had a great deal of

Heaven Sent

time in this dirty old mine shaft to think over my predicament."

"Who did it to you?" Zak pushed to his feet, his face flushed with anger, the veins in his neck protruding. "I'll kill him."

"I'm going to Kansas City," Phoebe announced, as if she hadn't heard Zak's threat. "A distant cousin of Mama's lives there. I'll claim to be a widow and—"

"Phoebe, you've never been away from home before," Matty objected.

"What else can I do? Except kill myself."

"Sister, no!"

"You shouldn't be talkin' that way, Phoebe," Zak scolded. "That ain't no way to talk."

"That's what you think because you don't understand," Phoebe told him with an impatient flick of her wrist.

"Then let me get this straight. Some devil stole your virtue and left you in the family way. Right or wrong?"

"You won't discuss this with anyone, will you?" Phoebe asked, turning tear-filled eyes to him. "We've been friends since we were knee high to grasshoppers."

"You're not goin' to Kansas City, and you're not gonna kill yourself, Phoebe Applebee. You're gonna marry me."

"What?"

"Marry you?"

"You might learn to ... care for me someday. Reckon your daddy won't be hesitatin' any longer about signing the water rights agreement either," he went on. "So don't think I'm doin' this just for you and your babe. Most likely your daddy will let me live—if I'm your husband."

Phoebe regarded him with awe and open admiration.

Sandra Madden

It was rare that Matty had ever seen her sister at a loss for words. This was one of those rare moments.

"Marry you?" Phoebe asked, her tone incredulous.

"Why not? I'm thinkin' we'll both get what we want. You'll have a pa for your babe, and I'll have the prettiest girl in the territory as my wife . . . and the water rights, of course."

Matty watched her sister's slightly dumbfounded expression as she rolled the name over her tongue, trying it on for fit. "Phoebe Pearl Tyler."

"I'm gonna be a cattle baron someday, Phoebe. You'll see. And I'm gonna build you a new house. I'll make sure you don't want for nothin', and I'll do my level best to make you happy."

Matty crossed to his side and gave him a kiss on the cheek. "You're a good man, Zak."

But he only had anxious eyes for her sister. "What do you say, Phoebe?"

The sun had started to go down when the lone horseman galloped down the road leading to the Tyler ranch. He rode hard, like a man on the run from a posse.

Coop went into full alert, every nerve sharp and tingling. He watched the man slide down from his horse and dash up the ranch house steps. Tom Tyler came out of his chair, throwing down his pipe.

This was it. Something important was happening, the break Coop had been waiting for. He'd never seen the man before, but he had no doubt: Zak had returned.

The two men on the porch engaged in a flailing of arms and raised voices, though he couldn't hear what was said. The initial outburst was followed by a calmer

Heaven Sent

but hurried exchange. Soon the men strode off toward the stables.

Coop seized Traveler's reins, prepared to ride. In minutes, Tom and Zak Tyler emerged from the stables on horseback. Were they headed for the same place, or would they be headed in different directions? Who to tail? Father or son? If they split up, Coop could only follow one man. Who should it be?

In the early stages of his career as a Pinkerton, Coop had learned to go with his gut, often more reliable than reason. He swung into the saddle. If he didn't miss his guess, Zak had returned for some kind of help, and his father had agreed to supply it. If Tom Tyler hadn't known his son had kidnapped Phoebe, he certainly knew it now.

Coop couldn't help a caustic grin. More 'n likely two female Applebees proved too much to handle, and certainly more trouble than a man dare to leave alone for any amount of time.

As Coop guided Traveler down the hillside, he allowed himself a fleeting moment of sympathy for Zak Tyler. The man obviously hadn't known what he was letting himself in for until it was too late.

Coop waited, concealed by the brush alongside the road, until the men came into sight. He waited until they'd passed before taking up pursuit. The Tylers rode together a stretch. Coop figured they'd gone more than a mile south, heading in the direction of the Silver Star, before they split up.

Tom left the main road, directing his mount up into the hills, and Zak galloped on toward the Silver Star, or town. The old man didn't appear to be in the same hurry as his son. On a hunch, Coop decided he'd follow the old man, tail him carefully at a distance.

Sandra Madden

He told himself no harm had come to Matilda Rose. These men were frustrated, angry neighbors, not ruthless sidewinders. But she had a leaky mouth. Coop knew well enough she could make a man crazy. The thought of anyone hurting the little spitfire, for any reason, caused his stomach to tighten, his heart to pound.

A knot the size of a wagon wheel rose in his throat and he was sweating as if it were a hundred degrees in the shade. Why didn't Tom Tyler go any faster? Did the old man even know where he was going?

Apparently, he did. A little more than halfway up the steep incline, Tom slowed and soon dismounted. He tied his horse to a tree and continued upward on foot. Coop followed suit, Colt drawn and ready. He hung back, not wanting Tom Tyler to hear his approach, the snap and crunch of thick brush beneath his feet that couldn't be avoided.

At the top of the hill lay a level clearing, and what looked like the opening of an old mine shaft. Miners in '48 must have sought gold here, as they did everywhere else in the state.

He watched Tom slow, looking all around him, to make sure he hadn't been followed. Coop ducked behind the thick trunk of a sycamore. The old rancher entered the mine shaft with a step that seemed unsure.

Dodging from tree to tree, Coop rushed up to the clearing. Gun drawn, he stood to one side and carefully stuck his neck out. He peered inside. At first glance he could see nothing but silhouettes. But he could hear Tom Tyler, and quickly made out several figures.

"Ladies, I am downright sorry about this. I had no notion Zak would go do somethin' so all-fired foolish." Clucking his tongue against the roof of his mouth, Tyler removed a bandanna from across the young blond girl

Heaven Sent

sitting on the bedroll next to Matilda Rose. "Miss Phoebe, are you all right?"

Coop hardly recognized Phoebe Applebee. She looked like many pretty young women. There just wasn't any one thing particularly memorable about her.

The sisters had been tied together, back to back. Phoebe sat on a thick bedroll, while Matilda Rose sat on the dirt floor. Tyler made no motion to remove Matilda Rose's gag.

Phoebe nodded. She appeared a might dazed to Coop. "Yes, sir, Mr. Tyler. I'm just fine."

"Would you like a drink of water?"

"Yes, sir."

"Zak asked me to stay with you until he got back."

"I know. He said he didn't want any harm to come our way while he was gone."

"Your daddy is never gonna forgive us for this."

"He might."

"Miss Matty, I reckon I should remove your gag too, but I'd like you to promise me to save your tongue-lashin' for another time."

She nodded her head vigorously.

"This wasn't my idea, you know. I didn't even know about it 'til a while back."

Matilda Rose released a long whoosh of breath and tossed her head. "Thank you, Tyler. Tarnation, I haven't gone that long without speakin' in some time."

Tyler stepped back warily. "Don't know why he tied you up."

She smiled at the old man. "Zak was just making sure the plans didn't change, I reckon."

"He made loose knots. We're fine," Phoebe assured Tyler.

"Right as rain," Matilda Rose agreed.

Sandra Madden

"He only did what he had to do," Phoebe added.

What the hell was going on? Coop strode forward to the center of the mine shaft entrance. Planting his feet and assuming a fierce scowl, he aimed his Colt at old Tom Tyler.

"Throw your gun toward me, Tyler. Nice and easy, now."

"Cooper T.!" Matilda Rose's face lit up, shining like a band new star. "I knew you'd find me."

He couldn't allow her apparent joy to influence him. He was a professional, doing a job. And he was confused. "Now that I have, you've got thirty seconds to tell me: What's happening here?"

"Oh, my stars," Phoebe murmured. "It's the drummer."

"Pinkerton," Matilda Rose corrected.

"And you must be the lady who accused me of something I didn't do."

"I am sorry about that, sir. How could I have known my sister would go after you?"

"How could you?"

"I . . . I have confessed to Matty that I made a terrible mistake."

Coop gave Matilda Rose his biggest I-told-you-so grin.

"If you will erase that arrogant grin, I will apologize again," she huffed. "I will apologize a hundred times if that will untie me."

"Precious," he drawled, enjoying the moment, "I have to think on it."

"What?"

"It's comforting to know you are bound to one spot where you can't get in any trouble."

"Please, Cooper T."

Heaven Sent

"First, I have a little business with your neighbor, here."

She rolled her eyes and sighed, as if he were hopeless.

Tom Tyler stepped back as Coop approached. "I swear I didn't know nothin' about this 'til—"

Coop cut him off. "I believe you, Tom. But I need to know where your boy went. When is he coming back?"

"He rode to Santa Barbara proper. Don't know how long it will take him."

"We're all going to wait for Zak to return, Cooper T.," Matilda Rose informed him. "But it will be so much more comfortable if my hands are untied."

"What do you mean you're going to wait for Zak? I figure on taking him in on my way to San Francisco."

Not that there was much chance the agency would want to see him in San Francisco at this point.

"No! You can't." Matilda Rose's little sister got up and started toward Coop. "I'm going to marry Zak Tyler."

"Dangdest thing I ever heard," Tom Tyler grumbled. "You're what?"

"Can't you see how perfect it is? Daddy won't be able to kill Zak now. And don't you think the water rights will make a nice wedding gift?" Matilda Rose asked.

"I've known Zak all my life," Phoebe added. "But I didn't know he had it in him to do such a daring thing. Zak has shown a lot of courage to defy my daddy. He risked his neck to protect his land . . . for what he believes in."

Confused, Coop rubbed the back of his neck. "What are you saying? Zak's a hero?"

Hands on hips, Phoebe announced defiantly, "Zak Tyler loves me and I will make him a good wife."

"Matilda Rose?" Coop needed someone to explain

what was going on here. "Has there been a kidnapping?"

"Yes and no. But there will definitely be a wedding. Zak went for a preacher," she told him. "I'm stayin' with my sister until Phoebe and Zak are man and wife. Our story is gonna be that Zak and Phoebe ran off to Montecito to get married."

"How are you going to explain the notes demanding water rights in return for Phoebe?"

"A ruse to throw Daddy off the trail. To keep him busy here. Zak and Phoebe were afraid he'd stop the wedding if he knew what they were really about."

"Why would they be afraid?"

"Daddy suspects anyone having under a two-hundred-thousand acre spread to be a fortune hunter."

Tom Tyler gave a disgusted wave of his hand. "Uriah's full of outlandish ideas. No use waitin' in this place. We can go down to the ranch and have some vittles. No tellin' if Zak will get back before mornin'."

"The whole family is loco. And Zak must be too, to want to marry one of you," Coop muttered as he untied Matilda Rose.

The ride to the Tylers' ranch was abnormally quiet. What had begun as a kidnapping would soon end with a wedding. Case closed.

Coop realized he would be leaving tomorrow, and wondered why he didn't feel relief.

The Tyler ranch house was small but comfortable. One large room, dominated by a rock fireplace, served as a living and dining area. Worn but comfortable furnishings filled the room. Tom Tyler's sister Hilda kept house and cooked.

Tall and thin, with deep-set brown eyes and tight lips, Hilda made no secret of the imposition of three

Heaven Sent

unexpected dinner guests. Nevertheless, she put out a fine spread of hearty beef stew and steaming biscuits. Without Uriah there to object, the rest of the Applebees and Tylers celebrated the end of the feud. Coop found himself at the table enjoying a true family dinner.

Tom chewed on Coop's ear for over an hour, telling him more than he ever wanted to know about raising cattle. Matilda Rose paid more attention to picking the potatoes from her stew than she did to Coop, which he found slightly disturbing.

When old Tom paused for breath, Coop turned his attention to Matilda and Phoebe, who discussed Phoebe's upcoming nuptials.

"Doesn't seem fair," Phoebe pouted, "that I can't have the wedding I've been dreaming about since I was a little girl."

"We'll throw you a big party in a few weeks after we make the announcement," Matilda Rose soothed. "A shindig bigger than anyone around these parts has ever seen."

Her sister brightened. "Of course! We'll decorate and have music and a wedding feast, just as if I'd been married proper."

Coop shook his head. He'd rather be wed to a crazy cowgirl than a spoiled quilt maker. Now, what put that thought into his head? He was about to ask Tom Tyler for a stiff drink when the door was flung open.

"I'm back with the preacher," Zak declared, flushed from riding hard and beaming like a properly besotted bridegroom. "Found him on the road."

An anticipatory silence descended on the room as the burly figure behind Zak stepped through the door and into the light.

"Horace Hawkins!"

Chapter Nineteen

"You! Dear God!" The circuit rider's expression underwent a rapid series of changes, from saintly to nonplussed to an ugly sneer. Jabbing a hairy finger toward Matty as if he'd come face-to-face with the devil, he bellowed, "Not you again!"

Phoebe blinked in bewilderment. "Do you know this man, Matty?"

"He put me in jail."

"Sister!"

"She stole my horse!" Hawkins countered loudly.

"Because it was mine . . . ours . . . Billy's," Matty bit out angrily. "He took Feller. Took her in the middle of the night while Cooper T. and I were sleeping."

Phoebe's hands flew up to cover her mouth. Her blue eyes were wider than the saucers on the table. "Sister!"

"I didn't mean that how it sounded." Matty felt herself color. She didn't need a looking glass to know that a deep flush of embarrassment had settled on her

Heaven Sent

cheeks. She lowered her eyes to contemplate the tips of her new boots.

The circuit rider's voice deepened to a menacing rumble. His lips barely discernable above his bushy beard, he narrowed his accusing eyes on Matty. "This woman told me this man"—his reproachful gaze swept over to rest on Cooper T.—"was her brother."

"Sister!" Phoebe squealed, yet again.

"However, I wouldn't be a bit surprised to discover it was just another lie."

"Lie!" Matty blurted. "Look who's talkin'! This is one preacher who's as crooked as a snake in a cactus patch."

"Matilda Rose, now don't get yourself all agitated."

Coop's admonition came too late. All horns and rattles, Matty made ready to tear into the supercilious preacher. "He took Billy Bowed-Legs's horse while we were sleepin' and then claimed we owed Feller to him for pullin' one of Cooper T.'s teeth."

"Did you think I can provide my services without payment, young lady?" Hawkins asked indignantly. "How could I afford to spread the word if that were so? How would I live without food and drink? Without a horse, how would I travel to areas where most men fear to go?"

Matty rolled her eyes. Piqued beyond all endurance, she honed in on the hairy rider. "The problem is, Horace Hawkins, that you never told us. You never mentioned to Cooper T. that he owed you. You just rode off with our horse. I mean, Billy's horse."

"I'm a circuit rider. I ride."

"Does . . . does this mean you can't marry us?" Phoebe stammered.

Asserting himself as man of the house, soon to be

287

husband and father, Zak stepped forward. "Are you legal, circuit rider?"

"Indeed I am. I have the papers to prove it."

"And I'll bet he'll marry you in exchange for a horse," Matty snapped. "Because Billy Bowed-Legs's horse belongs with us."

Hawkins drew himself up. "A horse might be a suitable arrangement, along with a meal and a room for the night."

"Agreed," Zak said. He gave Matty a wary sidelong glance. "Truce?"

"Truce," she conceded softly. If she said more, the preacher might not stay, might not marry Zak and Phoebe.

By the look on Zak's face, he would pay any price, do anything, to make Phoebe his as quickly as possible. Matty wondered if he feared Phoebe would change her mind about marrying him. Her sister was a lucky woman to be marrying a man who cared so much. Matty bit down on her lip.

As the others gathered around the table to discuss the morning wedding, Matty sidled up to Cooper T., who stood off by himself by the fireplace. "I reckon you'll be movin' on at first light."

"It's three hundred miles to San Francisco."

"Won't take long by steamer."

"No."

Getting over Cooper T. would take longer than traveling a few hundred miles. Matty reckoned she'd see his twinkling apple eyes and teasing, laughing mouth in her dreams for months, maybe years to come.

"You still wantin' to catch Jesse James?" she asked, hoping against hope he'd say no.

"The sidewinder is still on the loose," he replied.

Heaven Sent

"As soon as you put him behind bars, there'll be another train robber or murderer to take his place," she said. Any satisfaction that came to Cooper T. was bound to be short-lived. There would always be criminals to catch. Couldn't he see that?

He popped a toothpick in his mouth and clamped down. "Probably so."

"Probably."

The strained conversation came to an end. But Matty couldn't move from Cooper T.'s side. Desperate to commit every detail about him to memory, she closed her eyes and breathed in the scent of him, breathed deeply of his leathery, musky maleness. Her heart fluttered, an instant of gossamer flight.

He cleared his throat. "Your daddy's expecting word tomorrow. Do you think he's going to be so riled when he finds out about Zak and Phoebe's marriage that he kills somebody?"

"I don't think so."

"If you do, I'll stay to see it through. Be a kind of buffer 'til he gets hold of himself."

Matty forced a smile, forced her gaze to meet his, felt her belly flop at the moment of eye contact. "Thanks for offering, but Daddy will come around. Zak and Phoebe being married will give him an excuse to back down on the water rights. And I can't ask you to do more than you have for me, for us."

"I brought you home, like I said I would." Cooper T. looked down. Pressing his lips together, he rubbed the back of his neck. "Brought you a mite farther than the gates of the Silver Star."

"Yes, you did."

Was this good-bye, then? She couldn't bring herself to say the words.

Sandra Madden

"Most likely I'll see you in the morning before I leave," he said.

"We . . . we can say good-bye in the mornin'."

With eyes only for Cooper T., Matty memorized each tiny laugh line, each fleck of gold in his gaze. She didn't notice Phoebe flounce over to where they stood.

"Matty, I'm so tired I could collapse right here," she announced petulantly. "Come to bed with me."

Afraid to speak, fearing the tears in her heart would flow, Matty stood on her tiptoes and kissed Cooper T. lightly on the cheek. "Good night."

"Goodnight . . . precious."

Coop ambled out onto the porch and into the cool black night. Stars blanketed the sky, but none sparkled as bright as Matilda Rose's eyes when she was happy. She hadn't been happy tonight.

The air smelled of horse and hay and rich earth. A rising half moon promised a perfect night in this hillside paradise. But Coop felt tense, tighter inside than a man surrounded on all sides by rattlesnakes. He sat in one of the rockers, propping his feet on the rail. A couple of deep breaths and a cigar and he'd be relaxed again. He lit his cigar and stared into the night, stewing. A deep sense of melancholy crept along the edges of his emotions.

"Hey, Coop." Zak poked his head out the door. "Mind if I join you?"

"Hell no, Zak. It's your porch."

Zak sat in the rocker beside him and took the cigar Coop offered with a wide, grateful grin. "Don't mind if I do."

"Nice night," Coop commented.

"Sure is, just like it should be the night before a fella

Heaven Sent

gets hitched. Speakin' of which, I'd like to ask you a favor."

The knot in his stomach drew tight. "What's that?"

"Would you mind bein' my witness tomorrow? Pa could do it, but he ain't holdin' happy thoughts. Phoebe and me want to start fresh. We're aimin' to end the bad blood between the Tylers and the Applebees, and I'm thinkin' at least one neutral party witnessing our wedding and wishin' us well is a darn good way to start off." The rancher paused for breath. "You *do* wish us well?"

Coop couldn't reply fast enough. "You bet."

"This marriage is gonna be legal, aboveboard and forever."

His stomach relaxing, Coop smiled. "I'd be honored, Zak."

"Thank you. Thank you kindly, Coop. Can I get you a glass of Tyler wine? Sure would like to make a toast to tomorrow." He threw Coop a hound-dog smile. "Can't toast alone."

"Be glad to join you," Coop assured him. The obviously nervous man bolted from his chair and returned with mugs of wine faster than a calico girl working a whiskey mill.

Coop held out his mug. He wasn't much on making toasts. "To a long and happy marriage."

Zak grinned and gulped. When he sat down again he raised his mug toward Coop. "And here's hopin' someday you're as lucky as me and meet up with a sweet, pretty woman."

The knot in Coop's stomach tightened still another notch. He took a long swallow of the warm mellow wine. "Do folks in these parts like wine better than whiskey?"

Sandra Madden

"Naw, but most of us make our own wine so's we always got some on hand."

"This is good. Different from the Applebees' wine, which was good too."

"Yep." Leaning back, Zak laced his fingers together and rested his head against the pillow he'd made of his hands. "In this part of California, we've got the climate and soil to grow the best grapes in the country. Just a little difference in the plantin' and harvestin' can make a big difference in the taste."

"Is that right?" Unbidden, wild thoughts buzzed through Coop's head.

"More than once I thought about growin' more vines than what we needed. Thought about makin' some big old vats and goin' into the wine-makin' business myself."

"Why haven't you?"

"Got too much on my hands with the cattle," Zak answered with a grimace. "Pa doesn't do that much 'round here anymore. Maybe someday. Someday I'll do it."

"I noticed the grapes over at the Applebees were mostly ripe. Is it time for picking?"

Zak blew out a stream of smoke. "Most folks will be harvestin' their grapes in a couple of weeks. We harvest in August, plant in March. But if a man's growin' for business, he's workin' in the vineyards almost year-round. It takes a lot of work, and it's risky."

Coop lowered his feet from the rail. Sitting straight, he leaned toward Zak. "Risky? How so?"

"There's a lotta risks in growin'. For one, the quality of the grapes depends some on the weather. The size of the grapes and the sugar in 'em has as much to do with the weather as the soil. Hell, whether or not you've got grapes at all depends on the weather. And we can't control the weather."

Coop stared at the ash at the end of his cigar. "No. No, we can't."

" 'Course too, they get diseases that rot 'em sometimes."

"Wine-making sounds to be a challenging enterprise."

"You interested?" Zak asked.

"Well now, I've had some experience in bottling and selling . . . alcohol," Coop hedged.

"Wine?"

"No, but I could probably learn the grape end of it."

"A smart man like you? I reckon so."

Once behind closed doors, Phoebe dissolved into tears. After days of spunky defiance, she'd reverted to her former self.

"What am I going to do? Oh, Matty, what am I going to do?" she cried, perched on the edge of the bed.

"About what? I thought you were happy with your decision to marry Zak."

"But do you think I should marry him?"

Matty lacked the patience or desire to deal with Phoebe's fears tonight. With her own heart breaking, how could she help her sister?

"Do you want to marry the barber?" she asked more sharply than she'd intended.

"Oh, no!"

"Do you want to marry the minister's son? The father of your child?"

"After what he's done to me? How could you ask, Matty? He seduced a young innocent girl—me—with promises he had no intention of keeping. I was a fool, but he is worse."

Matty sighed and sank to the bed beside her sister. "Are you goin' to be happy livin' with Zak?"

"I . . . I think so. Zak really cares for me. He'll be good to me. What more can a woman in my position ask?"

"What more can any woman ask than to be married to a man who loves her dearly?" Matty asked.

"I suppose so. But this just isn't like any of the dreams I've dreamed for so long. Just look at me; look at my dress. It's dirty and I haven't had a bath in days."

"Look, there's a pitcher and basin right over there for a nice sponge bath."

Phoebe got up and gingerly poured water from the pitcher into the basin. She stuck an index finger in the water. "It's not hot."

"I'll heat it."

"It's bad enough I'm not going to have a real wedding. But at least I could have a clean dress."

"No one's goin' to be lookin' at your dress," Matty assured her, growing more weary with the discussion by the moment. Had she been responsible for spoiling Phoebe?

"*I* will notice."

"Oh, Phoebe."

"Would you ride home and get me a dress, Matty? You could sneak in, and Daddy would never know. I know you can do it; I've seen you sneak in and out before. I know you've ridden out to check on the herds at night."

"You do?"

"So I know you can do it."

Obviously, Phoebe knew more than Matty had ever

Heaven Sent

given her sister credit for. One thing for sure, she'd never worry about fragile Phoebe again.

Matty stood up. Badly needing to be alone with her own troubled thoughts, she planned to slip out on the porch for a while. Since she'd first realized she loved Cooper T., she'd known she must watch him ride away someday. Someday was now. But how was she going to live without him?

"Matty?"

"You wash up and get into bed, Phoebe."

"Please, Matty, a girl only gets married once."

Coop overslept. He had meant to be up at dawn, but the strain of nonstop hours on stakeout had drained him more than he'd expected. He woke alone in the Tylers' bunkhouse feeling more lethargic than refreshed. Zak had given over his room in the house to Horace Hawkins and had stayed the night in the bunkhouse with Coop and the ranch hands. Matilda Rose and Phoebe had shared a spare room in the main house.

He'd almost finished dressing when Zak burst through the door. "It's time."

"Be right there."

"We're out under the sycamore, by my ma's flower garden. Ma's gone, but her flowers live on. Pa and I have seen to it."

Coop grinned as he watched Zak stride out the door, his happiness unbridled. These were good people. All of them. Tom and Zak, Phoebe and Uriah. Matilda Rose.

When he reached the garden he was surprised to see Phoebe dressed in a soft pink summer dress, carrying a bouquet of flowers, fresh-picked from the garden.

Matilda Rose stood beside Phoebe wearing the beautiful blue gown he'd given her in the City of Angels.

Damn! That meant the little vixen had returned to the Silver Star sometime during the night. Ridden alone at night. He could kill her for taking a risk like that. For what? Two dresses.

She smiled at him, a radiant, splendid smile.

His anger melted. In his eyes Matilda Rose was far more lovely than the bride. He couldn't take his gaze away from her. Her lavender-blue eyes rested on his, as big and beautiful as the forget-me-nots in the garden. His heart gave a wild lurch when she tossed the thick glossy mass of chestnut curls that tumbled to her shoulders.

Coop's gaze fell to the inviting glimpse of cleavage as her breasts rose and fell softly. He saw beyond the silky fabric of her dress to visualize the soft curves of her hips and legs. He felt the start of a dangerous fire in his loins.

How could he say good-bye to the girl he'd come to know better than himself? He'd laughed with Matilda Rose, suffered with her, broken bad jerky with her across a campfire, and worried over her when she was attacked by wasps and taken by Zak. How could he say good-bye?

But he had little time for further musings. Horace Hawkins did the only decent thing since Coop and Matilda Rose had made his acquaintance. He made the marriage ceremony simple and quick.

As soon as the circuit rider pronounced Zak and Phoebe man and wife, the groom planted a kiss on his bride. Phoebe appeared stunned at first . . . and then delighted.

But no one in the small wedding party could wait to celebrate the union. Hawkins mounted his new pinto

Heaven Sent

and, with a wave to Coop and a parting glare at Matilda Rose, rode off.

Zak and Phoebe prepared to ride to Montecito. They'd decided to spend a few days there to make certain Uriah had enough time to calm himself.

Taking the eldest Applebee daughter by the hand, Coop led her toward the stables.

"Matilda Rose, it's time to face your daddy."

"I reckon." She kicked at the ground in front of her. A little sullen, he thought.

"Are you ready to ride?"

She looked up at him with those great questioning eyes that caused his stomach to drop.

"I thought you were leavin'," she said.

And never see her again? Never touch her again? Never love her again?

"Can't let you break this news to Uriah all by yourself," he told her. "After all we've been through together, what kind of a man would I be to leave you now? Besides, the road to Santa Barbara takes me right by the Silver Star."

"I appreciate your . . . your kindness."

Kindness played no part in his decision.

"Did I mention how beautiful you look this morning?" he asked.

She lowered her eyes and fingered a piece of the soft blue skirt. "It's the dress."

"No, it's you."

"You don't see things like other men."

"Maybe not." With the crook of his finger beneath her chin, Coop raised Matilda Rose's head so that he could look in her eyes. "But I'd say that was in my favor."

She swallowed hard.

Sandra Madden

He talked on, saving her from having to answer him. The ache in his gut was so bad he could barely breathe. "Have to admit I'm curious. What made you wear your blue dress this morning?"

"Because I . . . I wanted you to remember me like this," she replied softly. "Looking like a woman."

Matty and Cooper T. kept a steady pace as they rode toward the Silver Star. Feller trotted behind, tied to Matty's saddle. At least, by bringing Billy's horse home, she had something that might give her father pleasure. She looked over her shoulder, wishing she might see Billy Bowed-Legs astride his horse. But Feller didn't even carry a saddle. First she had lost Billy, her beloved teacher, and soon Cooper T., who had become her best friend, would be gone.

Where would she find comfort after Cooper T. left?

Not with her sister. Phoebe would make her home with Zak and his father until the new house was built. From this day on, Matty would be more alone than ever.

"Rider ahead."

Matty brought Spirit to a stop. "Two other riders with him."

"Ever any trouble on this road?"

"No, but maybe today. Maybe now. It looks . . . it looks like Daddy."

Chapter Twenty

Uriah Applebee kicked up a mighty cloud of dust when he reined his horse to a stop dangerously close to Coop and Matilda Rose. The two Silver Star cowhands riding behind him created a new cloud just when Coop thought he could breathe again.

Matilda Rose coughed and waved at the dust.

Her father's felt hat flapped against his back. Riding into the wind as he had, his big head of white hair stood straight out and back. Coop thought the sorely riled old man looked like a lion.

He roared like one. "There you are! Where've you been? What in Sam Hill is goin' on?"

"Well, sir—"

"I see you bought back one daughter."

"Yes, sir."

"Daddy—"

Uriah leaned forward in his saddle, squinting his eyes

as if he couldn't see. "Is that a dress you're wearin', girl?"

"Yes, you know it is, Daddy. We have so much to tel—"

Uriah interrupted his daughter with a hoot and turned to Coop. "What have you done to her, son? I haven't seen Matty in a dress for two years or more."

"Daddy, please, let me explain—"

"Time for explainin' after you've told me what you've learned about Phoebe? Where's Zak holdin' her?"

Matilda Rose's eyes met Coop's.

"He... they... Zak and Phoebe are married, Daddy."

"What?" The old man practically jumped out of his saddle. "What'd you say, girl?"

"Zak didn't kidnap Phoebe. The notes were just... just part of their scheme, to throw us off their trail."

"What scheme? What trail?"

"The trail to Montecito. They didn't want you to interfere when they ran off to Montecito to get married."

Clearly bedeviled, the old man scratched the top of his head. "Tyler faked the kidnapping?"

Matilda Rose nodded her head slowly. "Phoebe is married to Zak now."

"They ran off to Montecito to get hitched?"

"That's right, Uriah." Coop thought he'd better speak up and take the heat off Matilda Rose for a few minutes.

"I'll be damned." The elder Applebee shook his head, leaned back in his saddle, and let out a long, low whistle. "Zak, you say?"

"Zak Tyler," Coop repeated. "He had me fooled,"

Uriah appeared more befuddled than angry. As well he should be, Coop thought.

Heaven Sent

"Fooled a Pinkerton, you say?"

Matilda Rose rolled her eyes.

"I never knew she had any interest in the boy," Uriah admitted. "Figured she wanted a professional man like John, the minister's son. While you were away, Matty, she took a shine to Bert, the barber."

"Zak's a good man, Daddy. You must think so or you wouldn't have wanted me to marry him. Remember? If Zak married me, you were willing to give the Tylers water rights."

"I remember. But why'd Phoebe and Zak go to all the trouble of stagin' a kidnappin'? Don't figure."

Coop had been afraid the old man would ask this question.

"Think about it," Matilda Rose replied, as if the answer was obvious. "Phoebe has always been drawn to the most dramatic ways of doin' things."

"It would have been a lot easier on all of us if she had come to me and said she wanted to marry him," Uriah retorted gruffly.

"She was afraid to do that. She reckoned you'd say no, what with you feudin' with the Tylers."

Her father looked off to the horizon and grunted.

Coop gave Matilda Rose a smile of encouragement. He was here for moral support. There was little more he could do but smile.

"Remember, you've been insisting all along that I get married first, Daddy. Phoebe just got tired of waitin' and took matters into her own hands."

"First time I've known her to take the reins. And look at what a sorry mess she made."

"I know she didn't mean to hurt you, Daddy."

"Well, I suppose that just does it."

301

Sandra Madden

Coop and Matilda Rose exchanged questioning glances.

Uriah scanned the spread of land before him. "Zak doesn't need the Silver Star. He's got a big enough ranch."

"Are you goin' to give him the water he needs?" Matty asked quietly.

"I reckon. Reckon I have to now. Same as I have to give you the Silver Star. Zak can't be runnin' both."

Except for a stomach flip-flop, Matty felt little emotion at all. After years of wheedlin' and wantin', she finally had what she wanted. Or so she'd thought. She forced a smile. "Do you mean it?"

" 'Course I do."

With his hands folded atop one another on his saddle horn, Cooper T. straightened in the saddle. "Well now, I guess everything has been resolved."

"Not quite." Uriah pulled an envelope from his shirt pocket. "This come for you. Delivered from the wire office in Santa Barbara."

Coop tore open the envelope, pulled out a scrap of paper, and read.

"What is it?" Matty asked, fearing the worst. The worst for Cooper T. would be to be fired. If that happened, she would be responsible.

"Take a look."

With a twinkle in his eye that caused her heart to skip an important beat, the good-looking Pinkerton passed the message to her. It came from the Territory headquarters of the Alan Pinkerton agency.

We are pleased to inform you that your request for transfer to the railroad division has been ap-

Heaven Sent

proved. Proceed directly to Kansas City, reporting there no later than the thirtieth of August.

Two weeks away. The job he'd talked about and dreamed of since the day she took him was his. Cooper T. would leave her now. She would never see him again.

He had places to go; she had a ranch to run.

Her eyes met his. *Don't go, don't go. I love you. Please, stay with me. Stay with me.*

Cooper T. regarded her stoically, a small smile hovering at his lips.

What *was* he thinking?

"Congratulations, Cooper T. When Jesse James hears the news, he'll be shakin' in his boots."

"Never figured the agency was going to accept all my excuses, but I guess I learned a little about selling myself when Angus had me peddling his snake oil . . . er, tonic."

Matty spoke over the sudden lump in her throat. "The Pinkerton Agency knows better than to lose a good man like you."

"Why, thank you, Matilda Rose." He tipped his hat and winked.

The wink did it. Her heart slowly started to crumble. Her body swelled up with a year's worth of tears. Not daring to speak, she nodded. Her lips quivered.

Cooper T. looked away quickly, turning his attention brusquely to Uriah. "Could I impose on your hospitality to spend one more night with you? I'll head out tomorrow."

What was she going to do? How was she going to live without Cooper T.?

"Hold on a minute, son."

Sandra Madden

"Yes, sir?"

"Seems to me we had an understanding. You're not goin' anywhere. You're bound to marry Matty."

"Marry me?" she cried, caught off guard. "No!"

The eyes of both Cooper T. and her father fixed on her, regarding Matty as if she'd just dropped from the sky. Her pulse beat so fast and furious, she was sure they could hear it in San Francisco.

"Cooper T. just won the job he's been wantin' forever, Daddy. And I have a ranch to run. Can't have a man slow me down."

She'd lie like Horace Hawkins rather than have Cooper T. marry her out of some sense of obligation. She knew him well enough by now to know that he'd do it. Cooper T. Davis was a man of integrity. She didn't dare look at him.

"You were on the trail alone with him too long," her father barked, his piercing blue eyes dark with disapproval, more for her outburst, Matty suspected. "When folks find out, your reputation will be ruined worse than it is now. If that's possible."

"Who's going to find out?" she cried. "Who? How? No one will know if you don't say anything. Only you and Phoebe even know I was gone. And Billy-Bowed Legs, who sure isn't about to say anything."

Uriah's considerable eyebrows bunched up in a puzzled, snowy-white frown. "You sure have yourself worked up, girl."

"Because nothing happened between Cooper T. and me on the trail, Daddy. Nothing. Isn't that right, Cooper T.?"

"Whatever you say . . . precious."

That wasn't the answer she'd expected. Why wasn't

Heaven Sent

he helping her argument? She sent him a withering look before turning back to her father.

"What man in his right mind would dare touch me? I slept with a Winchester at my side, a Colt tucked under my bedroll, and a derringer wedged in my boot."

"Nothing happened, eh?"

"Nothing. I swear on . . . on Billy Bowed-Legs's grave. So let Cooper T. be on his way. I'll . . . I'll know it when the right cowboy comes along."

"What's wrong with this one?"

"Daddy!" she yelped, exasperated beyond belief. "You are embarrassing me."

"Now you know how it feels."

"Harumpf!"

"Matilda Rose, would you mind answering your daddy. I'd like to know what my drawbacks are. Knowing might help me with the ladies in the future."

Cooper T. was beginning to rile Matty. Why didn't he just take the opportunity she was giving him while the gates were still open. He could make a run for it. It was a long way to Kansas City.

"Besides having someplace else to be, you're . . . you're arrogant," she sputtered, in a hasty explanation. "And a mite too proud for me. You smoke big old fat, smelly cigars and drink the devil's brew. Whiskey."

" 'Course he smokes cigars and drinks whiskey," her father blustered. "He's a man's man."

To prove his words, Uriah gave Cooper T. a manly slap on the back.

"I don't like his teasin' ways either. Furthermore, his best friends clear up and down the coast of California are strumpets."

Her father smiled.

Matty was running out of breath and ideas. Uriah

remained undaunted. Judging from a swift, sidelong glance, Cooper T. didn't appear to be offended by anything she'd said yet. She prepared to wound him—for his own good. He'd thank her someday when he was riding the rails, catching train robbers.

"Most of all I don't like how he spreads the mustard. Always speakin' such perfect English so no one will figure out that he's not had any schoolin' except in the back of a wagon."

That said, Matty ventured a look his way.

Cooper T.'s dark brow's dove into a tight-knit frown. His eyes deepened to jade green, his jaw set tight.

"Matty, you plain don't know a good man when you see one."

"Daddy—"

"Davis, forgive my daughter; she's a little highstrung, a little eccentric, but she'll make you a good wife in the long run. Her shortcomings are—"

"Shortcomings!"

"Shortcomings are due to not havin' a ma during a critical time of her raisin'," he continued undaunted. "It was just Billy and me bringin' up my girls, with Lupe helpin'."

Cooper T.'s impenetrable gaze locked on Matty. "I understand."

"Now let's ride back to the Silver Star, where we can have a long talk, Davis. Just you and me," he said pointedly, glowering at Matty.

"He has to go, Daddy."

"I have time to talk."

As soon as they'd reached the ranch house, Matilda Rose fled to the refuge of her room. Uriah invited Coop into his study.

"She's actin' strange, son. Even for her. I apologize."

Heaven Sent

"No need."

"Whiskey or wine?"

"Wine."

"Now I know Matty says you want to be in Kansas City, but I'm thinkin' otherwise."

"What makes you think otherwise?"

"The way you look at Matty. The way she looks at you. I may be an old man, but I know that look."

Coop sipped the wine, held the glass to the light. "I've been wanting to talk to you about Matilda Rose . . . among other things, Uriah."

He spent the next two hours in deep discussion with Uriah Applebee. For all his ornery ways, Uriah was a decent man, a man who'd been way over his head when left with two young girls to raise. He'd done the best he could, and Coop had to hand it to the rancher. In addition to bringing up his girls, Uriah had created a profitable paradise.

The two men shared dinner together when Matilda Rose refused to join them. Following an after-dinner cigar, Coop said good night. On the way to his room he stopped at Matilda Rose's bedroom door but heard not a sound.

Not too many minutes later, he soaked in a tub, prepared by Lupe with great care and generous smiles. Ostensibly, he was readying for his marriage in the morning. But Matilda Rose had made it plain she didn't want him.

The news of his transfer had come as a surprise. He'd believed he was about to be fired. Coop guessed the agency was hard pressed to find men willing to sit trapped in a train for hours on end, mile after mile, waiting for train robbers who came less often than rain.

He'd been homeless as a poker chip for most of his

life. And the thing he realized on stakeout was that he was tired of it. The time had come to make a change, 'cause he couldn't leave Matilda Rose. She'd stolen his heart and given him a reason to want something more.

An idea had been simmering in the back of his mind, and the more he thought on it, the more excited he'd become. Coop had no interest in cattle, but the potential of vineyards fascinated him.

All his life he'd worked for someone else; first Angus, then the army, and then the Pinkerton Agency. He knew about bottling and selling, and each day he grew more certain he could learn to grow the best grapes. He'd gone so far as to envision the future. In less than five years, Cooper's California wine would be at every table, in every saloon.

If he stayed on at the Silver Star, he could start his own business and build a life with Matilda Rose. Unfortunately, she didn't want a life with him.

Hard to believe she could so easily let go of what they had together. If she was so set against marrying him, did he detect a certain melancholy lurking deep in lavender-blue eyes?

He heard the soft knock on the door and figured it must be Lupe come to inquire about the bathwater. He should have finished bathing long ago. "Come in."

Head down, Matilda Rose walked slowly through the door, closing it quietly behind her. She appeared contrite, chastened. He'd never seen her like this. But then, he never knew what to expect from his Winchester woman.

She was still dressed in her feminine blue dress, her shining curls tumbled to her shoulders. Soap in midair, Coop stared. She was a vision of loveliness. Unable to

Heaven Sent

speak, barely able to breathe, he regarded her with a growing warmth—and wariness.

Matilda Rose lifted her head—and gasped. "You're in the bathtub! You're naked!"

"I . . . I thought you were Lupe," he explained, looking down, checking to make sure he was hidden beneath the water. "I was just getting out." He dropped the soap. It splashed.

She gasped. Again. "No!"

"If you'll just turn around and face the wall for a minute, Matilda Rose, I'll get out of here and get dressed. We need to talk."

She nodded her head. "All . . . all right."

The room was still except for the sloshing of bathwater. The light, fresh scent of soap laced the air, and shadows cast from candle and lantern light cavorted on the walls.

"No peeking now," he warned.

"You are too full of yourself, Cooper T.!" Matty snapped as she turned to face the wall.

At the sight of him sitting in the tub, a gentle trembling had started inside her. She closed her eyes and saw him still, even as she heard the final splash of water and knew he was out of the copper tub.

His hair, wet and slick, had been swept back away from his freshly shaven face. Every striking plane of him seemed more compelling flecked with beads of water. His green eyes glimmered in a beckoning, unsettling fashion. But it was the soapsuds bubbling across the wide expanse of his chest that had drawn her gaze and held her mesmerized. Cooper T.'s dark, thickly corded chest and shoulders had claimed her rapt attention once again.

The beauty and strength of his masculinity struck

Matty anew, and warmed her. Exactly the feeling she did not want to have.

"I'm decent." Cooper T.'s deep baritone cut through her musings in a soft, dry tone. "You can turn around now."

When she turned, he gave her a roguish wink and lifted a glass of wine as if he were toasting her.

"When one hears a knock, it's customary to ask who it is. You just shouted out to come in. I never would have if I'd known you were in the bath."

"Matilda Rose, I explained. I thought you were Lupe. Beautiful women don't usually come to my bedroom in the evening."

"I'll only stay a minute."

"Stay as long as you like."

"Are you drunk?"

"Hell no."

"You've been drinking a lot of wine lately, Cooper T. Don't think I haven't noticed, because I have."

He grinned.

Her stomach collapsed.

"Call it research, precious. Now, what can I . . . do for you?" The corner of his mouth turned up in a devastating crooked smile.

Her throat went dry.

He hiked an eyebrow. "Matilda Rose . . . ?"

"Yes. Yes, well . . . my daddy is a strong-willed man. We can't let him force us into a marriage neither of us wants."

"I agree."

"If you ride out before dawn tomorrow, you can be long gone before any preacher gets here. To make it easier, I made sure Traveler has been stabled in the first stall by the stable doors."

Heaven Sent

"Was it something I said?"

"What?"

"Why is it that you don't want anything to do with me all of a sudden?" His gaze locked on hers. His eyes weren't twinkling.

She tossed her head. "I know what you want and I know what I want. We're not ridin' on the same road, Cooper T."

"Are you sure you know what I want?"

"You're lookin' for the next great adventure. You'll always be lookin'. And maybe you'll find it now that you've won the job you've been hankerin' after." She sailed for the door. "I don't aim to be married to a man who is bein' forced or bribed to be my husband and made to settle down."

"Matilda Ro—"

"I said what I came to say. There isn't anything else." She spun on her heel and slammed the door behind her.

"Oh, yes there is," Coop whispered.

The next morning, after a night spent deep in thought, Coop strode out to the dining area. Uriah sat alone at the long pine table, chewing on a strip of bacon.

"Where's my bride, Uriah?"

The old man shook his head woefully. "She's gone. Took off again."

"She did?"

"Matty's not in her room. Her horse is gone. Sorry, Davis. Once again I'm apologizin' for my daughter's lack of manners. I should have stood guard outside her door."

"Has the preacher arrived?"

"Expectin' him any time now."

Sandra Madden

"Looks like I'll have to go after Matilda Rose."

"You know where she's hidin'?"

"Got an idea. Keep the preacher here. It may take me an hour or so, but I'll be back."

In the middle of a sleepless night, Matty had taken Spirit and walked her horse down past the vineyard to the cottage. In her cozy getaway she'd alternately paced and cried. Cooper T. had said all the right things last night except one. *I love you.* He hadn't said, "I love you."

He was just as afraid to attach himself to anyone as she had been. She cried herself through the night and watched the first light of day before she finally fell into an exhausted sleep.

"My Colt is pointed straight at you, so don't go making any strange moves."

The voice penetrating Matty's consciousness sounded mildly threatening. She was having a bad dream, one of many more nightmares to come, she was sure. Pulling the covers over her head, she rolled over away from the voice.

"It's time to wake up and come with me, nice and peaceable."

"Go away," she murmured.

"I'm not going anywhere without you. You stole something of mine, and now you have to pay."

Matty groaned and rolled over onto her back. Her head felt fuzzy, her legs mushy. If she didn't open her eyes, maybe she could still slip back into the numbing peace of sleep.

Suddenly the covers were yanked back.

"Get up, woman." A familiar voice growled soft and husky in her ear. "You stole my heart and there's only one thing left to do. You're gonna marry me."

Heaven Sent

Matty bolted up on the quilt-covered straw of her loft bed.

Cooper T. knelt beside her. His eyes twinkled mischievously. His mouth turned up in his most devastating grin. He held his Colt in hand . . . cocked.

"Wha . . . what are you doin'?" she demanded, dazed and disoriented.

"I'm taking you just like you took me."

"Takin' me?" she repeated. Her mind continued to tumble in hazy turmoil.

"Making you mine."

"Is your gun loaded?"

He shook his head and grinned.

He had a most seductive, winning smile. An unsettling flood of warmth spread through her. "How did you know where to find me?"

"You told me once, remember?"

"Oh."

"I know all your secrets, Matilda Rose. And you know mine . . . except for one."

She sucked in her breath, staring at the rugged, handsome man she loved with all her heart.

"Cooper T. . . ."

"Don't say a word." He gently brushed her lips with his fingertip.

Matty held her breath as he moved closer. Closer. Closer still, until his mouth, warm and moist, rested on her ear.

"I love you," he whispered hoarsely.

Her heart hammered wildly. "Cooper T.—"

"Ssssh. Just listen. Hear me out. I knew you were trouble from the first time I looked into those big blue eyes of yours." He smiled softly, his eyes shining with love. He stroked her cheek with the back of his hand.

"Weeks ago, when I had the chance, I couldn't leave you. And I finally figured out why. You give me excitement every day, Matilda Rose. Every hour is an adventure with you."

"Love me?" Light-headed and floating, she'd hardly heard anything else.

"I love you with every part of me," he said, gathering her into his arms. "With you I feel everything . . . the sun, the wind, the rain on my face, the preacher's wrath, the rustler's fist . . ."

"Cooper T.!"

Chuckling, he gave her a playful wink, but as his laughter faded, he grew serious. "Matilda Rose, without you I would feel nothing . . . again."

Her fingers played at the buttons on his shirt. "You know I didn't mean any of those things I said. I just didn't want you to feel forced to stay. I love you too much to make you unhappy."

"I know. I understand." He kissed her lightly, lovingly. "But I've found something I want to do here. I'm going to love you. And while you're out chasing cows, or children, I'm going to make the finest wine California has ever tasted."

She tugged at his sleeve, aiming to start on the children right away. At last she understood his interest in wine, his questions.

"Soon as we retrieve your wagon, are you goin' to be selling your wine from town to town?"

"No. Someone else will do that. I'm going to stay with you in a place of our own, right here on the Silver Star," he added.

"I know just the spot," she whispered. They were in it.

"You know, there's a preacher waiting up at the main

Heaven Sent

house to marry us," he reminded her when she slipped off his shirt and tossed it aside.

Her fingertips traced the strong outline of his jaw, fell to his bare chest, marveling at the miracle, the man.

She raised her eyes upward in a small gesture of thanks. Billy Bowed-Legs had watched over her well. Miracles didn't just happen. Cooper T. had been heaven-sent.

"Do you think the preacher can wait?" she asked softly.

With a sly smile, Cooper T. gathered her into his warm, strong arms. "Well now, I reckon."

Walker's Widow
Heidi Betts

Clayton Walker has been sent to Purgatory . . . but it feels more like hell. Assigned to solve a string of minor burglaries, the rugged Texas Ranger thinks catching the crook will be a walk in the park. Instead he finds himself chasing a black-masked bandit with enticing hips and a penchant for helping everyone but herself. Regan Doyle's nocturnal activities know no boundaries; decked out in black, the young widow makes sure the rich "donate" to the local orphanage. And the fiery redhead isn't about to let a lawman get in her way—even if his broad shoulders and piercing gray eyes are arresting. But caught in a compromising position, Regan recognizes that the jig is up, for Clay has stolen her heart.

__4954-6 $5.99 US/$7.99 CAN

Dorchester Publishing Co., Inc.
P.O. Box 6640
Wayne, PA 19087-8640

Please add $2.50 for shipping and handling for the first book and $.75 for each additional book. NY and PA residents, add appropriate sales tax. No cash, stamps, or C.O.D.s. All Canadian orders require $5.00 for shipping and handling and must be paid in U. S. dollars. Prices and availability subject to change. Payment must accompany all orders.

Name_____
Address_____
City_____ State_____ Zip_____
E-mail_____
I have enclosed $ _____ in payment for the checked book(s).
❏Please send a free catalog.
CHECK OUT OUR WEBSITE! www.dorchesterpub.com

Saddled
Delores Fossen

Getting a passionate man like Rio McCaine to do what she wants will be like breaking a stallion, Abbie realizes. It will take a lot of work. Easy enough to change her own appearance—to make herself seem more ladylike than perhaps she is, to present herself as the type of girl a man might want to marry—but to get Rio to do everything she wants, she'll have to resort to a lie. Or two. And if she wants to save her sister from the Apaches and keep her inheritance for her own, this half-Comanche gunslinger is the only answer. Still, while Abbie is relatively wily when it comes to getting what she wants, there are a few things that can throw her for a loop....Like what will happen when her handsome husband realizes he's been tricked? Abbie has a feeling it'll be like riding a bucking bronco—and part of her shivers in pleasure at the thought.

___52430-9 $4.99 US/$5.99 CAN

Dorchester Publishing Co., Inc.
P.O. Box 6640
Wayne, PA 19087-8640

Please add $2.50 for shipping and handling for the first book and $.75 for each book thereafter. NY, NYC, and PA residents, please add appropriate sales tax. No cash, stamps, or C.O.D.s. All orders shipped within 6 weeks via postal service book rate. Canadian orders require $2.50 extra postage and must be paid in U.S. dollars through a U.S. banking facility.

Name_____
Address_____
City_____ State_____ Zip_____
I have enclosed $ _____ in payment for the checked book(s).
Payment <u>must</u> accompany all orders. ❏ Please send a free catalog.
CHECK OUT OUR WEBSITE! www.dorchesterpub.com

Desert Bloom
Ronda Thompson

For Lilla Traften, the Texas Panhandle is nothing but hot cactus and dirt, its inhabitants worse. Grady Finch, the rugged foreman of the WC Ranch may be devastatingly handsome, but he is tactless. Worse, the heat is getting to her; sunstroke is making her dream of Grady's hands upon her, of the sweaty love they might make in the dust. Hardly normal thoughts for a proper miss and charm-school teacher! Still, she can't help wondering what will win the heart of a man like Grady. She'll have to prove she can survive on her own. He'll have to see that not only the land can undergo transformation, but that Lilla, too, can flower in the desert.

___4943-0 $5.99 US/$6.99 CAN

Dorchester Publishing Co., Inc.
P.O. Box 6640
Wayne, PA 19087-8640

Please add $2.50 for shipping and handling for the first book and $0.75 for each additional book. NY and PA residents, add appropriate sales tax. No cash, stamps, or C.O.D.s. All Canadian orders require $5.00 for shipping and handling and must be paid in U.S. dollars. Prices and availability subject to change. **Payment must accompany all orders**.

Name _____
Address _____
City_____ State_____ Zip _____
E-mail _____
I have enclosed $_____ in payment for the checked book(s).
❑ Please send me a free catalog.
CHECK OUT OUR WEBSITE at www.dorchesterpub.com!

In Trouble's Arms
Ronda Thompson

Loreen Matland is very clear. If the man who answers her ad for a husband is ugly as a mud fence, she'll keep him. If not, she'll fill his hide full of buckshot. Unfortunately, Jake Winslow is handsome. Lori knows that good-looking men are trouble, and Jake proves no exception. Of course, she hasn't been entirely honest with him, either. She has difficulties enough to make his flight from the law seem like a ride through the prairie. But the Texas Matlands don't give up, even to dangerous men with whiskey-smooth voices. And yet, in Jake's warm strong arms, Lori knows he is just what she needs—for her farm, her family, and her heart.

Lair of the Wolf

Also includes the sixth installment of *Lair of the Wolf*, a serialized romance set in medieval Wales. Be sure to look for future chapters of this exciting story featured in Leisure books and written by the industry's top authors.

___4716-0 $5.99 US/$6.99 CAN

Dorchester Publishing Co., Inc.
P.O. Box 6640
Wayne, PA 19087-8640

Please add $1.75 for shipping and handling for the first book and $.50 for each book thereafter. NY, NYC, and PA residents, please add appropriate sales tax. No cash, stamps, or C.O.D.s. All orders shipped within 6 weeks via postal service book rate. Canadian orders require $2.00 extra postage and must be paid in U.S. dollars through a U.S. banking facility.

Name_____
Address_____
City_____ State_____ Zip_____
I have enclosed $_____ in payment for the checked book(s).
Payment <u>must</u> accompany all orders. ❏ Please send a free catalog.

ATTENTION BOOK LOVERS!

Can't get enough of your favorite **ROMANCE**?

Call **1-800-481-9191** to:

✷ order books,

✷ receive a **FREE** catalog,

✷ join our book clubs to **SAVE 20%!**

Open Mon.-Fri. 10 AM-9 PM EST

Visit **www.dorchesterpub.com**
for special offers and inside
information on the authors you love.

We accept Visa, MasterCard or Discover®.
LEISURE BOOKS ❤ LOVE SPELL